HOSTILIS INTERRUPTUS

The advantage of a longer stride meant that Lioren went through the entrance seconds ahead of the Nidian and had the first sight of the two writhing, bloody bodies locked together in mortal combat on the floor. Moving forward, he quickly interposed his medial arms between the tightly pressed bodies. Only then did he discover that they were not two males fighting to the death, but a male and female indulging in a sexual coupling.

  Loiren released them and backed away, but suddenly they broke apart and launched themselves at him. The weight of their combined attack toppled him over backward. Within moments he was fighting for his life . . .

By James White
Published by Ballantine Books:

AMBULANCE SHIP
ALL JUDGMENT FLED
CODE BLUE—EMERGENCY!
THE DREAM MILLENNIUM
FEDERATION WORLD
FUTURES PAST
THE GENOCIDAL HEALER
HOSPITAL STATION
MAJOR OPERATION
SECTOR GENERAL
THE SILENT STARS GO BY
STAR HEALER
STAR SURGEON

THE GENOCIDAL HEALER

James White

A Del Rey Book
BALLANTINE BOOKS · NEW YORK

To Jeff
aka Jeffrey McIlwain, MD, FRCS
who is also great with sick refrigerators
In Appreciation

A Del Rey Book
Published by Ballantine Books

Library of Congress Catalog Card Number: 91-93043

ISBN 0-345-37109-7

Manufactured in the United States of America

First Edition: February 1992

Cover Art by Bruce Jensen

Chapter 1

THEY had assembled in a temporarily unused compartment on the hospital's eighty-seventh level. The room had seen service at various times as an observation ward for the birdlike Nallajims of physiological classification LSVO, as a Melfan ELNT operating theater, and, most recently, as an overflow ward for the chlorine-breathing Illensan PVSJs, whose noxious atmosphere still lingered in trace quantities. For the first and only time it was the venue of a military court and, Lioren thought hopefully, it would be used to terminate rather than extend life.

Three high-ranking Monitor Corps officers had taken their seats facing a multispecies audience that might be sympathetic, antagonistic, or simply curious. The most senior was an Earth-human DBDG, who opened the proceedings.

"I am Fleet Commander Dermod, the president of this specially convened court-martial," it said in the direction of the recorder. Then, inclining its head to one side and then the other, it went on. "Advising me are the Earth-human Colonel Skempton of this hospital, and the Nidian, Lieutenant-Colonel Dragh-Nin, of the Corps's other-species legal department. We are here at the behest of Surgeon-Captain Lioren, a Tarlan BRLH, who is dissatisfied with the verdict of a previous Federation civil-court hearing of its case. The Surgeon-Captain is insisting on its right as a serving officer to be tried by a Monitor Corps military tribunal.

"The charge is gross professional negligence leading to the deaths of a large but unspecified number of patients while under its care."

Without taking its attention from the body of the court, and seeming deliberately to avoid looking at the accused, the fleet commander paused briefly. The rows of chairs, cradles, and

1

other support structures suited to the physiological requirements of the audience held many beings who were familiar to Lioren: Thornnastor, the Tralthan Diagnostician-in-Charge of Pathology; the Nidian Senior Tutor, Cresk-Sar; and the recently appointed Earth-human Diagnostician-in-Charge of Surgery, Conway. Some of them would be willing and anxious to speak in Lioren's defense, but how many would be as willing to accuse, condemn, and punish?

"As is customary in these cases," Fleet Commander Dermod resumed gravely, "the counsel for the defense will open and the prosecution will have the last word, followed by the consultation and the agreed verdict and sentence of the officers of this court. Appearing for the defense is the Monitor Corps Earth-human, Major O'Mara, who has been Chief of the Department of Other-Species Psychology at this hospital since it first became operational, assisted by the Sommaradvan, Cha Thrat, a member of the same department. The accused, Surgeon-Captain Lioren, is acting for and is prosecuting itself.

"Major O'Mara, you may begin."

While Dermod had been speaking, O'Mara, whose two eyes were recessed and partially hidden by thin flaps of skin and shadowed by the gray hair which grew in two thick crescents above them, had looked steadily at Lioren. When it rose onto its two feet, the prompt screen remained unlit. Plainly the Chief Psychologist intended speaking without notes.

In the angry and impatient manner of an entity unused to the necessity for being polite, it said, "May it please the court, Surgeon-Captain Lioren stands accused, or more accurately stands self-accused, of a crime of which it has already been exonerated by its own civil judiciary. With respect, sir, the accused should not be here, we should not be here, and this trial should not be taking place."

"That civil court," Lioren said harshly, "was influenced by a very able defender to show me sympathy and sentiment when what I needed was justice. Here it is my hope that—"

"I will not be as able a defender?" O'Mara asked.

"I *know* you will be an able defender!" Lioren said loudly, knowing that the process of translation was removing much of the emotional content from the words. "That is my greatest concern. But why are you defending me? With your reputation and experience in other-species psychology, and the high standards of professional behavior you demand, I expected you to understand and side with me instead of—''

"But I am on your side, dammit—'' O'Mara began. He was silenced by the distinctively Earth-human and disgusting sound of the fleet commander clearing its main breathing passage.

"Let it be clearly understood,'' Dermod said in a quieter voice, "that all entities having business before this court will address their remarks to the presiding officer and not to each other. Surgeon-Captain Lioren, you will have the opportunity to argue your case without interruption when your present defender, be he able or inept, has completed his submission. Continue, Major.''

Lioren directed one eye toward the officers of the court, another he kept on the silent crowd behind him, and a third he fixed unwaveringly upon the Earth-human O'Mara, who, still without benefit of notes, was describing in detail the accused's training, career, and major professional accomplishments during his stay at Sector Twelve General Hospital. Major O'Mara had never used such words of praise to or about Lioren in the past, but now the things it was saying would not have been out of place in a eulogy spoken over the mortal remains of the respected dead. Regrettably, Lioren was neither dead nor respected.

As the hospital's Chief Psychologist, O'Mara's principal concern was and always had been the smooth and efficient operation of the ten-thousand-odd members of the medical and maintenance staff. For administrative reasons, the entity O'Mara carried the rank of major in the Monitor Corps, the Federation's executive and law-enforcement arm, which was also charged with the responsibility for the supply and maintenance of Sector General. But keeping so many different and potentially antagonistic life-forms working together in harmony was a large job whose limits, like those of O'Mara's authority, were difficult to define.

Given even the highest qualities of tolerance and mutual respect among all levels of its personnel, and in spite of the careful psychological screening they underwent before being accepted for training in the Galactic Federation's most renowned multienvironment hospital, there were still occasions when serious interpersonal friction threatened to occur because of ignorance or misunderstanding of other-species cultural mores, social behavior, or evolutionary imperatives. Or, more dangerously, a being might develop a xenophobic neurosis which, if left untreated, would ultimately affect its professional competence, mental stability, or both.

A Tralthan medic with a subconscious fear of the abhorrent little predators which had for so long infested its home planet might find itself unable to bring to bear on one of the physiologically similar, but highly civilized, Kreglinni the proper degree of clinical detachment necessary for its treatment. Neither would it feel comfortable working with or, in the event of personal accident or illness, being treated by a Kreglinni medical colleague. It was the responsibility of Chief Psychologist O'Mara to detect and eradicate such problems before they could become life- or sanity-threatening or, if all else failed, to remove the potentially troublesome individuals from the hospital.

There had been times, Lioren remembered, when this constant watch for signs of wrong, unhealthy, or intolerant thinking which the Chief Psychologist performed with such dedication made it the most feared, distrusted, and disliked entity in Sector General.

But now O'Mara seemed to be displaying the type of uncharacteristic behavior that it had always considered as a warning symptom in others. By defending this great and terrible crime of negligence against an entire planetary population, a piece of wrong thinking without precedent in Federation history, it was ignoring and reversing the professional habits and practices of a lifetime.

Lioren stared for a moment at the entity's head fur, which was a much lighter shade of gray than he remembered, and wondered whether the confusions of advancing age had caused it to succumb to one of the psychological ills from which it had tried so hard to protect everyone else. Its words, however, were reasoned and coherent.

". . . At no time was it suggested that Lioren was promoted beyond its level of competence," O'Mara was saying. "It is a Wearer of the Blue Cloak, the highest professional distinction that Tarla can bestow. Should the court wish it I can go into greater detail regarding its total dedication and ability as an other-species physician and surgeon, based on observations made during its time in this hospital. Documentation and personal affidavits provided by senior and junior Monitor Corps officers regarding its deservedly rapid promotion after it left us are also available. But that material would be repetitious and would simply reinforce the point that I have been making, that Lioren's professional behavior up to and, I submit, while committing the offense of which it is charged, was exemplary.

"I believe that the only fault that the court will find in the accused," O'Mara went on, "is that the professional standards it has set itself, and until the Cromsag Incident achieved, were unreasonably high and its subsequent feelings of guilt disproportionately great. Its only crime was that it demanded too much of itself when—"

"But there *is* no crime!" O'Mara's assistant, Cha Thrat, broke in loudly. It rose suddenly to its full height. "On Sommaradva the rules governing medical practice for a warrior-surgeon are strict, stricter by far than those accepted on other worlds, so I fully understand and sympathize with the feelings of the accused. But it is nonsense to suggest that strict self-discipline and high standards of professional conduct are in any sense bad, or a crime, or even a venial offense."

"The majority of the Federation's planetary histories," O'Mara replied in an even louder voice, the deepening facial color showing its anger at this interruption from a subordinate, "contain many instances of fanatically good political leaders or religious zealots which suggest otherwise. Psychologically it is healthier to be strict in moderation and allow a little room for—"

"But surely," Cha Thrat broke in again, "that does not apply to the truly good. You seem to be arguing that good is . . . is *bad*!"

Cha Thrat was the first entity that Lioren had seen of the Sommaradvan DCNF classification. Standing, it was half again as tall as O'Mara, and its arrangement of four ambulatory limbs, four waist-level heavy manipulators, and a further set for food provision and fine work encircling the neck gave it a shape that was pleasingly symmetrical and stable—unlike that of the Earth-humans, who always seemed to be on the point of falling on their faces. Of all the beings in the room, Lioren wondered if this entity would be the one who best understood his feelings. Then he concentrated his mind on the images coming from the eye that was watching the officers of the court.

Colonel Skempton was showing its teeth in the silent snarl

Earth-humans gave when displaying amusement or friendship, the Nidian officer's features were unreadable behind their covering of facial fur, and the fleet commander's expression did not change at all when it spoke.

"Are the counsels for the defense arguing among themselves regarding the guilt or otherwise of the accused," it asked quietly, "or simply interrupting each other in their eagerness to expedite the case? In either event, please desist and address the court one at a time."

"My respected colleague," O'Mara said in a voice which, in spite of the emotion-filtering process of translation, sounded anything but respectful, "was speaking in support of the accused but was a trifle overeager. Our argument will be resolved, in private, at another time."

"Then proceed," the fleet commander said.

Cha Thrat resumed its seat, and the Chief Psychologist, its face pigmentation still showing a deeper shade of pink, went on, "The point I am trying to make is that the accused, in spite of what it believes, is not totally responsible for what happened on Cromsag. To do so I shall have to reveal information normally restricted to my department. This material is—"

Fleet Commander Dermod was holding up one forelimb and hand, palm outward. It said, "If this material is privileged, Major, you cannot use it without permission from the entity concerned. If the accused forbids its use—"

"I forbid its use," Lioren said firmly.

"The court has no choice but to do the same," Dermod went on as if the Surgeon-Captain had not spoken. "Surely you are aware of this?"

"I am also aware, as, I believe, are you, sir," said O'Mara, "that if given the chance the accused would forbid me to say or do anything at all in its defense."

The fleet commander lowered its hand and said, "Nevertheless, where privileged information is concerned, the accused has that right."

"I dispute its right to commit judicial suicide," said O'Mara, "otherwise I would not have offered to defend an entity who is so highly intelligent, professionally competent, and completely stupid. The material in question is confidential and restricted but not, however, privileged since it was and is available to any accredited authority wishing for complete psychological data on a candidate before offering to employ it in a position of importance, or advancement to a level of greater responsibility. Without false modesty I would say that my department's psych profile on Surgeon-Captain Lioren was what gained its original commission in the Monitor Corps and probably its last three promotions. Even if we had been able to monitor closely the accused's psych profile following its departure from the hospital there is no certainty that the Cromsag tragedy could have been averted. The personality and motivations of the entity who caused it were already fully formed, stable, and well integrated. To my later regret I saw no reason to alter them in any way.''

The Chief Psychologist paused for a moment to look at the beings crowding the room before returning its attention to the officers of the court. Its desk screen came to life, but O'Mara barely glanced at the upward march of symbols as it continued speaking.

''This is the psych record of a being with a complete and quite remarkable degree of dedication to its profession,'' the major said. ''In spite of the presence of fellow Tarlans of the female sex at that time, there are no social or sexual activities listed or, indeed, any indication that it wished to indulge in either. Self-imposed celibacy is undertaken by members of several intelligent species for various personal, philosophical, or religious reasons. Such behavior is rare, even unusual, but not unsane.

''Lioren's file contains no incidents, behavior, or thinking with which I could find fault,'' O'Mara went on. ''It ate, slept, and worked. While its colleagues were off duty, relaxing or having fun, it spent its free time studying or acquiring extra experience in areas which it considered of special interest. When promotion came, it was intensely disliked by the subordinate medical and environmental maintenance staff on its ward because it demanded of them the same quality of work that it required of itself, but fortunate indeed were the patients who came under its care. Its intense dedication and inflexibility of mind, however, suggested that it might not be suitable for the ultimate promotion to Diagnostician.

''This was not the reason for it leaving Sector General,'' O'Mara said quickly. ''Lioren considered many of the hospital staff to be lax in their personal behavior, irresponsible when off duty, and, by its standards, nonserious to a fault, and it wished to continue its work in an environment of stricter discipline. It fully deserved its Corps promotions, including the command of the rescue operation on Cromsag that ended in disaster.''

The Chief Psychologist looked down at its desktop, but it was not seeing the prompt screen, because for some reason it had closed its eyes. Suddenly it looked up again.

''This is the psych profile of an entity who had no choice but to act as it did,'' O'Mara resumed, ''so that its actions in the circumstances were proper. There was no carelessness on its part, no negligence, and therefore, I submit, no guilt. For it was only after the few survivors had been under observation here for two months that we were able to unravel the secondary endocrinological effects of the disease Lioren had been treating. If any offense was committed, it was the minor one of impatience allied to Lioren's firm belief that its ship's medical facilities were equal to the task demanded of them.

''I have little more to say,'' the major continued, ''except to suggest to the court that its punishment should be in proportion to the crime and not, as the accused believes and the prosecution will argue, the results of that crime. Catastrophic and horrifying though the results of the Surgeon-Captain's actions have been, the offense itself was a minor one and should be treated as such.''

While O'Mara had been speaking, Lioren's anger had risen to a level where it might no longer be controllable. Brown blotches were appearing all over his pale, yellow-green tegument, and both sets of outer lungs were tightly distended to shout a protest that would have been too loud for proper articulation and would probably have damaged the sound sensors of many of those present.

''The accused is becoming emotionally distressed,'' O'Mara said quickly, ''so I shall be brief. I urge that the case against Surgeon-Captain Lioren be dismissed or, failing that, that the sentence be noncustodial. Ideally the accused should be confined to the limits of this hospital, where psychiatric assistance is available when required, and where its considerable professional talents will be available to our patients while it is—''

''No!'' Lioren said, in a voice which made those closest to him wince and the translator squawk with sound overload. ''I have sworn, solemnly and by Sedith and Wrethrin the Healers, to forgo the practice of my art for the rest of my worthless life.''

''Now that,'' O'Mara replied, not quite as loudly as Lioren, "would indeed be a crime. It would be a shameful and unforgivable waste of ability of which you would be inarguably guilty."

"Were I to live a hundred lifetimes," Lioren said harshly, "I could never save a fraction of the number of beings I caused to die."

"But you could *try*—" O'Mara began, and broke off as once again the fleet commander raised his hand for silence.

"Address your arguments to the court, not each other," Dermod said, looking at them in turn. "I shall not warn you again. Major O'Mara, some time ago you stated that you had little more to say. May the court now assume that you have said it?"

The Chief Psychologist remained standing for a moment; then it said, "Yes, sir" and sat down.

"Very well," the fleet commander said. "The court will now hear the case for the prosecution. Surgeon-Captain Lioren, are you ready to proceed?"

Lioren's skin showed an increasing and irregular discoloration caused by the deep emotional distress that even the earliest and innocent memories evoked, but his surface air sacs had deflated so that he was able to speak quietly.

"I am ready."

Chapter 2

THE Cromsag system had been investigated by the Monitor Corps scout ship *Tenelphi* while engaged on a survey mission in Sector Nine, one of the embarrassing three-dimensional blanks which still appeared in the Federation's charts. The discovery of a system containing habitable planets was a pleasant break in the boring routine of counting and measuring the positions of a myriad of stars, and when they found one displaying all the indications of harboring intelligent indigenous life, their pleasure and excitement were intense.

The pleasure, however, was short-lived.

Because a scout ship with a complement of only four entities did not have the facilities to handle a first-contact situation, the regulations forbade a landing, so the crew had to content themselves with conducting a visual examination from close orbit while trying to establish the natives' level of technology by analyzing their communications frequencies and any other electromagnetic radiation emanating from the planet. As a result of their findings, *Tenelphi* remained in orbit while it recklessly squandered its power reserves on the ship's energy-hungry subspace communicator on increasingly urgent distress messages to base.

The Monitor Corps's specialized other-species contact vessel, *Descartes*, which normally made the initial approach to newly discovered cultures, was already deeply involved on the planet of the Blind Ones, where communications had reached the stage where it was inadvisable to break off. But the situation on the new planet was not a problem of First Contact but of insuring that enough of the natives would survive to make any kind of contact possible.

The Emperor-class battleship *Vespasian*, which was more than capable of waging a major war although in this instance it was expected to end one, was hastily converted to disaster-relief mode and dispatched to the region. It was under the command of the Earth-human Colonel Williamson, but in all matters pertaining to relief operations on the surface it was the Tarlan subordinate, Surgeon-Captain Lioren, who had the rank and the sole responsibility.

Within an hour of the two vessels matching orbits, *Tenelphi* had docked with *Vespasian* and the scout ship's captain, the Earth-human Major Nelson, and its Nidian medical officer, Surgeon-Lieutenant Dracht-Yur, were in the operations room giving the latest situation report.

"We have recorded samples of their radio signals," Major Nelson reported briskly, "even though the volume of traffic is unusually small. But we were unable to make any sense of it because our computer is programmed for survey work with just enough reserve capacity to handle the translation requirements of my crew. As things stand, we don't even know if they know we are here—"

"*Vespasian*'s tactical computer will translate the surface traffic from now on," Colonel Williamson broke in impatiently, "and the information will be passed to you. We are less interested in what you did not hear than in what you saw. Please go on, Major."

It was unnecessary to mention a fact known to everyone present, that while Williamson's tremendous capital ship had the bigger brain, Nelson's tiny and highly specialized survey vessel had eyes that were second to none.

"As you can see," Nelson went on, tapping the keys that threw the visuals onto the room's enormous tactical display screen, "we surveyed the planet from a distance of five diameters before moving in to map in more detail the areas that showed signs of habitation. It is the third planet, and so far as we know the only life-bearing one, of a system of eight planets. Its day is just over nineteen hours long, surface gravity one and one-quarter Earth-normal, the atmospheric pressure in proportion, and its composition would not seriously inconvenience the majority of our warm-blooded oxygen-breathers.

"The land surface is divided into seventeen large island continents. All but the two at the poles are habitable, but only the largest equatorial continent is presently inhabited. The others show signs of habitation in the past, together with a fairly high level of technology that included powered surface and air transport, with radiation traces suggesting that they had fission-assisted electricity generation. Their towns and cities now appear to be abandoned and derelict. The buildings are undamaged, but there are no indications of industrial or domestic wastes either in atmosphere or on the ground, no evidence of food cultivation, and the road surfaces, street paving, and a few of the smaller buildings have been broken up and damaged due to the unchecked growth of plant life. Even in the inhabited areas of the equatorial continent there is similar evidence of structural and agrarian neglect with the associated indications of—"

"Obviously a plague," Lioren said suddenly, "an epidemic for which they have little natural immunity. It has reduced the planetary population to the extent that they can no longer fully maintain all their cities and services, and the survivors have collected in the warmer and less power-hungry cities of the equator to—"

"To fight a bloody war!" the scout ship's medic, Dracht-Yur, broke in, its snarling Nidian speech making an angry accompaniment to the emotionless translated words. "But it is a strange, archaic form of warfare. Either they love war, or hate each other, very much. Yet they seem to have an inordinate respect for property. They don't use mass-destruction weapons on each other; there is no evidence of aerial bombing or artillery, even though they still have large numbers of ground and atmosphere vehicles. They just use them to transport the combatants to the battleground, where they fight at close quarters, hand to hand and apparently without weapons. It is savage. Look!"

Vespasian's tactical screen was displaying a series of aerial photographs of tropical forest clearings and city streets, sharp and clear despite massive enlargement and the fact that they had been taken from a vertical distance of fifty miles. Normally it was difficult to obtain much information on the body mass and physiological details of a native life-form from orbit—although a study of the shadow it cast could be helpful—but, Lioren thought grimly, far too many of these creatures had been obliging enough to lie flat on the ground dead.

The pictures shocked but did not sicken the Surgeon-Captain as they did Dracht-Yur, because the Nidian medic belonged to one of those strange cultures who reverenced the decomposing remains of their dead. Even so, the number of recently and not so recently dead lying about in the streets and forest clearings was bound to pose a health risk.

Lioren wondered suddenly whether the surviving combatants were unwilling or simply unable to bury them. A less sharp moving picture showed two of the creatures fighting together on the ground, and so gentle were the blows and bites they inflicted on each other that they might have been indulging publicly in a sexual coupling.

The Nidian seemed to be reading Lioren's mind, because it went on. "Those two look as if they are incapable of seriously damaging each other, and at first I assumed this to be a species lacking in physical endurance. Then other entities were seen who fought strongly and continuously for an entire day. But you will also observe that the bodies of these two show widespread patches of discoloration, while a few of the others have skins without blemish. There is a definite correlation between the degree of physical weakness and the area of discoloration on the body. I think it is safe to assume that these two are seriously ill rather than tired.

"But that," Dracht-Yur ended in an angry growl, "doesn't stop them from trying to kill each other."

Lioren raised one hand slightly from the tabletop, middle digits extended in the Tarlan sign of respect and approval. But the two officers gave no indication of understanding the significance of the gesture, which meant that they had to be complimented verbally.

"Major Nelson, Surgeon-Lieutenant Dracht-Yur," Lioren said, "you have both done very well. But there is more that you must do. Can I assume that the other members of your crew have also had the opportunity of observing the situation below and have discussed it among themselves?"

"There was no way of stopping them—" Nelson began.

"Yes," Dracht-Yur barked.

"Good," Lioren said. "*Tenelphi* is detached from its current survey duty. Transfer its officers to *Vespasian*. They will join the crews of the first four reconnaissance vehicles to go down as advisors since they know more, perhaps only a little more, about the local situation than we do. This ship will remain in orbit until the most effective rescue site has been chosen . . ."

At times like these Lioren was reluctant to waste time on politeness, but he had learned that, where Earth-human senior officers in particular were concerned, time wasted now would help expedite matters later. And Colonel Williamson was, after all, *Vespasian*'s commander and nominally the senior officer.

"If you have any comments or objections so far, sir," Lioren said, "I would be pleased to hear them."

Colonel Williamson looked at Nelson and Dracht-Yur briefly before returning its attention to Lioren. The scout-ship officers were showing their teeth, and a few of the colonel's were also visible as it said, "*Tenelphi* will not be able to resume its survey mission until we have topped up its consumables, and I would be surprised if its officers objected to any break in that deadly dull routine. You are making friends, Surgeon-Captain. Please continue."

"The first priority is to end the fighting," Lioren said, "and only then will it be possible to treat the sick and injured. This forced cessation of hostilities will have to be achieved without inflicting additional casualties or causing too much mental distress among the population. To a culture at the prespaceflight level of technology, the sudden arrival among them of a vessel of the size and power of *Vespasian*, and the visually monstrous entities it contains, would not be reassuring. The first approach will have to be made in a small ship by people who, for psychological reasons, must be of equal or lesser body mass than they are. And it will have to be done covertly, in an isolated area where there are few natives or, ideally, only one whose temporary withdrawal from among its friends will arouse minimum distress . . .''

The vehicle chosen for the mission was *Vespasian*'s short-range communications vessel, which was equally capable of space operations or extended aerodynamic maneuvering in atmosphere. It was small but comfortably appointed, Lioren thought, if one happened to be an Earth-human, but at present it was overloaded and overcrowded.

They descended steeply out of the orange light of sunrise into an uneven blanket of dark, predawn cloud, thrusters shut down and velocity reduced so that they would not cause unnecessary distress by dragging a sonic shock wave in their wake, and the ship was darkened except for the radiation from its infrared sensors, which the natives might or might not be able to see.

Lioren stared at the enhanced picture of the forest clearing with its single, low-roofed dwelling and outbuildings rushing up at them. Without power their ship was gliding in too steeply and much too fast and with the flight characteristics, it seemed, of an aerodynamically clean lump of rock. Then three small areas of vegetation were flattened suddenly and driven downward into shallow craters as the ship's pressor beams reached out to support it on immaterial, shock-absorbing stilts. The touchdown was silent and sudden but very gentle.

Lioren turned a disapproving eye toward the pilot, wondering, not for the first time, why some experts felt it necessary to display their expertise so dramatically; the boarding ramp slid out before he could think of words that were both complimentary and critical.

They wore heavy-duty space suits with the air tanks and helmet visors removed, confident that this makeshift body armor would protect them against any bare-handed attack by an intelligent life-form that used only natural weapons. The five Earth-humans and three Orligians in the party ran to search the outbuildings while Dracht-Yur and Lioren moved quickly toward the house, which, in spite of the early hour, had its internal lighting switched on. They circled the house once, keeping below the level of the closed and uncurtained windows, to stop at the building's only entrance.

Dracht-Yur focused its scanner on the door mechanism and the life-sensor on the spaces beyond; then it used the suit radio to say quietly, "Beyond the door there is a large room, presently unoccupied, and three smaller compartments opening off it. The first is empty of life, the second contains traces which are not moving and positioned so closely together that I can't be sure whether there are two or three entities, who are making the low, untranslatable noises characteristic of sleep. Maybe they are sick or wounded. The third room contains one being whose movements appear slow and deliberate, and the sounds from that compartment are quiet but distinct, like the intermittent contact between cooking utensils. The overall indication is that the occupants are unaware of our presence.

"The door mechanism is very basic," the Nidian medic continued, "and the large metal bar on the inside has not been engaged. You can simply lift the latch and walk in, sir."

Lioren was relieved. Breaking down the door would have made the job of convincing these people of his good intentions much more difficult. But with anything up to four natives in the house and only one overeager but diminuitive Nidian in support, Lioren was unwilling to enter just then. He remained silent until the others arrived to report that the outhouses contained only agricultural implements and nonsapient farm animals.

Quickly he described the layout of the house, then went on. "The greatest risk to us is the group of three or four beings occupying the room directly opposite this entrance, and they must not be allowed to leave it until the situation has been explained to them. Four of you guard the interior door and four the window in case they try to escape that way. Dracht-Yur and myself will talk to the other one. And remember, be quiet, careful, and nonaggressive at all times. Do not damage furniture or artifacts, and especially not the beings themselves, or do anything to suggest that we are not their friends."

He unlatched the door quietly and led the way inside.

An oil-burning lamp hung from the center of the ceiling, illuminating walls hung with a few pictorial carvings and what seemed to be displays of dried, aromatic vegetation, although to his Tarlan olfactory sensors the aroma was anything but pleasant. Against the facing wall there was a long dining bench with four high-backed chairs pushed under it. A few smaller tables and larger, more heavily padded chairs were visible, plus a large bookcase and other items which he could not immediately identify. The majority of the furniture was of wood and strongly but not expertly built, and a few of the items showed signs of being mass-produced. Plainly they were the very old, scratched, and dented legacies of better times. The middle of the room was uncluttered and covered only by a thick carpet of some fabric or vegetable material that deadened the sound of their feet as they crossed it.

All three of the internal doors had been left ajar, and from the room occupied by the single native the quiet noises of cooking utensils making contact with crockery were accompanied by a soft, wailing sound that was untranslatable. Lioren wondered if the entity was in pain from illness or wounds, or was perhaps indulging in its version of mouth music. He was about to move in to confront the native when Dracht-Yur grasped one of his medial hands and pointed toward the door of the other occupied room.

One of the Earth-humans had been gripping the door mechanism tightly to prevent it being opened from within. Now it held out its free hand waist high with three digits extended, then lowered it palm downward to show two digits at hip level, and brought it down almost to its knee joint before showing one digit. For an instant it released the door handle, pressed both palms together and brought its hands to one side of its face, then inclined its head and closed both of its eyes.

For a moment Lioren was completely baffled by the gestures until he remembered that the Earth-human DBDG classification, and quite a few other life-forms, adopted this peculiar position while asleep. The rest of the hand signals could only mean that the room contained three children, one of whom was little more than an infant, and that they were all asleep.

Lioren dipped his head Earth-human fashion in acknowledgment, relieved that the children could be easily contained in their room so that there would be no possibility of uninformed and terrified escapees spreading panic throughout the area. Feeling pleased and much more confident, he moved forward to open communication with what, judging by the sounds emanating from the food-preparation room, was almost certainly the only adult in the house.

The entity had its back turned toward the entrance, showing him a three-quarters rear profile as it busied itself with some task that was concealed by its upper torso. Because of the absence of individually mobile eye mountings in its cranium and the consequent loss of all-around vision, Lioren was able to watch it for a moment without it being able to see him.

Its bodily configuration more closely resembled Lioren's own than those of the Earth-humans, Nidians, or Orligians accompanying him, which should greatly reduce the visual shock of first contact. Except for the possession of three sets of limbs— two ambulators, two medial heavy manipulators, and two more at neck level for eating and to perform more delicate work, rather than the Tarlan's three sets of four—and a cranium covered by thick, blue fur that continued in a narrow strip along the spine to the vestigial tail, the general physical characteristics were remarkably similar. Its skin showed areas of pale yellow discoloration that were symptomatic of the plague that, with the savage and barbaric war, was threatening to sweep its planet free of intelligent life. The creature's physiological classification was DCSL, and curing its medical condition, at least, would be relatively simple once he obtained its cooperation.

Gently at first but with increasing firmness Lioren began clapping two of his guantleted, medial hands together to attract its attention, and when it swung around suddenly to face him, Lioren said, "We are friends. We have come to—"

It had been supporting a large bowl partially filled with a pale gray semiliquid material between its body and one medial hand, while the other medial hand was holding and pouring the contents of a smaller bowl into the first. Both containers, Lioren had time to note, were thick-walled and seemed to be made of a hard but very brittle ceramic, as was proved by the way they shattered when dropped onto the floor. The noise was loud enough to waken the three youngsters in the other room, and one of them, probably the infant, began making loud, frightened sounds which did not translate.

"We will not harm you," Lioren began again. "We have come to help cure you of the terrible disease which—"

The creature made a high-pitched gobbling sound which

translated as, "The children! What have you done to the children?" and hurled itself at Lioren and Dracht-Yur.

It was not a bare-handed attack.

From the number of kitchen implements lying on the tabletop nearby it had snatched up a knife, which it swung at Lioren's chest. The blade was long and pointed, serrated along one edge and sharp enough to leave a deep scratch in the fabric of Lioren's heavy-duty space suit. But the creature was a quick learner, because the second blow was a straight-armed jab which might have penetrated if Lioren had not grasped the creature's wrist in two medial hands and used a third to prise the weapon from its fingers, taking a small, incised wound to one of his own digits in the process, while at the same time holding off its two upper hands, which seemed intent on tearing holes in his face.

The violence of its attack sent Lioren staggering backward into the other room, and he had a glimpse of the diminutive Dracht-Yur diving at the creature's legs and wrapping its short, furry arms tightly around them. The creature overbalanced and all three of them crashed to the floor.

"What are you waiting for, immobilize it!" Lioren said sharply. Then with a sudden feeling of concern for the being, he said, "As yet I am unfamiliar with your internal physiology, and I trust that the weight of my body against your lower thorax is not causing damage to underlying organs."

The creature's response was to struggle even harder against the Earth-human, Orligian, and Tarlan hands holding it down, and only a few of the sounds it was making were translatable. Looking at the obviously confused and terrified being, Lioren spoke silent and highly critical words to himself. This, his first contact with a member of a newly discovered intelligent species, had not been handled well.

"We will not harm you," Lioren said, trying to sound reassuring in a voice louder than that of the creature and those of the three children in the other room, all of whom were awake and contributing their own untranslatable sounds. "We will not harm your children. Please calm yourself. Our only wish is to help you, all of you, to live out your lives free of war and the disease which is affecting you . . ."

It must have understood his translated words, because it had grown silent as he was speaking, but its struggle to free itself continued.

"But if we are to find a cure for this disaster," Lioren went on in a quieter voice, "we will have to isolate and identify the pathogen within your body causing it, and to do this we require specimens of your blood and other body fluids . . ."

They would also be needed to prepare large quantities of safe anesthetics, tranquilizing gases and synthetic food suited to the species metabolism if the war as well as the disease was to be checked with minimum delay and loss of life. But this did not seem to be the right moment to tell it all of the truth, because its efforts to break free had intensified.

Lioren looked at Dracht-Yur and indicated one of the native's medial arms where muscle tension and elevated blood pressure had caused one of the veins to distend, making it an ideal site for withdrawing blood samples.

"We will not harm you," Lioren repeated. "Do not be afraid. And please stop moving your arm."

But the large, glittering, and multibarreled instrument that the Nidian medic had produced, while absolutely painless in use, was not an object to inspire confidence. If their positions had been reversed, Lioren knew, he would not have believed a single word he was saying.

Chapter 3

WITH a few violent exceptions, the subsequent contacts with the planet's natives, whose name for their world was Cromsag, went more easily. This was because *Vespasian*'s transmitter had matched frequencies with the Cromsaggar broadcast channels to explain in greater detail who the off-world strangers were, where they had come from, and why they were there. And when the great capital ship landed and began to disgorge and erect prefabricated hospitals and food-distribution centers for the war's survivors, the verbal reassurances were given form and substance and all hostility against the strangers ceased.

But that did not mean that they became friends.

Lioren was sure that he knew everything about the Cromsaggar, with the exception of how their minds worked. From recently dead cadavers abandoned in the war zones he had obtained a complete and accurate picture of their physiology and metabolism. This had enabled their injuries to be treated with safe medication and their war to be ended ingloriously under blankets of anesthetic gas. The scout ship *Tenelphi* had been pressed into service as a fast courier vessel plying between Cromsag and Sector General. It carried specimens requiring more detailed study in one direction and the findings of Head of Pathology Thornnastor, which more often than not agreed with Lioren's own, in the other.

But the Cromsaggar disease was proving difficult for even Diagnostician Thornnastor to isolate and identify. Living rather than dead specimens were required for study, if possible displaying the symptomology from onset to the preterminal stage of the condition, and *Rhabwar*, the hospital's special ambulance ship, was dispatched to obtain them. And even more baffling than the plague, to which the victims invariably succumbed before reaching middle age, was their mental approach to it.

One plague victim had agreed to talk to Lioren about itself, but its words had merely added to the Surgeon-Captain's confusion. He knew the patient only by its case file number, because the Cromsaggar considered their written and spoken symbol of identity to be the most important of personal possessions, and even though this one was close to termination it would not divulge its name to a stranger. When Lioren asked it why many of the Cromsaggar had attacked off-worlders with any weapon that came to hand, but fought among themselves only with teeth, hands and feet, it said that there was no honor or gain in killing a member of one's own race unless it was with great effort and extreme personal danger. For the same reason they always stopped short of killing a very sick, severely weakened, or dying adversary.

Taking the life of another intelligent entity, Lioren firmly believed, was the most dishonorable act imaginable. In his position he should respect the beliefs of others, regardless of how strange or shocking they might be to one of his strict Tarlan upbringing, but he could not and would not respect this one.

Changing the subject quickly, he asked, "Why is it that after you fight, the injured are taken away to be cared for while the dead remain untouched where they fall? We know that your people have some knowledge of medicine and healing, so why do you allow the dead to remain unburied, to risk the spread of further pestilence into your already plague-ridden population? Why do you expose yourselves to this totally unnecessary danger?''

The ravages of the disease, which had covered the entire epidermis in patches of livid camouflage, had left the patient very weak, and for a moment Lioren wondered if it was able to reply, or even if it had heard the questions. But suddenly it said, ''A decomposing corpse is indeed a fearful risk to the health of those who pass nearby. The danger and the fear are necessary.''

''But *why*?'' Lioren asked again. ''What do you gain by deliberately subjecting yourselves to fear and pain and danger?''

''We gain strength,'' the Cromsaggar said. ''For a time, for a very short time, we feel strong again.''

''In a very short time,'' Lioren said with the confidence of a healer backed by all the resources of Federation medical science, ''we will make you feel well and strong without the fighting. Surely you would prefer to live on a world free of war and disease?''

From somewhere within its wasted body the patient seemed to gather strength. It said loudly, ''Never in the memories of those alive, or in the memories of their ancestors, has there been a time without war and disease. The stories told of such times, when the planetwide ruins of towns and cities were populated by healthy and happy Cromsaggar, are stories told only to comfort small and hungry children, children who soon grow large enough to fight and to disbelieve these stories.

''You should leave us, stranger, to survive as we have always survived,'' it went on, straining to raise itself from the litter. ''The thought of a world without war is too frightening to contemplate.''

He asked more questions, but the patient, although fully conscious and displaying a slight improvement in its clinical condition, would not speak to him.

There was no doubt in Lioren's mind that a medical cure would quickly be discovered for the condition affecting the ten thousand-odd surviving Cromsaggar. But he was less sure whether a species which fought wars using only the natural

weapons provided by evolution, because that made them feel
good for a while, was worth saving. The strict rules of engagement that governed the fighting did not make the situation any
less barbaric. They did not fight weaker opponents or children
or the very few who were advanced in years, but only because
the element of personal risk, and presumably the emotional reward, was reduced. He was glad that his only responsibility was
the return of the plague sufferers to bodily health and not the
curing of what appeared to be the even more diseased minds
inhabiting those bodies.

And yet there had been occasions when, in an effort to give
his patients something other than their own distressing clinical
condition to think about, he had tried to explain star travel and
the Galactic Federation to them. He had described the bewildering variety of shapes and sizes that intelligent life could take,
and tried to make them understand that they lived on one inhabited world of many hundreds. He found those frightening and
inexplicable minds of theirs had displayed an agility and a level
of intelligence, although not the degree of education and knowledge, that was almost the equal of his own.

At those times there had been a small and transient improvement in their clinical condition, and that had made Lioren wonder if their craving for the danger and emotional excitement of
war and single combat might not someday be fulfilled by the
many and even more difficult challenges of peace. But they refused, or perhaps were psychologically unable because of cultural conditioning, to divulge personal information about their
social behavior, moral strictures, or feelings on any subject unless, as in the present case, the patient was gravely ill and its
mental resistance low.

The truth was that Lioren did not know how his patients felt,
about themselves or anyone or anything else, and the stock question of the attending physician, "How do you feel?," was never
answered.

Rhabwar was due in two days' time, and he decided that this
particular patient would be among those transferred to the ambulance ship for investigation and treatment at Sector General,
and that he would ask for a consultation with the vessel's senior
medical officer.

Doctor Prilicla was a Cinrusskin, and, as a member of the
Federation's only empathic species, it knew how everyone felt.

Lioren asked that the meeting take place on *Rhabwar*'s casualty deck, rather than summoning Prilicla to the overcrowded sick bay of *Vespasian*, for reasons both practical and personal. The level of background emotional radiation from patients was much higher on *Vespasian* and would doubtless have distressed his visitor—it did no harm to show consideration to a professional colleague. On the ambulance ship there was less likelihood of his uncertainties regarding the Cromsaggar becoming known to his subordinates. It was his firm belief that a leader should display certainty at all times to the led if he was to receive their respect and total obedience.

Perhaps the empath held the same belief, but it was more likely that Prilicla had detected Lioren's emotional radiation at a distance, correctly analyzed it, and insured that their meeting would be private. He was grateful but not surprised. It was in the other's own selfish interest to minimize the generation of unpleasant emotional radiation around it, because to do otherwise would be to expose itself to exactly the same degree of unpleasantness.

The Cinrusskin positioned itself at eye level above one of the treatment tables, an enormous, incredibly fragile flying insect rendered small only by Lioren's greater body mass. From its tubular, exoskeletal body there projected six pencil-thin legs, four even more delicately fashioned manipulators, and four sets of wide, iridescent, and almost transparent wings that were beating slowly as, with the aid of the gravity nullifiers strapped to its body, it maintained a stable hover. Only on Cinruss, with its thick atmosphere and gravitational pull of one-eighth standard G, could a species of flying insect have evolved intelligence, civilization, and star travel, and Lioren knew of no race within the Federation who did not consider them to be the most beautiful of all intelligent life-forms.

From one of the narrow openings in the delicate, convoluted eggshell that was its head came a series of musical trills and clicks which translated as "Thank you, friend Lioren, for the complimentary feelings you are harboring, and for the pleasure of meeting you in person for the first time. I also detect strong emotional radiation which suggests that the purpose of our meeting is professional and urgent rather than social.

"I am an empath, not a telepath," it ended gently. "You will have to tell me what is troubling you, friend Lioren."

Lioren felt sudden irritation at the other's continuing use of the word "friend." He was, after all, the medical and administrative director of the disaster relief operation on Cromsag, and a Surgeon-Captain in the Monitor Corps, while Prilicla was a civilian Senior Physician at Sector General. His irritation was making the empath's whole body tremble and causing its hovering flight to become less stable. He suddenly realized that he was attacking a being with a weapon, his feelings, against which it had no defense.

Even the pathologically warlike Cromsaggar would scorn to attack such a weak and defenseless enemy.

Lioren's irritation quickly changed to shame. This was a time to forget the feelings of justified pride in his high rank and in the many professional accomplishments that had earned it. Instead he should try, as he had often done in the past, to make the most effective use of the abilities of a subordinate whose feelings were easily hurt, and to control his emotions.

"Thank you, friend Lioren, for the mental self-discipline you have just displayed," Prilicla said before he could speak. It settled like a feather onto the top of the examination table, no longer trembling, and added, "But I detect strong background emotional radiation that you are finding more difficult to control and that, I feel sure, concerns the Cromsaggar. My own feelings of concern over the situation here are strong, perhaps as strong as yours, and shared feelings about other persons or situations cause me lesser discomfort. So if there is some way that I can help you please do not hesitate to speak."

Lioren felt renewed irritation at being given permission to discuss the Cromsaggar when his only purpose in coming here had been to do so, but the feeling was faint and transient. As he began to speak, the Surgeon-Captain knew that he was briefly verbalizing his latest report, copied to his Monitor Corps superiors and to Prilicla itself, that *Rhabwar* would be carrying back to Thornnastor, but it was necessary that the empath be acquainted with the current position if it was to understand the importance of the later questions.

He described the continually expanding search that had brought back data fit only for industrial archeologists. There were no recent life signs. Many of the abandoned cities and mining and manufacturing complexes in the north and south temperate regions were many centuries old, and so well constructed that only a moderate effort would be required to restore them because the mineral wealth of the planet was far from exhausted. But the effort had not been made because the race's energies had been directed into fighting, so much so that many of them no longer grew food or had the strength to forage for that which grew wild, and the population had contracted into one region so that they could continue fighting without having to travel far to do so.

"When we stopped the war," Lioren went on, "or rather, when our sleep bombs halted the hundreds of small gang and two-person conflicts, there was an estimated surviving population of just under ten thousand entities, a number which included all the adults, their young, and a few newly born infants. But recently they have begun dying at the rate of about one hundred every day."

Prilicla had begun to tremble again. Lioren was unsure whether it was in response to his emotional radiation or its own reaction to the news of the increasing number of fatalities. He tried to make his mind as well as his voice calm and clinical as he continued.

"In spite of our supporting them with shelters, clothing, and synthetic nutrient, even going so far as to gather supplies of local food that they were too weak to harvest for themselves, the deaths continue. Adult fatalities are invariably due to the plague, sometimes expedited by the debilitating effect of war injuries, and the children succumb to other diseases for which we have no specifics as yet. The Cromsaggar accept our help and our food, but only their young appear grateful for it. They show no interest in what we are trying to do for them. I feel that the adults tolerate us as an additional and unwelcome burden that they can do nothing about. My own feeling is that they are disinterested in their own survival and want to be left alone to commit racial suicide in the bloodiest fashion possible, and there are times when I feel that such a warlike and individually violent race should not be restrained from doing so. I do not know what they themselves feel, about anything."

"And you would like me to use my empathic faculty," Prilicla asked, "to tell you what they feel?"

"Yes," Lioren said, with so much feeling that the Cinrusskin trembled for a moment. "I hoped that you, Doctor, might have detected urges, instincts, feelings about themselves, their off-

spring, or their present situation. My ignorance regarding their
thinking and motivations is total. I would like to be able to do
or say something to them that, as with an emotionally disturbed
entity about to jump from a high building, would make them
want to live instead of die. What is it that they fear, or need,
that would make them want to survive?''

"Friend Lioren," Prilicla said without hesitation, "they fear
death, like every other self-aware creature, and they want to
survive. There were no indications, even in the most serious
cases, of a wish for individual death or racial self-destruction,
and they should not be—''

"I am sorry," Lioren broke in. "My earlier remark about
allowing them to commit racial suicide—''

"They were words spoken because of helplessness and frus-
tration, friend Lioren," Prilicla said, in the gentlest of interruptions, "that were completely contradicted by your underlying
emotional radiation at the time. There was no need for an apology then or for your embarrassment now.

"And I had been about to say," it went on, "that the Cromsaggar should not be criticized for their lack of cooperation, and
the strong feelings of ingratitude until we know why they feel
so ungrateful. These feelings were strongly present in all of the
adult patients I monitored during transportation to Sector General and while I was present at the subsequent attempts to question them. They know we are trying to help them, but will not
help us with clinical or personal information about themselves.
When the interrogation was intensified they became agitated and
fearful, and a marked if temporary remission of symptoms was
observed at these times.''

"I have made the same observation," Lioren said, "and assumed that it was the transfer of focus from a material condition
to an immaterial one, the psychological mechanism which can
sometimes make faith healing effective. I did not consider it an
important datum.''

"You are probably correct," Prilicla said. "But Chief Psychologist O'Mara is of the opinion that the marked remission
due to the fear stimulus, combined with their fanatical refusal
to communicate with us beyond the exchange of a few words,
indicates the presence of an extremely strong and deep-rooted
conditioning about which the Cromsaggar, as individuals, may
be unaware. Friend O'Mara likens it to the racial group psycho-

ses afflicting the Gogleskans, and says that it is trying to probe
a very sensitive area that is surrounded by a very thick wall of
mental scar tissue, and advises everyone concerned to proceed
slowly and carefully.''

The Gogleskan psychosis forced them into avoiding direct
physical contact with each other for the greater part of their adult
lives, which was certainly not the problem with the Cromsaggar.
Trying to control his feelings of impatience, Lioren said, ''If we
do not quickly find a cure for this plague, your Chief Psychologist will run out of subjects for his slow and careful investigation. What progress has been made since your last visit?''

''Friend Lioren,'' Prilicla said gently, ''significant progress
has been made. However, I sense and wholly agree with your
need to avoid wasting time, so I suggest that Pathologist Murchison makes its report to you in person rather than having it
relayed through myself, since you will doubtless have questions
and I, because of my selfish need to surround myself with pleasant emotional radiation, have the unfortunate habit of accentu-
ating the positive aspects of any situation.''

Lioren's original reason for wanting a private meeting with
Prilicla no longer seemed valid, and he could not reject the
other's suggestion without seriously embarrassing both himself
and the empath. He had the feeling, which was no doubt shared
by the empath, that somehow he had lost the initiative.

Pathologist Murchison was a warm-blooded oxygen-breather
of physiological classification DBDG with a body that, although
considerably shorter and less massive than Lioren's own, had
the soft, lumpy and top-heavy aspect of many of the Earth-
human females. It was Thornnastor's principal assistant, when
not required for special ambulance-ship duty, and its words were
clear and concise and its manner respectful without being sub-
servient. It also had the slightly irritating habit of answering
questions before Lioren could ask them.

The identification, isolation, and neutralization of other-
species pathogens, Pathologist Murchison said, was a routine
procedure for Thornnastor's department, but the behavioral
characteristics of the Cromsaggar virus—its mechanisms of
transmission, infection, incubation, and propagation—remained
undetectable to all of the normal investigative techniques. It was
only in recent days, when the discovery had been made that the

virus was either inherited at conception or transmitted by the mother prior to birth, that some progress had been made.

"The effects on the adult Cromsaggar are known to you," Murchison went on, "and the present indications are that every member of the species is infected. In the preterminal stage there is a livid rash and skin eruptions covering most of the body, accompanied by progressive and massive debilitation and lassitude which is sometimes overcome, temporarily, by strong emotional stimuli such as fear and danger. The effects on the children are less apparent and this led to the initial assumption that the young were immune, which they are not.

"We have since discovered," it continued, "that severe debility and lassitude are also present in the young, although it is difficult to be precise since we have no idea of how active a young, noninfected Cromsaggar should be. And, incredible though it might seem, neither can we be precise about the ages of these child patients. There is physiological and verbal evidence which suggests that many of them are not nearly as young as they appear, and that our age estimates should be extended by a factor of two or three because, in addition to its general debilitating effect, the plague retards the overall physiological development and greatly delays the onset of puberty. Probably there are psychological effects, as well, which might explain their grossly antisocial adult behavior, but again, this must remain speculative since you have yet to find a normal, disease-free Cromsaggar."

"I doubt whether such an entity exists," Lioren said. "But you spoke of having verbal as well as physiological evidence. These people absolutely refuse to give information about themselves. How was it obtained?"

"A large proportion of the cases you sent us were young or, as we now know, not yet physically mature," Murchison replied. "The adult patients remain completely uncooperative, but O'Mara was able to open dialogue with a few non-adults, who were much less reticent about themselves. Because of this immature viewpoint, adult motivations still remain unclear, and the picture of the Cromsaggar culture that is emerging is confusing and fraught with—"

"Pathologist Murchison," Lioren interrupted, "my interest is in the clinical rather than the cultural picture, so please confine yourself to that. My reason for asking *Rhabwar* to transfer so many young or not so young patients to the hospital was that they were among the large numbers left parentless or without adults to care for them. As well as suffering from undernourishment or exposure, conditions which are treatable, they displayed symptoms of respiratory distress associated with elevated temperature, or a wasting disease affecting the peripheral vascular and nervous systems. If Thornnastor's investigation into the plague is showing no results, what of these other and, I would think, clinically less complex conditions which seem to affect only the young?''

"Surgeon-Captain Lioren," the pathologist said, using Lioren's name and rank for the first time, "I did not say that no progress is being made.

"All of the non-adult cases are being investigated and significant progress is being made," it went on quickly. "In one of them, the condition presenting respiratory distress symptoms, there has been a minor but positive response to treatment. But the main effort is being directed toward finding a specific for the adult condition, because it has become evident that if the massive debilitation and growth-retarding effects of the plague were removed, the diseases currently afflicting the pre-adult Cromsaggar would be countered by their bodies' natural defense mechanisms and would no longer be life-threatening.''

If that much was known, Lioren thought, then progress was indeed being made.

"The trials conducted so far," Murchison continued, "have been inconclusive. Initially the medication was introduced in trace quantities and the patients' condition monitored routinely for fifty standard hours before the dosage was increased, until on the ninth day, within a few moments of the injection being given, both patients lost consciousness."

It paused for a moment to look at Prilicla then, seeming to receive a signal undetectable by Lioren, resumed. "Both patients were placed in isolation some distance from the others and each other. This was done so as to minimize same-species interference in their emotional radiation. Doctor Prilicla reported that the level of unconsciousness was extraordinarily deep, but that there was no sign of the subconscious distress that would have been present had they been drifting into termination. It suggested that the unconsciousness might be recuperative since it had many of the characteristics of sleep following a lengthy period of physical stress and that nutrient should be given intra-venously. A few days after this was done there was a minor remission of symptoms in both cases, and evidence of slight tissue regeneration, although both patients remained deeply un-conscious and in a critical condition.''

"Surely that means—!'' Lioren began, and broke off as Mur-chison held up one hand as if it and not himself had the rank. But suddenly he was too excited to verbally tear its insubordinate head off as he should.

"It means, Surgeon-Captain,'' Murchison said, "that we must proceed very carefully and, if the first two test subjects regain consciousness rather than drifting into termination, we must closely monitor their clinical and psychological condition before the trial is extended to the other patients. Diagnostician Thornnastor and everyone in its department believes, and Doc-tor Prilicla feels sure, that we are on the way to finding the cure. But until we are certain we must exercise patience for a time until—''

"How much time?'' Lioren demanded harshly.

Prilicla's fragile body was shaking as if a strong wind was blowing through the casualty deck, but Lioren could no more have controlled the emotional storm of impatience, eagerness, and excitement that raged within him than he could have flown on the empath's fragile wings. He would apologize to Prilicla later, but now all that he could think of was the steadily dwin-dling number of Cromsaggar who still clung to life on this plague world, and who might now have a chance to remain alive. More quietly, he asked, "How long must I wait?''

"I don't know, sir,'' the pathologist said. "I only know that *Tenelphi* has been ordered to remain at flight readiness at Sector General until the medication has been approved for general use, so as to bring you the first production batch without delay.''

Chapter 4

RHABWAR departed with its casualty deck filled principally with non-adult Cromsaggar. There were many adult cases in *Vespasian*'s sick bay—and in the widely dispersed medical stations that Lioren visited every day—who were in a much more serious condition, but the future survival of any species lay with its young, and those fortunate enough to be under the care of Thornnastor would be the first to be cured.

He ignored the polite but increasingly sarcastic messages from Colonel Skempton, the administrative head of Sector General, reminding him that the hospital was unable to accept the entire Cromsag population, depleted though it might be, for hospitalization, and that they had already received more than enough members of that species for the purposes of clinical investigation. The entire *Rhabwar* crew would have been aware of Skempton's uncoded messages and the pressure on ward accommodation that had prompted them, but Prilicla had raised no objections to transporting the additional twenty patients.

Prilicla must be the least objectionable entity in the known galaxy, Lioren thought, unlike the Cromsaggar, who were his patients but who would never be his friends—unless there was a species-wide personality reconstruction by the Galactic Federation's many deities, of whose existence he had the gravest doubts.

Nevertheless, he spent all of his time, when he was not engaged in eating or sleeping, visiting the worst of his massively unlikable patients or encouraging the two hundred Corps medics and food technicians scattered across the continent who were trying, not always with success, to keep them alive. Always he hoped for a change of attitude, a willingness to talk to him and give information that would enable him to help them or that a tiny crack would show in their impenetrable wall of noncooperation, but in vain. The Cromsaggar, adult and young alike, continued dying at a steadily increasing rate because, like Sector General, he did not have the facilities to feed intravenously the entire population.

Occasionally, and in spite of the surface and orbital surveillance, they managed to die at each others' hands.

It had happened while he had been flying over one of the forest settlements that had long since been searched and declared empty of intelligent life, but that must have been because the occupants had taken to the trees to elude the searchers. Lioren spotted the small-scale war being waged by six of them in a grassy clearing between two buildings. By the time the flier, which would have carried a crew of four Nidians had it not been for his long Tarlan legs, had circled back to land and Dracht-Yur had helped him extricate himself from the tiny vessel's seating, the hand-to-hand fighting was over and four Cromsaggar lay still on the ground.

In spite of the numerous bites and digitally inflicted wounds covering the bodies, they were able to identify them as three dead males and one female whose life expectancy would be measured in seconds. Dracht-Yur pointed suddenly to the ground nearby where two separate trails of crushed and blood-spattered grass converged toward the open door of one of the buildings.

The advantage of a longer stride meant that Lioren went through the entrance seconds ahead of the Nidian, and his first sight of the two writhing, bloody bodies locked together in mortal combat on the floor reinforced the anger and disgust he felt at such animal behavior between supposedly intelligent beings. Moving forward, he quickly interposed his medial arms between the tightly pressed bodies and tried to push them apart. Only then did he make the disconcerting discovery that they were not, as he had first thought, two males fighting each other to the death but a male and female indulging in a sexual coupling.

Lioren released them and backed away quickly, but suddenly they broke apart and launched themselves at him just as Dracht-Yur arrived and blundered into his rear legs. The weight of the combined attack toppled him over backward so that he sprawled flat on the floor with the two Cromsaggar on top of him and the Nidian somewhere underneath. Within moments he was fighting for his life.

After the first few days on Cromsag had shown the natives to be too severely weakened by the plague to warrant the use of heavy protective suits, all Corps personnel had taken to wearing their cooler and less restrictive shipboard coveralls, which gave protection only against the sun, rain, and insect bites.

It was with a sense of outrage that Lioren realized that for the first time in his life the hands—not to mention the feet, knees, and teeth—of another person had been raised in anger against him. On Tarla disputes were not settled in this barbaric fashion. And even though the number of his limbs equaled the total of theirs, they did not behave like plague-weakened Cromsaggar. They were inflicting serious damage to his body and causing him more pain than he had ever thought it possible to feel.

As he fended off the more disabling body blows and tried desperately to keep the two Cromsaggar from pulling off his dirigible eye-supports, Lioren was aware of Dracht-Yur wriggling from underneath him and crawling toward the door. He was pleased when his attackers ignored it, because the Nidian's small, furry limbs had neither the muscle power nor the reach to make a useful contribution to the struggle. A few seconds later he caught a glimpse of the Nidian's head enclosed by a transparent envelope, heard the expected soft explosion of a bursting sleep-gas bulb, and felt the bodies of his attackers go suddenly limp and collapse on top of him before rolling slowly onto the floor.

For the few moments that the bodies, covered as they were by livid patches of discoloration and the oozing sores characteristic of preterminal plague victims, made heavy and almost intimate contact with him, it was a great relief to remember that one world's pathogens were ineffective against the members of off-planet species.

Designed as it was for maximum effect on the Cromsaggar metabolism, the anesthetic gas produced similar if less immediate results on other warm-blooded oxygen-breathers. Lioren was unable to move, but he was aware of the Nidian growling and barking urgently into its headset while it applied dressings to the worst of his wounds. Presumably it was telling the pilot of their flier to send for medical assistance, but his own translator pack had been damaged in the struggle and he could not understand a word. This did not worry him unduly, because the intense discomfort of his many injuries had faded to the mildest

of irritations and the hard floor beneath him felt like the softest
of sleeping pits. But his mind was clear and seemed unwilling
to follow his body into sleep.

Interrupting the two Cromsaggar in the sex act had been a
serious mistake, but an understandable one because none of his
people had witnessed the occurrence of anything like a sexual
coupling since arriving on Cromsag, and everyone, himself included, had assumed that the species had become too physically
debilitated by the plague to make much of such activity possible.
And their reaction, the sheer strength and ferocity of their attack, had surprised and shocked him.

During the very short breeding season on Tarla such activity,
especially among the aging who had been lifemates for many
years, was a cause for celebration and public display rather than
a matter for concealment—although he knew that many species
within the Federation, races who were otherwise highly intelligent and philosophically advanced, considered the mating process to be a private matter between the beings concerned.

Naturally, Lioren had no personal experience in this area,
since his dedication to the healing arts precluded him indulging
in any pleasure which would allow emotional factors to affect
the clinical objectivity of his mind. If he had been an ordinary
Tarlan male, an artisan or a member of one of the noncelibate
professions interrupted in similar circumstances, there would
have been a verbal impoliteness, but certainly not violence.

Distressing and distasteful as the incident had been, Lioren's
mind would not rest in its search to find a reason for such an
unreasonable reaction, however alien or uncivilized that reason
might be. Could it be that, gravely ill and seriously injured as
they had been in the fighting outside, they had crawled into the
house to seek a moment of mutual pleasure together before dying? He knew that the coupling must have been by mutual agreement, because the Cromsaggar mechanics of reproduction were
physiologically too complicated for the attentions of one partner
to be forced on another.

That did not rule out the possibility that the coupling was the
end result of the fighting, the bestowal of a female's favor on a
warrior victorious in battle. There were many historical precedents for such behavior, although not, thankfully, in the history
of Tarla. But that reason was unsatisfactory because both male
and female Cromsaggar fought, although not each other.

Lioren made a mental note to prepare a detailed report of the incident for the cultural contact specialists who would ultimately have to produce a solution to the Cromsaggar problem, if any of the species survived and it was invited to join the Federation.

The four separate images of the room, including the one of Dracht-Yur working on the other casualties, that his immobilized eyes were still bringing him dimmed suddenly into blackness, and he remembered a feeling of mild irritation before he fell asleep in midthought.

Dracht-Yur confined him to the sick bay on *Vespasian* until the worst of his injuries healed, reminding him, as only a hairy, small-minded, and sarcastic dwarf of a Nidian could, that until then the relationship between them was one of doctor and patient and that in the present situation it was the Surgeon-Lieutenant who had the rank.

It could not, however, no matter how often it stressed the advisability of post-trauma rest and mental recuperation, bind Lioren's jaw closed or keep him from setting up a communication system by his bedside.

Time passed like a pregnant *strulmer* climbing uphill, and the medical situation on Cromsag worsened until the daily death rate climbed from one hundred to close on one-fifty, and still *Tenelphi* did not come. Lioren sent a necessarily brief hyperspace radio signal to Sector General, prerecorded and repeated many times so that its words could be reconstructed after fighting their way through the interference of the intervening stars, requesting news. He was not surprised when it was ignored, because the expenditure of power needed for a lengthy progress report would have been wasteful indeed. All that he was telling them was that he and the medical and support personnel on Cromsag were beginning to feel so helpless and angry and impatient that the condition verged on the psychotic, but the hospital probably already knew that.

Five days later he received a reply stating that *Tenelphi* had been dispatched and was estimating Cromsag in thirty-five hours. It was carrying medication, as yet incompletely tested for long-term effects, which was a specific against the grosser, more life-threatening symptoms of the plague, and that the details of the pathological investigation and directions for treatment accompanied the medication.

During the excitement that ensued Lioren went over his plans for fast distribution. Dracht-Yur relented to the extent of allowing him to transfer from sick bay to the communications center of *Vespasian*, but not to risk compounding his injuries by traveling the air or surface of Cromsag in vehicles totally unsuited to the Tarlan physiology. But the general feeling of relief and euphoria lasted only until the arrival of *Tenelphi*.

The scout ship carried more than enough of the antiplague specific, which required only a single, intravenous application, to treat every Cromsaggar on the planet, but Lioren was forbidden to use it until additional field trials had been carried out.

According to Chief Pathologist Thornnastor, the physiological results following a minimum dosage had been very good, but there were indications of possibly damaging side effects. Symptoms of mental confusion and periods of semiconsciousness had been observed. These might prove to be temporary, but further investigation was required.

The single injection was followed by a slight but continuing reduction in symptoms, a slow improvement in the vital signs, and evidence of tissue and organs regeneration throughout the body in the days which ensued. During the periods of semiconsciousness the test subjects had requested and consumed food in quantities which, considering stomach size and the clinical condition of the patients involved, seemed unusually large. There was a steady increase in body weight.

The non-adult subjects had responded in similar fashion, including the periods of unconsciousnessness interspersed with episodes of semiconsciousness and mental confusion, except that with the young the food demand in relation to their smaller size had been greater. Daily measurement had shown a steady increase in growth, both in body mass and limb dimensions.

It was thought probable that with the gradual remission of the condition the non-adult patients, whose physical growth had been retarded by the plague, were returning to optimum size for their ages. The periods of unconsciousness and impaired thinking were in response to a demand by the body for maximum rest during these periods of regeneration and were of little clinical importance. The medication was being used in minimum quantities, but a very small increase in the dosage of one test subject resulted in a strengthening and acceleration of the effects already noted. In spite of the excellent physiological results so far, the associated episodes of mental confusion were cause for concern lest a side effect of the medication led to long-term brain damage.

Thornnastor apologized for sending medication that it had not completely cleared for use, but said that Lioren's hyperspace radio signals had emphasized the urgency of the situation, and in order to save a few days' transit time between the medication's approval and its administration to the patients the final tests should be made concurrently on Cromsag and in Sector General.

"I have been instructed to conduct tests on a maximum of fifty Cromsaggar," Lioren said, when he was relaying Thornnastor's report to his senior medical officers. "The subjects are to include the widest possible variation in age and clinical condition, as well as minor variations in the dosage administered within that number. We are to pay particular attention to the mental state of these subjects during their periods of semiconsciousness, in the hope that their degree of confusion will be lessened when they are on their home world among others of their kind rather than in the strange and doubtless unsettling environment of Sector General. The initial test period will require ten days, followed by a further—"

"In ten days we would lose a quarter of the remaining population," Dracht-Yur broke in suddenly, its barking speech sounding angry even through the translator, "which has already shrunk to two-thirds of the number alive when *Tenelphi* found this Crutath-accursed planet. They're dying out there like, like . . ."

"That was my thought exactly," Lioren said, omitting the reprimand the Nidian deserved for its bad manners, and making a mental note to check on the meaning of the word "Crutath." "It is a thought which all of you share. But it is not because of our common feelings that I will disobey Thornnastor and ignore its recommendations. The decision is not yours. I will, of course, listen to your professional advice and accept it if it has merit, but the instruction to proceed and the responsibility for everything that ensues as a result will be entirely mine.

"This is what I am planning to do . . ."

There was no criticism of his plan because he had formulated it with great care and attention to detail, and—strangely, since it was coming from subordinates to a superior—the advice offered by many of them was personal rather than professional. They advised that he obey Thornnastor, but compromise by testing a few hundred, perhaps a thousand subjects instead of a mere fifty, saying that the course he was advocating would do nothing for any hopes he might have for future advancement. Lioren felt a strong temptation to do as they suggested, if only out of respect for the words of an entity said to be the foremost pathologist in the Federation rather than out of any selfish concern over his future career, but he was not sure that Diagnostician Thornnastor fully appreciated the urgency of the Cromsaggar problem. The hospital's Chief of Pathology was a perfectionist who would never allow imperfect work to leave its department, and giving Lioren permission to assist with the test program was probably the only compromise that it was capable of making. But a great, hulking Tralthan whose data-crammed mind, it was said, permanently accommodated the brain recordings of at least ten other-species medical authorities could be forgiven for a certain amount of mental confusion.

The Cromsaggar death rate was climbing steadily toward two hundred a day, and treating a mere fifty of them with an unnecessary degree of caution when virtually the entire population could be given the chance to live instead of dying in a lingering and painful manner was, to Lioren's mind, a great and a cowardly and a completely unacceptable wrong.

In this desperate situation he could accept imperfections even if Thornnastor's department could not. The psychological effects that accompanied the cure might be temporary, and even if they were not then they, too, might be curable in time. But if the worst should happen and permanent mental harm was the result, it was highly unlikely that the condition would be transmitted to an offspring, because O'Mara itself had stated that the damage was nonphysical. Any Cromsaggar child born of cured but mentally deficient parents would grow up healthy and sane.

Or as sane, Lioren thought, as it was possible for any member of this bloodthirsty race to be.

He had told his staff that it must be an operation combining maximum effort with maximum urgency, and that every single Cromsaggar on the planet must be treated for effect rather than submitting them to time-wasting trials, and within an hour of the meeting's end the plan was being implemented. On foot to the patients who were being housed close to the grounded *Ves-*

pasian, and by surface or air transport to the more distant shelters, the medication and supplies of synthetic nutrient were being distributed by every Monitor Corps entity available, which meant all but the capital ship's watch-keeping and communications officers and those charged with the maintenance of the air and surface vehicles. Lioren, whose injuries were still hampering his mobility, divided his attention between communications and the sick bay, where he was the only medic on duty.

The dosage administered varied in proportion to the age, body mass, and clinical condition of the patients. With the very young it was triple that recommended for trial purposes by Thornnastor, and, making due allowance for the potency of the medication, for those close to termination it was massive. Priority should have been given to the more serious cases, but there was so much variation in the degree of illness within small groups that it saved time if everyone was treated as and when they were encountered.

It quickly developed into a routine that was too frenetic to be described as boring. A few words of explanation and reassurance would be given, the single injection administered, and food and water placed within easy reach of the patient, who was usually too ill to make anything but a verbal objection; then it would be on to the next one.

By the end of the third day the entire population had been treated and the second phase began, that of visiting the patients, on a daily basis if possible, to replenish the consumables and observe and report on any change in their clinical condition. The medical and support staff worked day and night, eating infrequently of the same bland, synthetic food supplied to their patients and sleeping hardly at all. Increasing fatigue caused a forced landing and two ground-vehicle accidents, none of which involved fatalities, so that the ship's hospital no longer held only plague victims.

On the fourth day one of his adult Cromsaggar in sick bay terminated, but the number of deaths outside the ship went down to one hundred and fifteen. On the fifth day the figure had dropped to seven, and there were no fatalities reported on the sixth day.

Except for the difference in scale and the continuing effort needed to keep the widely dispersed patients supplied with food, the situation in sick bay reflected the clinical conditions outside.

As Thornnastor had predicted, a gradual remission in external symptoms was apparent and the food requirement of the adult patients had increased, and the fact that all of the food had been synthesized made no difference to their appetites. Much as he wanted to monitor their progress internally, they would not cooperate and refused to allow him to so much as touch them. With all of his medical staff and the majority of the ship's crew scattered across the continent, he thought it better not to force the issue, especially as the patients were growing stronger with every day that passed. In spite of the differences in body mass, the young were eating more than the adults, and, as Thornnastor had also observed, their rate of physical growth was phenomenal.

It was obvious that, in order to cause such a massive retardation of growth, the disease, which the Cromsaggar had acquired prenatally, must have involved the entire endocrine system. Now that the process was being reversed and they were not only growing but maturing, another, nonclinical change was occurring. The young patients who, once their initial fear had given way to curiosity and they had grown accustomed to his strange body and multiplicity of limbs, had spoken to him freely and with the unguarded enthusiasm of children were becoming increasingly reticent.

They were speaking to him less because, Lioren observed, their recovering elders were talking to them more. And they talked only when he was not present.

By then his Monitor Corps patients had been well enough to be discharged to continue their recuperation in their own quarters, so he did not know what the Cromsaggar talked about until one day, after replenishing the food supply and his few words of friendship and reassurance had been ignored, he deliberately left one of the sick-bay senders switched on Transmit so that he would be able to listen to them from his own quarters.

In the manner of all eavesdroppers, he fully expected to overhear unkind things about himself and the bad dreams from the sky, which was the literal translation of the Cromsaggar name for their rescuers. But he was completely wrong. Instead, they talked and chanted and sang together so that his translator was unable to separate the individual voices. It was only when a single Cromsaggar spoke out alone, an adult addressing one or more of the young, that Lioren realized what he was hearing.

It was part of an initiation ceremony, a preparation and for-
malized sex instruction given to the newly mature before entry
into adult life, including the behavior expected of them thereafter.

Lioren broke the connection hastily. The rite of passage into
adulthood was a highly sensitive area in the cultures of many
intelligent species, and one into which he was not qualified to
delve. If he were to continue listening out of mere lascivious
curiosity, he might find that he no longer respected himself.

He was relieved, nevertheless, that with the exception of two
very small children who were little more than infants, the sick
bay held only male Cromsaggar.

During the days that followed there were no organic fatalities
reported, but the air and surface vehicles, which had been in
continuous operation over eight days and nights, had not fared
so well. The food synthesizers on *Vespasian* and in the outlying
medical stations were running at maximum safe overload, a
condition that was not recommended for more than a few hours
at a time. All of the organic components were displaying signs
of stress and severe fatigue but were operating at close to optimum efficiency, even though they rarely talked to each other
and seemed to be asleep on their feet. It was becoming clear to
everyone concerned that the operation was a success and that
no member of the patient population was about to die, and that
knowledge was both the fuel and the lubrication which kept
them working.

It was irritating to all of them, but not important, that the
Cromsaggar showed no gratitude for what was being done for
them apart from demolishing the previous day's food supply.
The brief explanation of the treatment and reassurance regarding
their ultimate cure that was given at every visit to replenish
stores was ignored. The patients were not actively hostile, unless one of the medics tried to check on their vital signs or obtain
a blood sample, whereupon they reacted violently toward the
person concerned.

An ungrateful and unlikable race, Lioren thought, not for the
first time. But it was their physiology rather than their psychology which was his problem, and the problem was being solved.

From Sector General there was a continuing silence.

He could imagine Thornnastor's slow, careful progress, with
its relatively few patients, toward a stage in the treatment which

Lioren had already surpassed with the entire planetary population. It was no reflection on the Tralthan pathologist, who was,
after all, the entity responsible for producing the cure for the
plague. But if Lioren had not ignored its recommendations and
risked the displeasure of his superiors, many hundreds of Cromsaggar would have died by now. And without false modesty on
his part, the solution he had devised for the problem had been
truly elegant.

His calculated variation in the dosage administered, based as
it had been on age, body mass, and clinical factors, had insured
that the young and old alike were progressing toward a complete
cure at the same time. In spite of his insubordination, he was
sure that his action would merit praise rather than censure.

Early on the following day he sent a brief message to the
Monitor Corps base on Orligia, and copied to Sector General,
requesting additional food synthesizers and spares for the air
and ground transport units, adding that there had been no Cromsaggar fatalities for eight days and that a full report accompanied
by a medical officer with firsthand experience of the situation
was being sent with *Tenelphi* to the hospital. The request for
synthesizers combined with the sudden drop in the death rate
would tell Thornnastor what Lioren had done, and the scout
ship's medical officer would be able to fill in the details.

Dracht-Yur had been working well and very hard, and ordering its return to normal duties on *Tenelphi* would be both a rest
and a well-deserved reward for its efforts. It would also remove
the Surgeon-Lieutenant from the scene and thereby make it possible for Lioren, whose injuries were healing well, to escape the
little Nidian's irksome medical quarantine.

Before retiring that night Lioren posted the usual guard outside the sick bay, an unnecessary precaution because none of
the Cromsaggar had shown any interest in what lay beyond the
entrance, but necessary in Captain Williamson's opinion in case
one of the young ones decided to go exploring and injured itself
on ship equipment. Tomorrow he would fly to the outlying medical shelters and, for the first time since his embarrassing mishap
with the mating Cromsaggar, view the situation for himself.

He would be seeing, Lioren told himself with mixed feelings
of pleasure, pride, and self-congratulation, the final stages of
the cure of Cromsag.

Before he was due to board his flier next morning he visited sick bay to check on the condition of his patients, only to find the deck and walls splattered with Cromsaggar blood and all of the adults dead. The entrance guard, after succumbing to a violent attack of nausea, reported hearing quiet voices and chanting that had continued far into the night, followed by a period of unbroken silence which it had attributed to them being asleep. But from the condition of the bodies it was clear now that they had instead been fighting and silently kicking, biting, and tearing the lives out of each other until only two of the female infants survived.

Lioren was still trying to recover from the shock, and make himself believe that he was not asleep and having a particularly horrendous dream, when the wall speaker beside him came to sudden, noisy life. It said that he should go at once to the communications center and that the bloody, self-inflicted massacre in sick bay had been repeated all over Cromsag.

Very soon it became clear that Surgeon-Captain Lioren was responsible not for curing but for killing a planetary population.

Chapter 5

WHEN Lioren finished speaking there was complete stillness in the room. Even though all present were already aware of every harrowing detail of the Cromsag Incident and his responsibility for it, the mere repetition was enough to shock any civilized being into silence.

"The guilt in this matter is entirely mine," Lioren resumed, "and lest there be any doubt about this in anyone's mind, I ask Thornnastor, the Diagnostician-in-Charge of Pathology, to give its evidence."

The Tralthan lumbered forward on its six elephantine feet to take the witnesses position, and, fixing one eye each on the president of the court, Lioren, O'Mara, and its printed notes, it began to speak. Within a few minutes Fleet Commander Dermod was holding up one hand for silence.

"The witness is not obliged," it said, "to relate its evidence in such clinical detail. No doubt its medical colleagues would find it interesting but it is not understandable by the court. Please simplify your language, Diagnostician Thornnastor, and go to the explanation of why the Cromsaggar acted as they did."

Thornnastor stamped its two medial feet in a gesture which suggested impatience, but whose exact significance would have been clear only to another Tralthan, and said, "Very well, sir . . ."

Because of the more cautious approach to the trial program at Sector General and the consequently slower progress toward a complete cure, Thornnastor explained, the hypersignal from *Vespasian* was received in time to prevent a repetition of the catastrophe that had occurred on Cromsag. All of the Cromsaggar had been dispersed and confined to single quarters, and the Department of Other-species Psychology had intensified its efforts to overcome the fanatical noncooperation of the patients so that they would answer questions about themselves.

It was only when the decision had been made, very reluctantly and only after lengthy consideration of possible psychological damage, to tell the patients the whole truth of what had happened on their home planet, including the fact that they were the sole surviving adult members of their race, that they began to talk about themselves. There was much anger and recrimination, understandably, but enough information was provided to make possible the formation of a theory which was supported by the archeological evidence.

The best estimate was that the plague had made its first appearance just under one thousand years ago, when the Cromsaggar level of technological and philosophical advancement included atmospheric flight and a culture that no longer practiced war. No information was available regarding the origin and evolution of the disease other than that it was transmitted by either parent during sexual coupling and, in the beginning, its effects had been mild and embarrassing rather than life-threatening. The majority of the Cromsaggar did not travel widely, and they took their sexual bondings, once formed, very seriously and did not stray in this respect, either. A number of the more farsighted Cromsaggar formed communities that were plague-free, but the mating process depended on emotional rather than medical factors and eventually the disease broached this immaterial defense. Another three centuries were to pass before the plague spread unchecked across all of Cromsag to infect every member of the population, adult and child alike. By that time it had increased in virulence, and deaths in middle age were becoming common.

The continuing efforts of the medical scientists were of no avail, and by the end of the following century their civilization had receded to pretechnology levels with no hope of a revival, and it was rare for anyone to live more than a decade past maturity. As a race, the Cromsaggar were facing extinction, a very early extinction because of the effect of the plague on the birth rate.

"The complete symptomology of the disease," Thornnastor said, "including the endocrinological involvement with its effect on the sufferers' rate of growth and maturation, has already been studied and can be discussed at length, but I shall summarize and simplify for the benefit of the court.

"Among the adults of both sexes," it went on, "the visually and tactually unpleasant skin condition was one factor in the reducing birth rate, but it was a minor one. Even if the tegument of both partners was flawless and aesthetically pleasing, the greatly reduced performance of the endocrine system is such that the act of sexual coupling and conception is impossible without an abnormal level of prior emotional stimulation."

Thornnastor paused. It did not possess the kind of features which could change expression, but it was as if the mind-pictures it was seeing inside its great, immobile dome of a head had made further speech impossible for a moment. Then it went on. "Efforts were made to circumvent this difficulty by medical means, and by the use of substances derived from naturally occurring vegetation which heightened the senses or had hallucinatory effects. These methods proved ineffective and were discarded because of problems of irreversible addiction, death from overdose, and seriously deformed and nonviable offspring. The solution that was ultimately found was nonmedical and involved a deliberate regression in social behavior to the dark ages of their history.

"The Cromsaggar went to war . . ."

It was not a war fought for reasons of territorial expansion or trade advantage, and neither was it fought at a distance from fortified positions or by warriors acting in concert or protected by armored machines or equipment, and it was a war not waged to the death because there was no intention on either side of killing an opponent who might very well be a family member or a friend. In fact, there were no sides because it was fought hand to hand between pairs of unarmed individuals, and it was a war whose sole purpose was to cause the maximum of fear, pain, and danger, but if possible, not death to the combatants. There was no threat or danger from a beaten and seriously wounded opponent and, even though they had been trying desperately to kill each other moments before, the vanquished were left where they lay, hopefully to recover from their wounds to fight and instill fear in an opponent another day.

Life was rare and precious to the Cromsaggar, rarer and more precious with every dwindling generation that passed; otherwise they would not have tried so hard to keep their race alive.

For it was only by overloading the sensorium with pain and intense muscular effort and subjecting themselves to the highest possible levels of emotional stress that endocrine systems rendered dormant by the effects of the plague could be roused into something like normal activity, and remain so, aside from the wounds that had been sustained, for the time necessary for a successful coupling and procreation to take place.

But in spite of the terrible solution that had been found, adult deaths from the plague continued to rise and the birth rate to fall. The population contracted in numbers and territory occupied, moving to one continent so as to conserve what little was left of their civilization and resources and to be within easy fighting distance of each other. There was archeological evidence to suggest that in the beginning the Cromsaggar were not warlike, but the need to fight and often kill each other so that their race as a whole could survive made them so, and by the time *Tenelphi* discovered them, the practice of hand-to-hand combat among all adults had been conditioned into the race for many centuries.

"Even though the decision was taken for the best of all clinical reasons, that of saving many lives," Thornnastor went on, "without prior knowledge of this conditioning, the effect of introducing a complete and short-duration cure for the plague could not have been foreseen. It is probable, and Chief Psychologist

O'Mara agrees with me in this, that the Cromsaggar who had been treated were aware of feeling better and stronger than they had ever felt before, and subconsciously they must have realized that it was no longer necessary for them to fight and place themselves in the greatest possible danger in order to achieve sexual arousal. But for many centuries they had been taught from an early age that single combat between members of one's own sex invariably preceded coupling with one of the opposite, a level of conditioning with the strength of an evolutionary imperative. And so, the more their clinical condition improved the greater was their urge to fight and procreate. The many young, whose physical development had been retarded by the effects of the plague and who had suddenly come to maturity, felt the same compulsion to fight.

"But the real tragedy," the Tralthan continued, "lay in the fact that individually and as a group they were fully cured, and stronger than any Cromsaggar had been since the coming of the plague. Previously they had been weak, diseased, and able to expend only a small fraction of the physical effort of which they were now capable. Their newfound strength reduced the personal fear of pain and death, and made it difficult to calibrate the levels of damage inflicted on and by opponents who were so strong and evenly matched. The result was that they killed each other, every single adult on Cromsag, leaving only the infants and children alive.

"Briefly and simply," Thornnastor ended, "that is the background to the Cromsag Incident."

The silence that followed Thornnastor's words lengthened and deepened until the faint, bubbling sound made by the refrigerated life-support system of an SNLU in the audience seemed loud. It was like the Tarlan Silence of Remembrance after the passing of a friend, except here it was the population of a world that had died and it seemed that no person present was going to break it.

"With respect to the court," Lioren said suddenly, "I ask that the trial be ended here and now, without further argument and waste of time. I stand accused of genocide through negligence. I am guilty without doubt or question and the responsibility and the guilt are entirely mine. I demand the death penalty."

O'Mara rose to his feet before Lioren had finished speaking.

The Chief Psychologist said, "The defense would like to correct the accused on one very important point. Surgeon-Captain Lioren did not commit genocide. When the incident occurred it reacted quickly and correctly in the circumstances, by warning the hospital and organizing the rescue and care of the newly orphaned Cromsaggar children, this in spite of the fact that many of its own people had been so taken by surprise that they were unable to use the gas in time, and who were seriously injured in attempts to stop the fighting. During this period the Surgeon-Captain's behavior was exemplary and, although the witnesses are not here present, their evidence was presented to and accepted by the civil court on Tarla and is on record—"

"The evidence is not disputed," Lioren broke in impatiently. "It is not relevant."

"As a result of this timely warning and subsequent actions," O'Mara continued, ignoring the interruption, "the adult Cromsaggar under treatment here were separated before they could attack each other, and the young, both here and on Cromsag, were saved. Altogether thirty-seven adults and two hundred and eighty-three children, with a roughly equal distribution of sex, are alive and well. I have no doubt that, after a lengthy period of reeducation, resettlement, and specialized assistance in breaking their conditioning, Cromsag will be repopulated, and, now that the plague has been removed, its people will return to living together in peace.

"It is understandable that the accused should feel an overwhelming guilt in this matter," the psychologist went on in a quieter voice. "Had that not been so, it would not have caused this court-martial to be convened. But it is possible that the great guilt that it feels over the Cromsag Incident, together with its urgent need to discharge that guilt and its impatience to receive punishment for the alleged crime, has caused it to exaggerate its case. As a psychologist I can understand and sympathize with its feelings, and with its attempts to escape the burden of its guilt. And I am sure that there is no need to remind the court that, among the sixty-five intelligent species who make up the Galactic Federation, not one of them practices judicial execution or physical chastisement during confinement."

"You are correct, Major O'Mara," the fleet commander said. "The reminder is unnecessary and time-wasting. Make your point briefly."

The color of O'Mara's facial skin deepened slightly, and it said, "The Cromsaggar are not extinct, and they will continue to survive as a race. Surgeon-Captain Lioren is guilty of exaggeration, but not genocide."

All at once Lioren felt anger, despair, and a terrible fear. He kept one eye on O'Mara and directed the other three individually toward the officers of the court and forced calmness and clarity onto his mind as he said, "The exaggeration, this small inaccuracy that was intended only as a simplification of a terrible truth, is unimportant because the enormity of my guilt is beyond measure. And I should have no need to remind Major O'Mara of the punishment, the destruction of a medic's professional future rather than life, which is meted out to any member of the staff whose carelessness or lack of observation leads to the clinical deterioration or death of a patient.

"I am guilty of negligence," Lioren went on, wishing that the translator could reproduce the desperation in his voice, "and the defense counsel's attempt to belittle and excuse what I have done is ridiculous. The fact that others, including the hospital personnel concerned with the trials of the medication, were also surprised by the Cromsaggar behavior is not an excuse. I should not have been surprised, because all the information was available to me, all the clues to the puzzle were there if I had correctly read the signs. I did not read them because I was blinded by pride and ambition, because a part of my mind was thinking that a rapid and total cure would enhance my professional reputation. I did not read them because I was negligent, unobservant, and mentally fastidious in refusing to listen to patients' conversations relating to Cromsaggar sex practices which would have given a clear warning of what was to happen, and because I was impatient of superiors who were advocating caution—"

"Ambition, pride, and impatience," O'Mara said, rising quickly to its feet, "are not crimes. And surely it is the degree of professional negligence, if any, that the court must punish, not the admittedly terrible and far-reaching effects of what is at most a minor transgression."

"The court," Fleet Commander Dermod said, "will not allow counsel to dictate to it, nor will it allow another such interruption of the prosecution's closing statement. Sit down, Major. Surgeon-Captain Lioren, you may proceed."

The guilt and the fear and the desperation were filling Lioren's mind so that the finely reasoned arguments he had prepared were lost and forgotten. He could only speak simply of how he felt and hope that it would be enough.

"There is little more to add," he said. "I am guilty of a terrible wrong. I have brought about the deaths of many thousands of people, and I do not deserve to live. I ask the court for mercy, and for the death sentence."

Again O'Mara rose to its feet. "I am aware that the prosecution is allowed the last word. But with respect, sir, I have made a detailed submission regarding this case to the court, a submission which I have not had the opportunity of introducing for discussion."

"Your submission was received and has been given due consideration," the fleet commander said. "A copy was made available to the accused, who, for obvious reasons, chose not to introduce it. And may I remind defense counsel that it is I who will have the last word. Please sit down, Major. The court will confer before passing sentence."

The misty gray hemisphere of a hush field appeared around the three officers of the court, and it seemed that everyone else might have been enclosed in the same zone of silence as their eyes turned on Lioren. In spite of it being at extreme range for an empath, at the rear of the audience he could see Prilicla trembling. But this was not a time when he could control his emotional radiation. When he remembered the contents of O'Mara's submission to the court, he felt the most dreadful extremes of fear and despair overwhelming his mind and, for the first time in his life, an anger so great that he wanted to take the life of another intelligent being.

O'Mara saw one of his eyes looking in its direction and moved its head slightly. It was not an empath, Lioren knew, but it must be a good enough psychologist to know what was in Lioren's mind.

Suddenly the hush field went down and the president of the court leaned forward in its chair.

"Before pronouncing sentence," the fleet commander said, looking toward O'Mara, "the court wishes clarification and reassurance from defense counsel regarding the accused's probable behavior in the event of a custodial rather than the death sentence being imposed. Bearing in mind Surgeon-Captain

Lioren's present mental state, isn't it likely that either sentence would quickly result in the accused's death?''

O'Mara rose again. Its eyes were on Lioren rather than the fleet commander as it said, ''In my professional opinion, having observed the accused during its training here and studying its behavior subsequent to the Cromsag Incident, it would not. The Surgeon-Captain is an ethical and highly moral being who would consider it dishonorable to escape what it will consider to be a justly imposed punishment for its crime by means of suicide, even though a custodial sentence would be the harshest, in terms of continued mental distress, that could be imposed. However, as the court will recall from my submission, I prefer the term 'remedial' to 'custodial.' To reiterate, the accused would not kill itself but it would, as you have already gathered, be most grateful if the court would do the job for it.''

''Thank you, Major,'' the fleet commander said; then it turned to face Lioren.

''Surgeon-Captain Lioren,'' it said, ''this court-martial upholds the earlier verdicts of your own civil and medical courts on Tarla, your home world, and finds you guilty of an excusable error in observation and judgment which led, regrettably, to a major catastrophe. Although it would be kinder in the circumstances to do so, we will not depart from Federation judicial practice of three centuries, or waste a potentially valuable life should the therapy prove successful, by imposing the death sentence that you so plainly desire. Instead you are to be given a custodial and remedial sentence of two years, stripped of your Monitor Corps and medical rank, and forbidden to leave this hospital, which is an establishment large enough for your confinement not to prove irksome. For obvious reasons you are also forbidden access to the Cromsaggar ward. You will be placed in the charge and under the direction of Chief Psychologist O'Mara. In that time the major expects to bring about a psychological and emotional readjustment which will enable you to begin a new career.

''You have the court's deepest sympathy, ex-Surgeon-Captain Lioren, and its best wishes.''

Chapter 6

LIOREN stood on the clear area of floor in front of O'Mara's desk, surrounded on three sides by the strangely shaped furniture designed for the comfort of physiological classifications other than his own, and stared down at the psychologist with all of his eyes. Since the imposition of the sentence and a regimen that nothing in his power could change, the intensity of his feelings toward the stocky little biped with its gray head fur and eyes that never looked away had diminished from a life-threatening hatred to a level of dislike so deeply etched into Lioren's mind that he did not believe that it could ever be erased.

"Liking me is not a prerequisite of the treatment, fortunately," O'Mara said, seeming to read Lioren's mind; "otherwise Sector General would be without its medical staff. I have made myself responsible for you and, having read a copy of my written submission to the court-martial, you are aware of my reasons for doing so. Need I restate them?"

O'Mara had argued that the principal reason for what had happened on Cromsag had been due to certain character defects in Lioren, faults which should have been detected and corrected during its other-species medical training at Sector General, and this was an omission for which the Psychology Department was entirely to blame. That being the case, and bearing in mind the fact that Sector General was not a psychiatric hospital, Lioren could be considered as a trainee who had not satisfactorily completed its training in other-species relations rather than a patient, and be attached to the Psychology Department under O'Mara's supervision. In spite of his proven medical and surgical ability with many life-forms, as a trainee he would have less status than a qualified ward nurse.

"No," Lioren said.

"Good," O'Mara said. "I dislike wasting time, or people. At present I have no specific orders for you other than that you will move freely within the hospital, initially with an escort from this department, or, if there are times when this causes an unacceptable level of embarrassment or distress, you will perform routine office tasks. These will include you familiarizing yourself with the work of the department and the medical staff psych files, most of which will be opened to you for study. Should you uncover any evidence of unusual behavior, uncharacteristic reactions toward other-species staff members, or unexplained reductions in professional standards, you will report it to me, having first discussed it with one of your department colleagues to insure that it is worth my attention.

"It is important to remember," the psychologist went on, "that with the exception of a few of the most gravely ill patients, everyone in the hospital knows all about your case. Many of them will ask questions, polite and considerate questions for the most part, except the Kelgians, who do not understand the concept of politeness. You will also receive many well-intentioned offers of help and encouragement and much sympathy."

O'Mara paused for a moment; then, in a softer voice, it continued. "I shall do everything that I can to help you. Truly, you have suffered and are suffering a great mental anguish, and laboring under a burden of guilt greater than any I have encountered in the literature or in my own long experience; a load so heavy that any other mind but yours would have been utterly destroyed by it. I am greatly impressed by your emotional control and horrified at the thought of your present level of mental distress. I shall do everything possible to relieve it and I, too, who am in the best position of anyone other than yourself to understand the situation, offer you my sympathy.

"But sympathy," it went on, "is at best a palliative treatment, and one which diminishes in effect with repeated application. That is why I am applying it on this one and only occasion. Henceforth, you will do exactly as you are told, perform all the routine, menial, boring tasks set you, and you will receive no sympathy from anyone in this department. Do you understand me?"

"I understand," Lioren said, "that my pride must be humbled and my crime punished, for that is what I deserve."

O'Mara made an untranslatable sound. "What you think you

deserve, Lioren. When you begin to believe that you might *not*
deserve it, you will be well on the way to recovery. And now I
will introduce you to the staff in the outer office.''

As O'Mara had promised, the work of the office was routine
and repetitious, but during the first few weeks it was still too
new for him to find it boring. Apart from the periods spent
sleeping, or at least resting, or using his room's food dispenser,
Lioren had not left the department, nor had he exercised anything but his brain. His concentration on the new duties was
total, and as a result the quality, quantity, and his understanding
of the work increased to the point where it drew praise from
both Lieutenant Braithwaite and Trainee Cha Thrat, although
not from Major O'Mara.

The Chief Psychologist never praised anyone, it had told him,
because its job was to shrink heads, not swell them. Lioren
could not make any clinical or semantic sense of the remark and
decided that it must be what the Earth-human DBDGs called a
joke.

Lioren could not ignore his growing curiosity about the two
beings with whom he was spending so much time, but the psych
files of departmental personnel were closed to each other, and
they neither asked personal questions nor answered any about
themselves. Possibly it was a departmental rule, or O'Mara had
told them to keep a rein on their natural curiosity out of consideration for Lioren's feelings, but then one day Cha Thrat suggested that the rule did not apply outside the office.

''You should forget that display screen for a while, Lioren,''
the Sommaradvan said as it was about to leave for its midday
meal, ''and rest your mind from Cresk-Sar's interminable student progress reports. Let's refuel.''

Lioren hesitated for a moment, thinking about the permanently crowded dining hall for the hospital's warm-blooded
oxygen-breathers and the people he would have to meet in the
busy corridors between. Lioren was not sure if he was ready for
that.

Before he could reply, Cha Thrat said, ''The catering computer has been programmed with a full Tarlan menu, synthetic,
of course, but much better than that tasteless stodge the room
dispensers dish out. That computer must be feeling hurt, ag-

grieved, even insulted at being ignored by the only Tarlan on the staff. Why not make it happy and come along?"

Computers did not have feelings, and Cha Thrat must know that as well as he did. Perhaps it was making a Sommaradvan joke.

"I will come," Lioren said.

"So will I," Braithwaite said.

It was the first time in Lioren's experience that the outer office had been left unattended, and he wondered if one or both of them were risking O'Mara's displeasure by doing so. But their behavior on the way to the dining hall, and the firm but unobtrusive manner in which they discouraged any member of the medical staff who seemed disposed to stop him and talk, made it plain that they were acting with the Chief Psychologist's approval. And when they found three vacant places at a table designed for the use of Melfan ELNTs, Braithwaite and Cha Thrat made sure that he remained between them. The other occupants, five Kelgian DBLFs noisily demolishing the character of some unnamed Charge Nurse as they were rising to leave, could not be avoided. Nothing was proof against Kelgian curiosity.

"I am Nurse Tarsedth," one of them said, turning its narrow, conical head to point in Lioren's direction. "Your Sommaradvan friend knows me well, since we trained together, but does not recognize me because it insists that, in spite of having four eyes, it cannot tell Kelgians apart. But my questions are for you, Surgeon-Captain. How are you feeling? Does your guilt manifest itself in bouts of psychosomatic pain? What therapy has O'Mara devised for you? Is it effective? If not, is there anything I can do to help?"

Suddenly Braithwaite started making untranslatable sounds, and its facial coloring had changed from pinkish yellow to deep red.

Tarsedth looked at it briefly, then said, "This often happens when the food and air passages share a common entrance channel. Anatomically, the Earth-human DBDG life-form is a mess."

Anatomically, Lioren thought as he tried hard to concentrate on the questioner in an attempt to avoid the pain that its questions were causing, the Kelgian was beautiful. It was physiological classification DBLF, warm-blooded, oxygen-breathing, multipedal, and with a long, flexible cylindrical body covered overall by highly mobile, silvery fur. The fur moved continually in slow ripples from its conical head right down to the tail, and with tiny cross-eddies and wavelets appearing as if the incredibly fine pelt were a liquid stirred by an unfelt wind. It was that fur which explained, and excused, the other's rude and direct approach to what it must know to be a sensitive subject.

Because of inadequacies in the Kelgian speech organs, their spoken language lacked modulation, inflection, and any emotional expression, but they were compensated by the fur, which acted, so far as another Kelgian was concerned, as a perfect but uncontrollable mirror of the speaker's emotional state. As a result the concept of lying or being diplomatic, tactful, or even polite was completely alien to them. A Kelgian said exactly what it meant or felt because its fur revealed its feelings from moment to moment, and to do otherwise would have been considered a stupid waste of time. The opposite also held true, because politeness and the verbal circumlocutions used by many other species simply confused and irritated them.

"Nurse Tarsedth," Lioren said suddenly, "I am feeling very unwell, but on the psychological rather than the physical level. The therapy O'Mara is using in my case is not yet clear to me, but the fact that I have visited the dining hall for the first time since the trial, even though accompanied by two protectors, suggests that it is beginning to work, or that my condition may be improving in spite of it. If your questions are prompted by more than mere curiosity and the offer of help intended to be taken as more than a verbal kindness, I suggest that you ask for details of the therapy and its progress, if any, from the Chief Psychologist."

"Are you stupid?" the Kelgian said, its silvery pelt tufting suddenly into spikes. "I would not dare ask a question like that. O'Mara would tear my fur off in small pieces!"

"Probably," Cha Thrat said as Tarsedth was leaving, "without benefit of anesthetic."

Their food trays slid from the table's delivery recess to the accompaniment of an audible signal that kept him from hearing the Kelgian's reply. Braithwaite said, "So that's what Tarlans eat," and thereafter kept its eyes averted from Lioren's platter.

In spite of having to eat and speak with the same orifice, the Earth-human kept up a continuous dialogue with Cha Thrat, during which they both left conversational gaps enticingly open so that Lioren could join in. Plainly they were doing their best both to put him at ease and keep his attention from the nearby tables where everyone was watching him, but, with a member of a species who had to make a conscious mental effort *not* to look in every direction at once, they were having little success. It was also plain that he was undergoing psychotherapy of a not very subtle form.

He knew that Cha Thrat and Braithwaite were fully informed about his case, but they were trying to make him repeat the information verbally so as to gauge his present feelings about himself and those around him. The method they were using was to exchange what appeared to be highly confidential and often personal information about themselves, their past lives, their personal feelings about the department and toward O'Mara and other entities on the hospital staff with whom they had had pleas- ant or unpleasant contact, in the hope that Lioren would recip- rocate. He listened with great interest but did not speak except in answer to direct questions from them or from staff members who stopped from time to time at their table.

Questions from the silver-furred Kelgians he answered as simply and directly as they were asked. To the shy well-wishings of a massive, six-legged Hudlar whose body was covered only by a recently applied coat of nutrient paint and the tiny ID patch of an advanced student nurse he replied with polite thanks. He also thanked an Earth-human called Timmins, wearing a Mon- itor Corps uniform with Maintenance insignia, who hoped that the Tarlan environment in his quarters had been properly repro- duced, and said that if there was anything else that would make him feel more comfortable he should not hesitate to ask for it. A Melfan wearing the gold-edged band of a Senior Physician on one crablike arm stopped to say that it was pleased to see him making use of the dining hall, because it had wanted to speak to the Tarlan but that, regrettably on this occasion, it was due in ELNT Surgery. Lioren told it that he intended using the dining hall regularly in the future and that there would be other oppor- tunities to talk.

That reply seemed to please Braithwaite and Cha Thrat, and when the Melfan Senior left them they resumed the conversation whose gaps Lioren steadfastly refused to fill. If he had chosen to speak and reveal his feelings just then, it would have been to say that, having been condemned to live for the terrible crime he had committed, he must accept as part of the punishment these constant reminders of his guilt.

He did not think they would be pleased to hear that.

The members of the Psychology Department, Lioren discovered, were free to move anywhere within the hospital and talk to or question, at any time which did not adversely affect the performance of the individual's professional duties, everyone from the lowest trainee nurse or maintenance person up to the near godlike Diagnosticians themselves, and it came as no surprise that their authority to pry into everyone else's most private and personal concerns made them very few friends among the staff. The surprises were the manner in which these multispecies psychologists were recruited and their prior professional qualifications, if any.

O'Mara had joined Sector General shortly before it had been commissioned, as a structural engineer, and the work it had done among the original staff and patients that resulted in its promotion to major and Chief Psychologist was no longer open for study, although there was a rumor that it had once wet-nursed an orphaned infant Hudlar unaided and without benefit either of heavy-lifting machinery or translation devices, but that story Lioren considered to be too wildly improbable to have any basis in fact.

From the words spoken and unspoken it seemed that Lieutenant Braithwaite's career had begun in the Corps's Other-Species Communications and Cultural Contact Division, where initially it had shown great promise and an even greater impatience with its superiors. It was enthusiastic, dedicated, self-reliant, and intuitive where its work was concerned, and whether its intuition proved trustworthy, as happened in the majority of cases, or unsafe, the result was deeply stressful to those in authority. Its attempt to expedite the First Contact procedure on Keran by circumventing the philosophically conservative priesthood caused a citywide religious riot in which many Keranni were killed and injured. Thereafter it was disciplined before being transferred to a number of subordinate administrative positions, none of which proved suitable either to Braithwaite or its superiors, before coming to Sector General. For a short time it was attached to the Maintenance Department's internal-communications section until, in an attempt to rewrite and simplify the multispecies translation program, it knocked down the main computer and left the entire hospital staff and patients unable to do anything but bark, gobble, or cheep unintelligibly at each other for several hours. Colonel Skempton had been less impressed by what Braithwaite had hoped to do than by the havoc it had caused, and was about to banish it to the loneliest and most distant Monitor Corps outpost in the Federation when O'Mara had intervened on its behalf.

Similarly, Cha Thrat's career had been beset by personal and professional difficulties. It was the first and so far only Sommaradvan female to qualify and practice as a warrior-surgeon, a position of great eminence in a profession which was otherwise exclusively male. Lioren was unsure of what a warrior-surgeon of that planet was supposed to be or do, but it had been able to treat successfully a member of an off-planet species, an Earth-human Monitor Corps officer very seriously injured in a flier crash, that Cha Thrat had encountered for the first time. Impressed by its surgical skills and flexibility of mind, the Corps had offered it the opportunity of training in multispecies surgery at Sector Twelve General Hospital. Cha Thrat had accepted because, unlike on its home world, the other-species doctors there would judge it on professional merit without caring whether it was male or female.

But the intense dedication and rigorous clinical disciplines of a warrior-surgeon of Sommaradva, which in many respects resembled those of Lioren's own Tarlan medical fraternity, were not those of Sector General. Cha Thrat did not go into the details of its misdemeanors, suggesting instead that any member of the staff would be eager to satisfy Lioren's curiosity in the matter, but the impression given was that as a trainee it had exercised its clinical initiative too freely, and too often proved its nominal superiors wrong. After one particular incident during which it had temporarily lost one of its own limbs, no ward in the hospital would accept it for training and it, like Braithwaite, had been transferred to Maintenance until a major act of insubordination warranted by the clinical situation at the time brought about its dismissal. And, again like Braithwaite, it was O'Mara who had kept Cha Thrat from leaving the hospital by recruiting it for the department.

As the conversation that was designed both to inform and to draw him out continued, Lioren felt a growing sympathy for these two entities. Like himself they had been cursed with too much intelligence, individuality, and initiative and had suffered grievously thereby.

Naturally, their crimes were insignificant compared with Lioren's own, because they were psychologically flawed misfits rather than criminals and not fully responsible for the wrongs they had done. But were they confessing those misdeeds to him in the form of an apparently unimportant exchange of gossip, ostensibly so that he would better understand them and the situation within the department? Or was it an attempt to assuage their own guilt by trying to help him? He could not be sure because they were concealing their true feelings, unlike himself, by talking too much rather than by remaining silent. The thought that they might not be suffering at all, that their efforts to help Lioren and their other department duties made them forget their past misdeeds came to trouble him, but he dismissed the idea as ridiculous. One could no more forget a past crime than one's own name.

"Lioren," Braithwaite said suddenly. "You are not eating and neither are you talking to us. Would you prefer to return to the office?"

"No," Lioren said, "not immediately. It is clear to me that this visit to the dining hall was a psychological test and that my words and behavior have been closely observed. You have also, almost certainly as part of the test, been answering questions about yourselves without my having to ask them, some of them personal questions which I would have considered it most impolite to ask. Now I will ask one question directly of you. As a result of these observations, what are your conclusions?"

Braithwaite remained silent, but with a small movement of its head indicated that Cha Thrat was to answer.

"You have heard and will understand," the Sommaradvan said, "that I am a warrior-surgeon forbidden to practice my true art and am not yet a fully-qualified wizard. For this reason the spells that I cast lack subtlety, as your words have already shown, and are quite transparent. There is a risk that my observations and conclusions, too, may be oversimplified and inaccurate. They are that my spell aimed at bringing you out of the seclusion of the office and your quarters to the dining hall was unsuccessful in that you reacted calmly and with no apparent emotional distress to the entities who approached you. It was unsuccessful in that it did not overcome your unwillingness to reveal personal feelings, which was another and more important purpose of the test. My conclusion is that any future visits to the dining hall should be unaccompanied unless the accompaniment be for social rather than therapeutic reasons."

Braithwaite nodded its head in the Earth-human gesture of silent agreement. "As the subject of this partially successful test, Lioren, what are your own conclusions about it? Express your feelings about that, at least, freely as would a Kelgian, and do not spare ours."

Lioren was silent for a moment, then said, "I feel curious as to why, in this age of advanced medicine and technology, Cha Thrat considers itself to be a wizard, unqualified or otherwise. I also feel surprise and concern regarding the personal information you have revealed to me. At the risk of being grossly offensive, I can only conclude that . . . Is the Psychology Department staffed with insubordinate misfits and entities with a history of emotional disturbance?"

Cha Thrat made an untranslatable sound and the Earth-human barked softly.

"Without exception," Braithwaite said.

Chapter 7

NEVER in all his long years as a student on Tarla and during his advanced training at Sector General had Lioren been given such a woolly-minded and imprecise set of instructions.

Surely Major O'Mara, who was reputed to possess one of the finest and most analytical minds in the hospital, should not be capable of issuing such instructions. Not for the first time Lioren wondered if the Chief Psychologist, charged as it was with the heavy responsibility of maintaining the mental health of close on ten thousand medical and maintenance staff belonging to sixty-odd different species, had been affected by one of the nonphysical maladies it was expected to treat. Or was it simply that Lioren, as the department's most recent and least knowledgeable recruit, had misunderstood the other's words?

"For my own mental clarification and to reduce the possibility of misunderstanding," Lioren said carefully, "may I repeat my instructions aloud?"

"If you think it necessary," the Chief Psychologist replied. From Lioren's growing experience of reading Earth-human voice sounds and the expressions on their flabby, yellow-pink faces, he knew that O'Mara was losing patience.

Ignoring the nonverbal content of the response, Lioren said, "I am to observe Senior Physician Seldal, for as long and as often as the subject's duty schedule and my other work allows, without drawing attention to the fact that it is under observation. I am to look for evidence of abnormal or uncharacteristic behavior even though you are aware that, to a Tarlan BRLH like myself, normal and characteristic behavior in a Nallajim of physiological classification LSVO would appear equally strange to me. I am to do this without any prior indication of what it is that I am to look for or, indeed, if there is anything to look for in the first place. If I am able to detect such behavior, I should try, covertly, to discover the reason for it, and my report should include suggestions for remedial treatment.

"But what," he went on when it was clear that the other was not going to speak, "if I cannot detect any abnormality?"

"Negative evidence," O'Mara said, "can also be valuable."

"Is it your intention that I proceed in complete ignorance," Lioren asked, anger making him forget for a moment the deference due to a nominal superior, "or will I be allowed to study the subject's psych file?"

"You may study it to your heart's content," O'Mara said. "And if you have no further questions, Charge Nurse Kursenneth is waiting."

"I have an observation and a question," Lioren said quickly. "This seems to me to be a particularly imprecise method of briefing a trainee on his first case. Surely I should be given some indication of what is wrong with Seldal. I mean, what did the Senior Physician do to arouse your suspicions in the first place?"

O'Mara exhaled noisily. "You have been assigned the Seldal case, and you have not been told what to do because I don't know what to do with it, either."

Lioren made a surprised sound which did not translate and said, "Does the possibility exist that the most experienced other-species psychologist in the hospital is faced with a case that it is incapable of solving?"

"Other possibilities you might consider," O'Mara said, leaning back into its chair, "is that the problem does not exist. Or that it is a minor one and so unimportant that no serious harm will result if it was to be mishandled by a trainee. It is also possible that more urgent problems are claiming my attention and this is the reason why you have been given this small and nonurgent one.

"For the first time you are being given access to the psych file of a Senior Physician," it went on before Lioren could reply. "It might also be that, as a trainee, you are expected to discover for yourself what it was that aroused my suspicions, and in the light of your subsequent investigation to decide whether or not they were justified."

Embarrassed, Lioren allowed his four medial limbs to go limp so that the fingertips touched the floor, the sign that he was defenseless before the just criticism of a superior. O'Mara would understand the significance of the gesture, but the Earth-human chose to ignore it and went on, "The most important part of our work here is to be constantly on the lookout for abnormal or uncharacteristic behavior in each and every member of the staff, whatever the species or circumstances, and ultimately to develop an instinct for detecting the cause of such trouble before it can seriously affect the being concerned, other staff members or patients. Are your objections based on an unwillingness to speak at length, rather than the necessarily brief conversations held in the dining hall, because the subject of your past misdeeds would be sure to come up and this would cause you severe emotional distress?"

"No," Lioren said firmly. "Any such discomfort would be as nothing compared with the punishment I deserve."

O'Mara shook its head. "That is not a good response, Lioren, but for now I shall accept it. Send in Kursenneth as you leave."

The Kelgian Charge Nurse undulated rapidly into the inner office, its silvery fur rippling with impatience, as Lioren closed the door behind him and dropped into his work position with enough force to make the support structure protest audibly. The only other person in the outer office was Braithwaite, whose attention was focused on its visual display. Muttering angrily, he bent over the console to key in his personal ID and departmental authorization with the request for the Seldal material, optioning for the printed rather than the Tarlan audio translation.

"Are you addressing me or yourself?" Braithwaite asked, looking up suddenly from its work and displaying its teeth. "Either speak a little louder so I can hear you, or more quietly so I can't."

"I am not addressing anyone," Lioren said. "I am thinking aloud about O'Mara and its unreasonable expectations of me. Mistakenly I assumed that I was speaking in an undertone, and I apologize for distracting you from your work."

Braithwaite sat back in its chair, looked at the closely printed sheets that were piling up on Lioren's desktop and said, "So he gave you the Seldal case. But there is no need to agitate yourself. If you can produce a result at all, you would not be expected to do so overnight. And if you should tire of delving into the not very murky recesses of a Nallajim Senior's mind, the latest batch of trainee progress reports from Cresk-Sar are on your desk. I would like you to update the relevant personnel files before the end of next shift."

"Of course," Lioren said. Braithwaite showed its teeth again and returned to its work.

Senior Physician Cresk-Sar had been his clinical tutor during his first year at the hospital and it was still a person totally impossible to please. Reading its characteristically pessimistic report on the apparent lack of progress of the current intake of student nurses, Lioren wondered for a moment whether he should give priority to the deadly dull but important material from the Senior Tutor or to the more interesting but probably less productive psych file on Seldal. Dutifully, as befitted the most junior member of the department, he decided on the former.

A few moments later, while he was reading the clinical competence appraisal and promotion options for a Kelgian student nurse whose name was familiar to him, he abruptly changed his mind and called up the Seldal file. He began studying it so closely that he scarcely noticed the departure of Kursenneth and the arrival of a Tralthan intern who lumbered into the inner office on its six massive feet. But the noise had caused Braithwaite to

look up, and Lioren made a polite, untranslatable sound designed to attract the lieutenant's attention.

"This is interesting," he said, "but the only parts that I fully
understand are the LSVO physiological and environmental data.
I don't know enough about Nallajim interpersonal behavior in
general and Seldal in particular to be able to detect any abnormality. It would be better if I was to observe Seldal directly for
a period, and talk to it if this can be done without arousing its
suspicions, so that I will have a clearer idea of the entity I am
investigating."

"It's your case," Braithwaite said.

"Then that is what I shall do," Lioren said, securing the
Seldal and Cresk-Sar material and preparing to leave.

"And I agree," the lieutenant said, returning to its work,
"that doing anything else is preferable to wading through Cresk-
Sar's god-awful boring progress reports . . ."

A quick reference to the senior staff duty roster told Lioren
that Seldal would be in the Melfan OR on the seventy-eighth
level. Allowing for traffic density in the intervening corridors
and a delay while changing into a protective envelope before
taking the shortcut through the level of the chlorine-breathing
Illensan PVSJs, he should be able to see the Senior Physician
before it left for its midday meal.

As yet Lioren had no clear idea of what he would do or say
when he was confronted with his first nonsurgical case, and on
the way there was no opportunity to think of anything other than
avoiding embarrassment or injury by tripping over or colliding
violently with staff members.

Theoretically the entities possessing the greater medical se-
niority had the right of way, but not for the first time he saw a
Senior belonging to one of the smaller physiological classifications take hasty evasive action when a six-limbed Hudlarian
FROB Charge Nurse with eight times the body mass and an
urgent task to perform bore down on it. In such cases it was
reassuring to see that the instinct for survival took precedence
over rank, although the ensuing contact was verbally rather than
physically violent.

With Lioren, however, there was no problem. His trainee's
armband indicated that he had no rank at all and should get out
of everyone's way.

Two crablike Melfan ELNTs and a chlorine-breathing Illensan PVSJ chittered and hissed their displeasure at him as he dodged between them at an intersection; then he jumped aside as a multiply absentminded Tralthan Diagnostician lumbered heavily toward him, and in so doing accidentally jostled a tiny, red-furred Nidian intern, who barked in reproof.

Even though their physiological classifications varied enormously, the majority of the staff were warm-blooded oxygen-breathers like himself. A much greater hazard to navigation were the entities traversing what was to them a foreign level in protective armor. The local protection needed by a TLTU doctor, who breathed superheated steam and whose pressure and gravity requirements were many times greater than the environment of the oxygen levels, was a great, clanking juggernaut which had to be avoided at all costs.

In the PVSJ transfer lock he donned a lightweight envelope and let himself into the yellow, foggy world of the chlorine-breathers. There the corridors were less crowded, and it was the spiny, membranous, and unadorned denizens of Illensa who were in the majority while the Tralthans, Kelgians, and a single Tarlan, himself, wore or in some cases drove protective armor.

The greatly reduced volume of pedestrian traffic gave Lioren a chance to think again about his strangely imprecise assignment, his department, and the work that he had been sentenced to perform.

Even if he was able to prove that O'Mara's suspicions were unfounded, investigating Seldal would be a unique experience for him. He would take the case very seriously indeed, regardless of its probable minor nature, and if his observations showed that Seldal really had a problem . . .

Lioren raised his four eyes briefly to offer up a prayer to his light-years-distant God of Tarla, in whose existence he no longer believed, pleading for guidance as to what was or was not abnormal behavior in one of the highly intelligent, three-legged, nonflying birdlike natives of Nallaji. He lowered his eyes in time to flatten himself against the wall as the mobile refrigerated pressure envelope belonging to an ultra-low-temperature SNLU rolled silently toward him from a side corridor. Irritated at his momentary lapse of attention, Lioren resumed his journey.

Until now the only abnormal and dangerous behavior he had identified, and it was a type all too prevalent in the hospital, was careless driving.

Chapter 8

LIOREN moved along the Melfan surgical ward at a pace which suggested that he knew where he was going and what he intended doing when he got there. The Illensan Charge Nurse on duty looked up from its desk, stirred restively within its protective envelope, but otherwise ignored him, and the other nurses were too busy attending to the post-op ELNTs even to notice his passing. But as he walked between the double line of padded support frames which were the Melfan equivalent of surgical beds it became clear that Senior Physician Seldal, in spite of its name appearing on the ward's staff-on-duty board, was not present. Neither was Student Nurse Tarsedth.

Among the Illensan, Kelgian, and Tralthan nurses working all around him a Nallajim would have been hard to miss, which meant that it must still be in the operating theater adjoining the ward. Lioren climbed the ascending ramp to the observation gallery—a large number of the medical staff were physiologically incapable of mounting stairs—and saw that he had guessed right. He also discovered that there were two other observers in the gallery. As he had hoped and half expected, one of them was Tarsedth, the Kelgian DBLF who had spoken to him during his first visit to the dining hall several days earlier.

"What are *you* doing here?" the Kelgian asked, its fur rippling with erratic waves of surprise. "After that mess you made on Cromsag they told us that you would be having nothing to do with other-species bloodletting."

Lioren thought that it was a particularly dishonorable thing to lie to a member of a species that was totally incapable of lying, so he decided on the compromise of not telling all of the truth.

"I still retain my interest in other-species surgery, Nurse Tarsedth," he said, "even though I am forbidden to practice it. Is the case interesting?"

"Not to me," Tarsedth said, returning its attention to the scene below them. "My principal interest here is in the OR staff procedure, artificial gravity controls, patient presentation, and instrument deployment, not all this surgical pecking at some hapless Melfan's innards."

The other occupant of the gallery, an FROB, vibrated its speaking membrane in the Hudlar equivalent of clearing its throat, and said, "I am interested in the surgery, Lioren. As you can see, the operation is nearing completion. But if there is any aspect of the earlier work of particular interest to you, I would be pleased to discuss it."

Lioren turned all of his eyes on the speaker but was unable, as were the majority of the hospital staff, to tell one Hudlar from another. The transparent eye casings were featureless, as were the squat, heavy body and the six tapering, immensely strong tentacles which supported it. The skin, which in appearance and texture resembled a seamless covering of flexible armor, was discolored by patches of dried-out, exhausted food, indicating that the being was urgently in need of respraying with nutrient. But it seemed to know Lioren, or knew of him. Was it possible that this friendly Hudlar, like Tarsedth, had spoken to him earlier?

"Thank you," Lioren said. Choosing his words carefully, he went on, "I am interested in Nallajim surgical procedure, and in particular how this one—"

"I thought all you Psychology people knew everything about everybody," Tarsedth broke in, strong emotion agitating its fur. "You've read Cresk-Sar's reports on us, so you know I am here, spending free time trying to familiarize myself with other-species OR procedures. You know that I'm trying to impress our noxious little Nidian tutor with my knowledge and interest in the subject so that it will approve my request for a posting to the new ELNT theater on fifty-three, and the early promotion that it would bring. I wouldn't be surprised if you were sent here by O'Mara or Cresk-Sar.

"You know everything," Tarsedth ended, its pelt spiking into worried peaks, "but Psychology people say nothing."

Lioren controlled his anger by reminding himself once again

that the Kelgian could not help expressing its true feelings, and his reply, so far as it went, was equally blunt and honest.

"I came here to watch Seldal at work," he said, "and I have no interest in your future plans or your method of furthering them. Cresk-Sar's latest report came in this morning, and from reading it and earlier reports I have been made aware of your progress in the most meticulous and boring detail. I am also aware that the material in your file is confidential to my department and must not be discussed with anyone outside it. However, I will say that you are—"

The Hudlar's speaking membrane vibrated suddenly as it said, "Lioren, be careful. If you have information which should not be divulged, even though the reasons appear to you to be unreasonable or administrative rather than therapeutic, please remember that you are once again a trainee and your future depends, like ours, in keeping our department heads happy or, at very least, not actively antagonistic toward us because of disobedience or insubordination.

"Tarsedth is trying very hard for this promotion," it went on quickly, "and it is irritated by what it considers to be the unnecessary secrecy regarding its chances. But it would not wish reassurance or otherwise if the information you gave it was to lead to your dismissal. Like the other nurse trainees, all of whom have discussed you at great length, Tarsedth believes that your only hope of coming to terms with your terrible problem is to remain within the hospital.

"Lioren," it ended, "please guard your tongue."

For a moment a sudden engagement of his emotions made it impossible for Lioren's speech centers to function. It seemed that the dislike of the medical staff for Psychology Department members was not general. But he must not forget that his purpose in coming here was to collect information on Seldal, and the best way of doing that might be to place these two entities under an obligation to him.

"As I was about to say," Lioren resumed, "I am forbidden to discuss restricted material, whether it refers to the inner workings of the mind of a nurse-in-training or that of the able and highly respected Senior Physician Cresk-Sar . . ."

Tarsedth made a sound which did not translate, but the uneven ruffling of its fur made it plain what the Kelgian thought of its principal tutor.

"However," he went on, "that does not preclude the discussion of such matters between yourselves, or of you producing theories regarding your possible future behavior based on past, firsthand knowledge of the entity concerned. You might begin by considering the fact that, for a great many years, Cresk-Sar has been noted for being the most dedicated, meticulous, professionally uncompromising, and personally unpleasant tutor on the staff. And that its trainees suffer the most extreme mental and emotional discomfort, but rarely fail their examinations. Perhaps because of the fear that they will disappoint it by failing to achieve their full potential, the most promising students are made to suffer the worst unpleasantness. You might also remember that Cresk-Sar is so single-minded about its teaching duties that it frequently interrupts and questions trainees regarding their progress during off-duty periods. You might also consider the probable effect on such a tutor of a hypothetical trainee who seems to be ambitious, dedicated, or stupid enough to spend free time, and even forgo a meal as you are doing, in furthering that ambition.

"Having weighed all these factors yourselves," Lioren added, "you might consider that our hypothetical trainee had nothing to worry about, and hypothetically I would be forced to agree with you."

"Lioren," Tarsedth said, its fur settling into slow, relieved waves, "you are breaking, or at least seriously deforming, the rules. And ambitious I may be but stupid I am not; I packed a lunch box. But this one—" It pointed its head in the Hudlar's direction. "—came away without its nutrient supply. It will have to be very polite and apologetic, whatever that means, to the Charge Nurse and ask for a quick spray, or it won't make our next lecture."

"I'm always polite and apologetic," the Hudlar said, "especially to Charge Nurses, who must grow a little tired of forgetful, starving FROBs turning up at odd times looking for a handout. It will be critical toward me, perhaps personally abusive, but it won't refuse. After all, a Hudlar collapsing from malnutrition in the middle of its ward would make the place look untidy."

He looked closely at the Hudlar, whose smooth and incredibly dense body was beginning to sag in spite of its six widely spaced tentacles. The FROB classification were native to a very heavy-gravity planet with proportionately high atmospheric pressure. The world's atmosphere resembled a thick, semiliquid soup laden with tiny, airborne food particles, which were ingested by an absorption mechanism covering its back and flanks, and, because the Hudlars were intensely energy-hungry creatures, the process was continuous. In other-world environments and at the hospital it had been found more convenient to spray them at frequent intervals with nutrient paint. It was possible that this one had found Seldal's procedure so interesting that it had allowed its energy reserves to run dangerously low.

"Wait here," Lioren said briskly, "while I ask Charge Nurse for a sprayer. It would be less troublesome for all concerned if you made the observation gallery untidy instead of collapsing in the main ward. And up here we won't risk spraying your smelly Hudlar nutrient onto its nice clean floor and patients."

By the time he returned with the nutrient tank and sprayer, the Hudlar's body had settled to the floor with its tentacles twitching feebly and only soft, untranslatable sounds coming from its speech membrane. Lioren used the sprayer expertly and accurately—in common with his fellow Monitor Corps officers, he had been taught to perform this favor for FROB personnel engaged in construction work in airless conditions—and within a few minutes it was fully recovered. Below them Seldal and its patient were no longer visible and the theater was emptying of its OR staff.

"That particular act of charity caused you to miss the end of the operation," Tarsedth said, ruffling its fur disapprovingly at the Hudlar. "Seldal has left for the dining hall and won't return until—"

"Your pardon, Tarsedth," the Hudlar broke in, "but you are forgetting that I recorded the procedure in its entirety. I would be happy to have both of you view a rerun in my place after lectures."

"No!" Tarsedth said. "Hudlars don't use beds or chairs and there would be nowhere for a soft body like mine, or even Lioren's, to relax. And my place is far too small to allow a couple of outsize *thrennigs* like you two inside. If it is that interested, Lioren can always borrow your tape sometime."

"Or both of you could come to my room," Lioren said quickly. "I have never seen a Nallajim surgeon perform and any comments you might make would be helpful to me."

"When?" Tarsedth said.

He had arranged a time suitable for all three of them when the Hudlar said quietly, "Lioren, are you sure that talking about other-species surgery will not cause you emotional distress or that gossiping, for that is what we will be doing, with people outside your department will not get you into trouble with O'Mara?"

"Nonsense!" Tarsedth said. "Gossiping is the most satisfying nonphysical activity between people. We'll see you then, Lioren, and this time I'll make sure my overweight friend here remembers to bring a spare nutrient tank."

When they had gone, Lioren returned the exhausted tank to the Charge Nurse, who needed to be reassured that the nutrient spray had not smeared the transparent wall of the observation gallery. He had often wondered why every ward's Charge Nurse, regardless of size, species, or environmental requirements, was so fanatically insistent that its medical domain was kept at all times neat, orderly, and scrupulously clean. But only now had he begun to realize that, regardless of what the subordinate nursing staff might think of it personally, the ward of a Charge Nurse who demanded perfection in the minor details was particularly well suited to dealing with major emergencies.

Lioren felt symptoms of a minor and nonpainful discomfort in his stomach that was usually attributable to excitement, nonphysical pleasure, or hunger—on this occasion he thought that it might be a combination of all three. He plotted a course that would take him as quickly as possible to the dining hall, intent on eliminating one of the possible causes, but he did not expect the symptoms to be entirely relieved, because he was thinking about his first nonsurgical case.

Abasing himself to the professional level of a couple of trainee nurses—and him a former Surgeon-Captain in the Monitor Corps—had not been as difficult as he had thought, nor had it shamed him to the degree he had expected and deserved. He was even pleased with himself for correctly deducing from Cresk-Sar's report that Tarsedth would be observing Seldal's operation. After lunch, in order to keep the entity Braithwaite happy, he would return to the office and deal with the remainder of the Senior Tutor's report.

Altogether it promised to be a long, busy day and an even longer evening, during which he would view the recording of

Seldal's operation and discuss the Nallajim's procedure at length. Having been told of Lioren's abiding interest in other-species surgery, the two nurses would be expecting many questions from him. In the circumstances it would be natural for the conversation to wander from the operation to the personality, habits, and behavior of the surgeon performing it. Everyone liked to gossip about their superiors, and the quantity of highly personal information available usually increased in direct proportion to the rank of the individual concerned. If he was careful, this information could be abstracted in such a way that neither his informants nor his case subject would be aware of what was happening.

As the beginning of a covert investigation, Lioren thought with a little shiver of self-congratulation, it was faultless.

Chapter 9

"WITH Nallajims," Tarsedth said while they were reviewing the Seldal operation late that evening, "I can never make up my mind whether I'm watching surgery or other-species cannibalism."

"In their early, precurrency days," the Hudlar said, the modulation of its speaking membrane suggesting that its words were not to be taken seriously, "that was the only way a Nallajim doctor could obtain its fee from a patient."

"I am filled with admiration," Lioren said, "that a life-form with three legs, two not-quite atrophied wings, and no hands at all could become a surgeon in the first place. Or, for that matter, perform any of the other delicate manipulatory functions which led to the evolution of intelligence and a technology-based culture. They began with so many serious physiological disadvantages that—"

"They do it by poking their noses into the most unlikely

places," Tarsedth said, its fur rumpling with impatience. "Do you want to watch the operation or talk about the surgeon?"

Both, Lioren thought, but he did not speak the word aloud.

The LSVO physiological classification to which Seldal belonged was a warm-blooded, oxygen-breathing species which had evolved on Nallaji, a large world whose high rotational velocity, dense atmosphere, and low gravity in the intensely fertile equatorial regions had combined to provide an environment suited to the proliferation of avian life-forms. It had been an environment which enabled airborne predators to evolve which were large both in variety and size, but so heavily armed and armored that they had gradually rendered themselves extinct. Over the millennia while this incredibly violent process was working itself out, the relatively tiny LSVOs had been forced out of the skies and their high, vulnerable nests and had taken to the shelter of the trees, deep gullies, and caves.

Very quickly they had to adapt to sharing the ground with the small animals and insects which had formerly been their prey.

Gradually the Nallajim had lost the ability for sustained flight, and as a species they had progressed too far along the evolutionary path for their wings to become arms, or even for their wingtips to subdivide into the digits suitable for the fabrication of tools or weapons. But it was the savage, mindless, and continuing threat from insects large and small who infested, and by their sheer numbers dominated, the land as the giant avians interdicted the air that brought about the minor changes in bone structure and musculature of the beak that caused the Nallajim to develop intelligence.

Handless but no longer helpless, they had been forced to use their heads.

On Nallaji, the winged insects that swarmed and stung their prey to death were outnumbered by those that burrowed and laid eggs deep within the sleeping bodies of their victims. The only way these burrowing insects could be removed was by pecking them out with the long, thin, flexible Nallajim beak.

From being a simple family and tribal debugging device, the LSVO beak progressed to a stage where it was capable of fabricating quite complex insect-proof dwellings, tools, insect-killing weapons, cities, and ultimately starships.

"Seldal is *fast*," Lioren said admiringly, after one particularly delicate piece of deep surgery, "and it gives remarkably few instructions to its OR staff."

"Use your eyes," Tarsedth said. "It doesn't have to talk to them because the staff are engaged in supporting the patient more than the surgeon. Look at the way its beak jabs all over that instrument rack. By the time it gave directions to a nurse and the correct instrument was stuck onto its beak, Seldal could have obtained the instrument unaided, completed the incision, and been ready for the next stage.

"With this surgeon," the Kelgian went on, "it is the choice and disposition of the racked instruments that is important. There is no juggling with clamps and cutters, no verbal distractions, no tantrums because an OR nurse is slow or misunderstands. I think I'd like to work with this birdbrained Senior Physician."

The conversation, Lioren thought, was moving away from Seldal's operation to the subject of Seldal itself, which was exactly what he had been hoping would happen. But before he could take advantage of the situation, the Hudlar, who was plainly another enthusiast where Nallajim surgery was concerned, tried to be helpful while displaying its own expertise.

"Its procedure is very fast and may seem to be confusing to you, Lioren," it said, "especially since you have told us that you have no prior surgical experience with Melfan ELNTs. As you can see, the patient's six limbs and all of the body are exoskeletal. The vital organs are housed within that thick, osseous carapace and are so well protected that traumatic injury rarely occurs although these organs are, unfortunately, subject to a number of dysfunctions which require surgical intervention . . ."

"You," Tarsedth broke in, its fur spiking with irritation, "are beginning to sound like Cresk-Sar."

"I'm sorry," the Hudlar said. "I only meant to explain what Seldal was doing, not bring back unpleasant memories of our tutor."

"Do not trouble yourself," Lioren said. The Hudlar FROBs were acknowledged to be the physically strongest life-forms of the Galactic Federation and with the least-pervious body tegument, but emotionally their skins were extremely thin. He added, "Please continue, so long as you don't ask questions afterward."

The Hudlar's membrane vibrated with an untranslatable

sound. "I won't. But I was trying to explain why speed is so important during Melfan surgery. The major internal organs float in a shock-absorbent fluid and are only tethered loosely to the interior walls of the carapace and underside. When the fluid is removed temporarily prior to surgery, the organs are no longer supported and they sink onto each other with consequent compression and deformation effects which include restriction of the blood supply. Irreversible changes take place which could result in termination of the patient if the situation is allowed to continue for more than a few minutes."

With an intensity that shocked his sensorium like a traumatic injury, Lioren found himself wishing suddenly for the impossible, for a recent past that had taken a different turning and would have allowed him to share this trainee's enthusiasm for other-species surgery rather than a demeaning and probably unproductive interest in the surgeon's mind. The thought that the pain, no matter how severe or often it came, would always be less than he deserved brought little comfort.

"Normally an ELNT surgical procedure requires a large operative field and many assistants," the Hudlar went on, "whose principal purpose is to support these no-longer-floating organs on specially shaped pans while the surgeon-in-charge performs the operation proper. This procedure has the disadvantages of requiring an unnecessarily large opening in the carapace to allow entry of the supporting instruments, and the healing of such a wound is slow and sometimes leads to unsightly scarring and discoloration where the section of carapace was temporarily removed. This can lead to severe emotional trauma in the patient because the carapace, the richness and graduations of its color and individuality in pattern, plays an important part in the courtship process. With a single Nallajim operating, however, the greater speed of this procedure combined with the smaller entry wound reduces both the size and the possibility of a disfigurement occurring postoperatively."

"A good thing, too," Tarsedth said, its fur rippling in vehement sympathy. Kelgian DBLFs had the same feelings about their mobile, silvery fur as the Melfan ELNTs about their beautifully marked carapaces. "But would you look at the way it is pecking at the operative field, sometimes with its naked beak, like a bloody astigmatic vulture!"

Seldal's instrument rack was suspended vertically just beyond the operative field, within easy reach of the surgeon's beak. Each recess contained specialized instruments with hollow, conical grips that enabled the Nallajim's upper, lower, or entire beak to enter and grasp, use, replace, or discard them with bewildering rapidity. Occasionally Seldal went in with nothing but the two, long, cylindrical lenses that extended from its tiny eyes almost to the tip of its beak—which had been strapped in position for the duration of the operation—to correct its avian tendency for long-sightedness. Its three claws were wrapped tightly around the perch attached to the operating frame, and the stubby wings fluttered constantly to give it additional stability when it jabbed with its beak.

"In early times," the Hudlar said, "both the eggs and the egg-laying insects which had to be removed from the patients were edible, and it was considered proper for the surgeon to ingest them. Melfan tissue would not be harmful to a Nallajim, and you will remember from basic training that any ELNT pathogens it contained would not affect or infect an entity who had evolved on a different world. But in a multispecies hospital like Sector General eating parts of a patient, however small, can be emotionally disturbing to onlookers, so you will note that all such material is discarded.

"The operation," the Hudlar went on, "is to remove—"

"It surprises me," Lioren broke in, again trying to guide the conversation back to the surgeon rather than its work, "that a same-species surgeon, Senior Physician Edanelt, for example, was not assigned to the case instead of a life-form who requires a Melfan Educator tape to—"

"That," Tarsedth said, "would be like expecting Diagnostician Conway to forgo all other-species surgery until it had first treated the Earth-human DBDGs in the hospital. Don't be stupid, Lioren. Operating on an other-species patient is far more interesting and exciting than one of your own kind, and the more physiological differences there are the greater the professional challenge. But you know all this already. On Cromsag you treated—"

"There is no need to remind me of the results," Lioren said sharply, irritated in spite of knowing that the other could not help being irritating. "I was about to say that Seldal, who has a beak and no arms, is showing no signs of mental confusion while its mind is partially under the control of a being accustomed to using six limbs all of which are capable of various degrees of manipulation. The psychological and emotional pressure, not to mention the input from its mind-partner's involuntary muscle system, must be considerable.''

"Yes," the Hudlar said. "Obviously it has good control of both minds. But I wonder how I, another six-limbed being, would feel if I had to take a Nallajim tape. I don't have a beak equivalent or even a mouth."

"Don't waste time worrying about it," Tarsedth said. "Educator tapes are only offered to those studious, highly intelligent, and emotionally stable types who are being considered for promotion to Senior Physician or higher. The way Cresk-Sar criticizes our work, can you imagine one of us ever being offered an Educator tape?"

Lioren did not speak. Much stranger things had happened in Sector General—the staff records showed that Thornnastor's principal assistant, the DBDG Earth-human Pathologist Murchison, had joined the hospital as a trainee nurse—but it was a strict rule of the department that the subject of a long-term promotion should not be discussed with trainees who were being considered for it nor, except in the most general terms, any of the problems associated with the Educator-tape system.

The major problem from which all the others stemmed was that, while Sector General was equipped to treat every known form of intelligent life, no single entity could hold in its mind even a fraction of the physiological data necessary for this purpose. Surgical dexterity was a product of aptitude, training, and experience, but the complete information covering the physiology of a given patient could only be transferred artificially by Educator tape, which was the brain record of some great medical authority belonging to the same species as that of the patient to be treated.

If a Melfan doctor was assigned to a Kelgian patient, it was given a DBLF tape until the treatment was complete, after which the mind recording was erased. The exceptions to this rule were the Senior Physicians of proven emotional stability such as Seldal, and the Diagnosticians.

The Diagnosticians were those rare beings whose minds were stable enough to retain permanently six, seven, and in one case up to ten physiology tapes simultaneously. To these data-crammed minds were given the initiation and direction of original research in xenological medicine in addition to the practice and teaching of their considerable art.

The tapes, however, imparted not only the physiological data required for treatment, but the entire memory and personality of the donor entity as well. In effect a Diagnostician, and to a lesser extent a Senior Physician, subjected itself voluntarily to an extreme form of multiple schizophrenia. The donor entities apparently sharing the host doctor's mind could be aggressive, unpleasant individuals—geniuses were rarely nice people—with all sorts of pet peeves and phobias. Normally these would not become apparent during the course of an operation or treatment because both host and donor minds were concentrating on the purely medical aspects of the work. The worst effects were felt when the possessor of the tape was sleeping.

Alien nightmares, Lioren knew from a few of his own tape experiences, were really nightmarish. And alien sexual fantasies were enough to make the host mind wish, if it was capable of wishing coherently for anything at the time, that it was dead. He could not even imagine the physical and emotional effect of the sensorium of an enormous, intelligent crustacean on the mind of a ridiculously fragile but equally intelligent bird.

He continued to watch the frenetically active Seldal while recalling the saying often repeated among the hospital staff that anyone who was sane enough to practice as a Diagnostician was mad, a remark reputed to have originated with O'Mara itself.

"Seldal's ELNT procedure fascinates me," Lioren said, firmly returning to the subject of his investigation. "It shows no hesitation whatever, no pauses for thought or reconsideration, none of the too-careful movements one sees with Educator-tape work. Is it like this with other life-forms?"

"With respect, Lioren," the Hudlar said, "at the speed it works would you notice an awkward pause if you saw one? We have watched it perform an Earth-human gastrectomy and, among others, do something to a DBLF that Tarsedth had better explain to you since the Kelgian reproductive mechanism is proving difficult for me to understand—"

"You should talk!" Tarsedth broke in. "Every time a Hudlar mother produces offspring it changes to male mode. That's— that's *indecent*!"

"Presumably these patients required only short-duration Educator taping," the Hudlar went on, "but Seldal accommodated itself to them without apparent difficulty. For the past six weeks it has been engaged principally on Tralthan surgery and says that it finds the work most interesting, stimulating, and comfortable, next to working on another Nallajim—''

"Another female Nallajim, it means," Tarsedth said, ruffling its fur in disapproval, or perhaps envy. "Do you know that in the three years that Seldal has been here it has been nested by nearly every female LSVO on the staff? What they see to ruffle their tail feathers in such a scrawny, self-effacing nonentity is beyond my understanding."

"Is my translator faulty," Lioren asked, trying to hide his excitement at acquiring this new and potentially useful datum, "or am I to understand that Seldal actually discussed its Educator-tape problems with a couple of trainees?"

"The discussion was perfunctory," the Hudlar said before Tarsedth could reply, "and was concerned with personal preferences rather than problems. Seldal is very approachable, for a Senior, and usually invites post-op questions from anyone who has been watching from the observation gallery. There wasn't time this morning or you could have asked questions yourself.

"In any case," it went on, turning itself ponderously to regard Tarsedth, "my interest in Seldal's love life, which seems to have become less gaudy in recent weeks, is at best academic. But even among my own species it is not uncommon for female-mode persons to be attracted to males who have personalities which are as shy and timid as that of Seldal. Such people are frequently more sensitive, unhurried, and interesting as lovers."

It returned its attention to Lioren and continued. "To modify a saying of one of our classmates, which seems to apply to activities associated with same-species reproduction, a faint heart sometimes wins the fair lady."

"It's talking about Hadley," Tarsedth explained, "an Earth-human trainee. It was supposed to have gone into the maintenance tunnels with . . ."

He had not heard that particular item of gossip before, probably because no official notice had been taken of the incident or the grapevine had been already overloaded with even more scandalous material that day. The story of Hadley's misdemeanor was followed by others, many of which had found their way to his department in the form of much less interesting psych-file updates which were, regrettably, free of Tarsedth's creative exaggeration. He was forced to use every verbal strategem he could devise to bring the conversation back to the Nallajim Senior and keep it there.

Lioren was discovering many interesting facts about Seldal's behavior, personality, and interests. It was information which he would not have been able to obtain from the Senior Physician's file. So far as his assignment was concerned, the evening was being spent profitably and, he thought with increasing feelings of guilt, very enjoyably.

Chapter 10

THE following morning's work period was sufficiently far advanced for his digestive system to begin complaining that it had nothing to engage its attention when Braithwaite walked slowly across to Lioren's desk. Placing its flabby pink hands palms downward on an uncluttered area of the work surface, it bent its arms so that its head was close to his and said quietly, "You haven't spoken a word for more than four hours. Is there a problem?"

Lioren leaned back, irritated by the uninvited close approach of the being, and by the fact that on several previous occasions it had criticized him for talking too much. Even though Braithwaite was showing concern and trying to be helpful, he wished that his immediate superior's behavior would not vacillate so. There were times when he much preferred the approach of O'Mara, who was, at least, consistently nasty.

At the adjacent desk, Cha Thrat was concentrating even more intently on its screen as it pretended not to listen. For some reason Lioren's problems, and some of his suggested solutions, had been a source of considerable amusement over the past few days, but this time it was going to be disappointed.

"The reason for my silence," he replied, "is that I was concentrating on clearing the routine work so as to have more time available for Seldal. There is no specific problem, merely a discouraging lack of progress in every direction.''

Braithwaite removed its hands from his desk and straightened up. Showing its teeth, it asked, ''In which direction are you progressing least?''

Lioren made the Gesture of Impatience with two of his medial limbs and said, ''It is difficult to quantify negative progress. Over the past few days I have observed Seldal's performance of major surgery and discussed the subject's behavior with other observers, during which information emerged which was not available from its psych file. The new material is based on unsupported gossip and may not be entirely factual. The subject is highly respected and popular among its medical subordinates. This popularity seems to be deserved rather than deliberately sought. I cannot find any abnormality in this entity.''

''Obviously that is not your final conclusion,'' said Braithwaite, ''or you wouldn't be trying to free more time for the investigation. How do you plan to spend this time?''

Lioren thought for a moment, then said, ''Since it will not always be possible to question observers or its OR staff without revealing the reason for my questions, I shall have to ask—''

''No!'' Braithwaite said sharply, the hairy crescents on its face lowering so that they almost hid its eyes. ''You must not question the subject directly. If you should discover anything amiss, report it to O'Mara and do or say nothing to Seldal itself. You will please remember that.''

''I am unlikely to forget,'' Lioren said quietly, ''what happened the last time I used my initiative.''

For a moment there was neither sound nor movement from Cha Thrat or Braithwaite, but the Earth-human's facial pigmentation was deepening in color. Lioren went on. ''I was about to say that I would have to question Seldal's patients, discreetly, in the hope of detecting by hearsay any unusual changes in the subject's behavior during its visits before and after surgery. For this I need a list and present locations of Seldal's post-op patients and the timing of its ward rounds so that I can talk to them without meeting the subject itself. To avoid comment by the ward staff concerned it would be better if someone other than myself requested this information.''

Braithwaite nodded its head. ''A sensible precaution. But what will be your excuse for speaking to these patients and for talking to them about Seldal?''

"The reason I shall give for visiting them," Lioren replied, "will be to ask for any comments or criticism they may have regarding the environmental aspects of their various recovery wards, since this is an important nonmedical aid to recuperation and the department carries out such checks from time to time. I shall not ask the patients about their medical condition or their surgeon. But I have no doubt that both subjects will arise naturally and, while pretending disinterest, I shall gather as much information as I can.''

"A finely woven, intricate, and well-concealed spell," Cha Thrat said before Braithwaite could speak. "My compliments, Lioren. Already you show promise of becoming a great wizard.''

Braithwaite nodded its head again. "You seem to be covering all eventualities. Is there any other information or help you need?''

"Not at present," Lioren said.

He was not being completely truthful, because he wanted clarification of Cha Thrat's compliment, which, to a highly qualified former medic like himself, had verged on the insulting. Perhaps "spell" and "wizard," which were words that Cha Thrat used frequently, had different meanings on Sommaradva than on Tarla. But it seemed that his curiosity was soon to be satisfied, because the Sommaradvan wanted to see a Tarlan trainee wizard at work.

The choice of the first patient was forced on him because the other two were beginning their rest periods and Psychology Department staff had no authority to intervene during clinical treatment, which included interrupting a patient's sleep. The interview promised to be the most difficult and delicate of the three cases Braithwaite had listed for him.

"Are you sure you want to talk to this one, Lioren?" Cha Thrat asked with the small upper-limb movements that he had learned signified deep concern. "This is a very sensitive case.''

Lioren did not reply at once. It was a truism accepted on every inhabited world of the Federation that medics made the worst patients. Not only was this one a healer of the highest professional standing, the interview would have to be conducted with great care because patient Mannen's condition was terminal.

"I dislike wasting time," Lioren said finally, "or an opportunity."

"Earlier today," Cha Thrat said, "you told Braithwaite that you had learned your lesson regarding the too-free use of initiative. With respect, Lioren, it was impatience and your refusal to waste time that caused the Cromsag Incident."

Lioren did not reply.

Mannen was an Earth-human DBDG, of advanced age for that comparatively short-lived species, who had come to Sector General after graduating with the highest honors at its home world's foremost teaching hospital. It had quickly been promoted to Senior Physician and within a few years to the post of Senior Tutor, when its pupils had included such present members of the medical hierarchy as Conway, Prilicla, and Edanelt, until it relinquished the position to Cresk-Sar on its elevation to Diagnostician. Inevitably the time had come when the establishment's most advanced medical and mechanical aids were no longer capable of extending its life, even though its level of mentation remained as sharp and clear as that of a young adult.

Ex-Diagnostician and current-patient Mannen lay in a private compartment off the main DBDG medical ward, with biosensors monitoring its vital signs and the usual life-support mechanisms absent at its own request. Its clinical condition was close to critical but stable, and its eyes had remained closed, indicating that it was probably unconscious or asleep. Lioren had been surprised and pleased when they found the patient unattended, because Earth-humans were numbered among the intelligent species who liked the company of family or friends at ending of life. But his surprise had disappeared when the ward's Charge Nurse informed them that the patient had had numerous visitors who had left or been sent away within a few moments of arrival.

"Let us leave before it awakens," Cha Thrat said very quietly. "Your excuse for being here, to ask if it is satisfied with the room's environmental system, is, in the circumstances, both ridiculous and insensitive. Besides, not even O'Mara can work a spell on an unconscious mind."

For a moment Lioren studied the monitor screens, but he could not recall the values he had learned so long ago regarding the measurement of Earth-human life processes. This room was a quiet and private place, he thought, in which to ask personal questions.

"Cha Thrat," he asked softly, "what precisely do you mean by working a spell?"

It was a simple question that required a long and complicated answer, and the process was neither shortened nor simplified by Cha Thrat breaking off every few minutes to look worriedly toward the patient.

The Sommaradvan culture was divided into three distinct levels of person—serviles, warriors, and rulers—and the medical fraternities responsible for their welfare were similarly stratified.

At the bottom were the serviles, people who were unwilling to strive for promotion and whose work was undemanding, repetitious, and completely without risk because in their daily lives they were protected against gross physical damage. The healers charged with their care were physicians whose treatments were purely medical. The second level, much less numerous than the serviles, were the warriors, who occupied positions of great responsibility and, in the past, considerable physical danger.

There had been no war on Sommaradva for many generations, but the warrior class had kept the name because they were the descendants of the people who had fought to protect their homelands, hunted for food, and raised defenses against predatory beasts while the serviles saw to their physical needs. Now they were the technicians, engineers, and scientists who still performed the high-risk or the most prestigious duties, which included the protection of rulers. For this reason the injuries sustained by warriors had usually been traumatic in nature, requiring surgical intervention or repair rather than medication, and this work was the responsibility of the warrior-surgeons. At the top of Sommaradva's medical tree were the ruler-healers, who had even greater responsibilities and, at times, much less reward or satisfaction in their work.

Protected against all risk of physical injury, the ruler class were the administrators, academics, researchers, and planners on Sommaradva. They were the people charged with the smooth running of the cities and the world, and the ills which affected them were principally the phantasms of the mind. Their healers dealt only in wizardry, spells, sympathetic magic, and all the other practices of nonphysical medicine.

86 JAMES WHITE

"Naturally," Cha Thrat said, "as our culture advanced socially and scientifically an overlapping of responsibilities occurred. Serviles occasionally fracture a limb, or the mental stresses encountered while studying for promotion sometimes threaten the sanity of the mind concerned, or a ruler succumbs to a servile digestive upset, all of which necessitates healers practicing above or below their class.

"Since earliest times," the Sommaradvan concluded, "our practitioners of healing have been divided into physicians, surgeons, and wizards."

"Thank you," Lioren said. "Now I understand. It is merely a matter of semantic confusion combined with a too-literal translation. To you a spell is psychotherapy which can be short and simple or long and complicated, and the wizard responsible for it is simply a psychologist who—"

"It is *not* a psychologist!" Cha Thrat said fiercely; then, remembering the patient, it lowered its voice again and went on, "Every non-Sommaradvan I have met makes the same mistake. On my world a psychologist is a being of low status who tries to be a scientist by measuring brain impulses or bodily changes brought about by physical and mental stress, and by making detailed observations of the subject's subsequent behavior. A psychologist tries to impose immutable laws in an area of nightmares and changing internal realities, and attempts to make a science of what has always been an art, an art practiced only by wizards.

"A wizard will use or ignore the instruments and tabulations of the psychologists," the Sommaradvan continued before Lioren could speak, "to cast spells that influence the complex, insubstantial structures of the mind. A wizard uses words, silences, minute observation, and most important, intuition, to uncover and gradually reorient the sick, internal reality of the patient to the external reality of the world. There is a great difference between a mere psychologist and a wizard."

The other's voice had been rising again but the sensors reported no change in the patient's condition.

It was obvious to Lioren that the Sommaradvan had few opportunities to talk freely about its home planet and the few friends it had left there or to relieve its feelings about the intolerance of its professional peers that had forced it to come to Sector General. It went on to relate in detail the disruption its particularly rigid code of professional ethics had caused throughout the hospital until its eventual rescue by the wizard O'Mara, and its own personal feelings and reactions to all these events. Plainly Cha Thrat wanted, perhaps badly needed, to talk about itself.

But confidences invited more confidences, and Lioren began to wonder if he, the one member of the Tarlan species on the hospital staff speaking like this to its only Sommaradvan, did not have the same need. Gradually there was developing a two-way exchange in which the questions and answers were becoming very personal indeed.

Lioren found himself telling Cha Thrat about his feelings during and after the Cromsag Incident, of the guilt that was terrible beyond words or belief, and of his helpless fury at the Monitor Corps and O'Mara for refusing him the death he so fully deserved and for sentencing him instead to the ultimate cruelty of life.

At that point Cha Thrat, who must have sensed his increasing emotional distress, firmly steered the conversation onto O'Mara and the Chief Wizard's reasons for taking them into its department, and from there to the assignment that had brought him here in the hope of gathering information from a patient who was plainly in no condition to give it.

They were still discussing Seldal and wondering aloud whether they should try talking to Mannen the next day, if it should survive that long, when the supposedly unconscious patient opened its eyes and looked at them.

"I, that is, we apologize, sir," Cha Thrat said quickly. "We assumed that you were unconscious because your eyes remained closed since our arrival and the biosensor readings showed no change. I can only assume that you realized our mistake, and because we were discussing matters of a confidential nature, you maintained the pretense of sleep out of politeness to avoid causing us great embarrassment."

Mannen's head moved slowly from side to side in the Earth-human gesture of negation, and it seemed that the eyes staring up at him were in some clinically inexplicable fashion younger than the rest of the patient's incredibly wrinkled features and time-ravaged body. When it spoke, the words were like the whispering of the wind through tall vegetation and slowed with the effort of enunciation.

"Another . . . wrong assumption," it said. "I am . . . never polite."

"Nor do we deserve politeness, Diagnostician Mannen," Lioren said, forcing his mind and his voice to the surface of a great, hot sea of embarrassment. "I alone am responsible for this visit, and the blame for it is entirely mine. My reason for coming no longer seems valid and we shall leave at once. Again, my apologies."

One of the thin, emaciated hands lying outside the bed covering twitched feebly, as if it would have been raised in a nonverbal demand for silence if the arm muscles had possessed sufficient strength. Lioren stopped speaking.

"I know . . . your reason for coming," Mannen said, in a voice barely loud enough to carry the few inches to its bedside translator. "I overheard everything . . . you said about Seldal . . . as well as yourself. Very interesting it was . . . But the effort of listening to you . . . for nearly two hours . . . has tired me . . . and soon my sleep will not be a pretense. You must go now."

"At once, sir," Lioren said.

"And if you wish to return," Mannen went on, "come at a better time . . . because I want to ask questions as well as listen to you. But the visit should not be long delayed."

"I understand," Lioren said. "It will be very soon."

"Perhaps I will be able to help you . . . with the Seldal business and in return . . . you can tell me more about Cromsag . . . and do me another small favor."

The Earth-human Mannen had been a Diagnostician for many years. Its help and understanding of the Seldal problem would be invaluable, especially as it would be given willingly and without the need of him having to waste time hiding the reason for his questions. But he also knew that the price he would have to pay for that assistance in inflaming wounds that could never heal would be higher than the patient realized.

Before he could reply, Mannen's lips drew back slowly in the peculiar Earth-human grimace which at times could signify a response to humor or a nonverbal expression of friendship or sympathy.

"And I thought I had problems," it said.

Chapter 11

LIOREN'S subsequent visits were lengthier, completely private, and not nearly as painful as he had feared.

He had asked Hredlichi, the Charge Nurse on Mannen's ward, to inform him immediately whenever the patient was conscious and in a condition to receive visitors, regardless of the time of the hospital's arbitrary day or night that should be. Before agreeing, Hredlichi had checked with the patient, who hitherto had refused visits from everyone except for the ward rounds of its surgeon, and been greatly surprised when Mannen agreed to receive nonmedical visits only from Lioren.

Cha Thrat had explained it was insufficiently motivated to be willing to interrupt its sleep or drop other, more urgent work at a moment's notice to pursue the Seldal investigation—which was, after all, Lioren's responsibility—although it would continue to assist Lioren in any other way which did not involve major personal inconvenience. As a result, the first visit to Mannen had been the only one at which the Sommaradvan had been present.

By the third visit, Lioren was feeling relieved that Mannen did not want to talk exclusively about the Cromsaggar, disappointed that his understanding of Seldal's behavior was no clearer, and embarrassed that the patient was spending an increasing proportion of each visit talking about itself.

"With respect, Doctor," Lioren said after one particularly argumentative self-diagnosis, "I am not in possession of an Earth-human Educator tape which would enable me to give an opinion in your case nor, as a member of the Psychology Department, am I allowed to practice medicine. Seldal is your physician-in-charge and it—"

"Talks to me as if . . . I was a drooling infant," Mannen broke in. "Or a frightened, terminal patient. At least you don't . . . try to administer . . . a lethal overdose . . . of sympathy.

You are here to . . . obtain information about Seldal and, in return, to satisfy my curiosity . . . about you. No, I am not so much afraid of dying . . . as having too much time to think about it."

"Is there pain, Doctor?" Lioren asked.

"You know there is no pain, dammit," Mannen replied in a voice made stronger by its anger. "In the bad old days there might have been pain, and inefficient painkilling medication that so depressed the functioning of the involuntary muscle systems that . . . the major organs went into failure and the medication killed the patient as well as its pain . . . so that its medic escaped with the minimum of ethical self-criticism and . . . its patient was spared a lingering death. But now we have learned how to negate pain without harmful side effects . . . and there is nothing I can do but wait to see which of my vital organs . . . will be the first to expire from old age.

"I should not," Mannen ended, its voice dropping to a whisper again, "have allowed Seldal loose in my intestines. But that blockage was . . . really uncomfortable."

"I sympathize," Lioren said, "because I, too, wish for death. But you can look back with pride and without pain to your past and to an ending that will not be long delayed. In my past and future lies only guilt and desolation that I must suffer until—"

"Do you really feel sympathy, Lioren?" Mannen broke in. "You impress me as being nothing but a proud and unfeeling . . . but very efficient organic healing machine. The Cromsag Incident . . . showed that the machine had a flaw. You want to destroy the machine . . . while O'Mara wants to repair it. I don't know which of you will succeed."

"I would never," Lioren said harshly, "destroy myself to avoid just punishment."

"To an ordinary member of the staff," Mannen went on, "I would not say such . . . personally hurtful things. I know you feel you deserve them . . . and worse . . . and you expect no apology from me. But I do apologize . . . because I am hurting in a way that I did not believe possible . . . and am striking out at you . . . and I ignore my friends when they visit me in case they discover . . . that I am nothing but a vindictive old man."

Before Lioren could think of a reply, Mannen said weakly, "I have been hurtful to a being who has not hurt me. The only recompense I can make is by helping you . . . with information on Seldal. When it visits me tomorrow morning . . . I shall ask it specific and very personal questions. I shall not mention . . . nor will it suspect your connection.''

"Thank you,'' Lioren said. "But I do not understand how you can ask—''

"It is very simple,'' Mannen said, its voice strengthening again. "Seldal is a Senior Physician and I was, until my summary demotion to the status of patient, a Diagnostician. It will be pleased to answer all my questions for three reasons. Out of respect for my former rank, because it will want to humor a terminal patient who wants to talk shop for what might well be the last time, and especially because I have not spoken a word to it since three days before the operation. If I cannot discover any helpful information for you after that exercise, the information does not exist.''

This terminally ill entity, in what might well be the last constructive act of its life, was going to help him with the Seldal assignment as no other person was capable of doing, simply because it had used a few impolite words to him. Lioren had always considered it wrong to become emotionally involved in a case, however slightly, because the patient's interests were best served by the impersonal, clinical approach—and Mannen was not even his patient. But somehow it seemed that the investigation into the Nallajim Senior's behavior was no longer his only concern.

"Thank you again,'' Lioren said. "But I had been about to say that I cannot understand why you are hurting in ways that you did not believe possible when your medication should render you pain-free. Is it a nonmedical problem?''

Mannen stared up at him unblinkingly for what seemed a very long time in silence, and Lioren wished that he was able to read the expression on its wasted and deeply wrinkled features. He tried again.

"If it is nonmedical, would you prefer I send for O'Mara?''

"No!'' Mannen said, weakly but very firmly. "I do not want to talk to the Chief Psychologist. He has been here many times, until he stopped trying to talk to a person who pretended to be asleep all the time and, like my other friends, stayed away.''

It was becoming clear that Mannen wanted to talk to someone, but had not yet made the decision to do so. Silence, Lioren thought, might be the safest form of questioning.

"In your mind," Mannen said finally, in a voice which had found strength from somewhere, "there is too much that you want to forget. In mine there is even more that I cannot remember."

"Still I do not understand you," Lioren said.

"Must I explain it as if you were a first-day trainee?" the patient said. "For the greater part of my professional life I have been a Diagnostician. As such I have had to accommodate in my mind, often for periods of several years, the knowledge, personalities, and medical experience of anything up to ten entities at a time. The experience is of many alien personalities occupying and—because these tape donors were rarely timid or self-effacing people—fighting for control of the host mind. This is a subjective mental phenomenon which must be overcome if one is to continue as a Diagnostician, but initially it seems that the host mind is a battleground with too many combatants warring with each other until—"

"That I do understand," Lioren said. "During my time here as a Senior I was once required to carry three tapes simultaneously."

"The host is able to impose peace and order," Mannen continued slowly, "usually by learning to understand and adapt to and make friends with these alien personalities without surrendering any part of his own mind, until the necessary accommodation can be made. It is the only way to avoid serious mental trauma and removal from the roster of Diagnosticians."

Mannen closed its eyes for a moment, then went on. "But now the mental battlefield is deserted, emptied of the onetime warriors who became friends. I am all alone with the entity called Mannen, and with only Mannen's memories, which includes the memory of having many other memories that were taken from me. I am told that this is as it should be because a man's mind should be his own for a time before termination. But I am lonely, lonely and empty and cared for and completely pain-free while I spend a subjective eternity waiting for the end."

Lioren waited until he was sure that Mannen had finished speaking; then he said, "Terminally aged Earth-humans, indeed the members of the majority of species, find comfort in the presence of friends at a time like this. For some reason you have chosen to discourage such visits, but if you would prefer the company of donor entities who were your friends of the mind, the answer is to reimpress your brain with Educator tapes of your choosing. I shall suggest this solution to the Chief Psychologist, who might—"

"Tear you psychologically limb from Tarlan limb," Mannen broke in. "Have you forgotten that you are supposed to be investigating Seldal, not one of its patients called Mannen? Forget about the tapes. If O'Mara ever found out what you, a psychology trainee, have been trying to do here, you would be in very serious trouble."

"I cannot imagine," Lioren said very seriously, "being in worse trouble than I am now."

"I'm sorry," Mannen said, raising one of its hands a few inches above the covers and then letting it fall again. "For a moment I had forgotten the Cromsag Incident. A tongue-lashing from O'Mara would be insignificant compared to the punishment you are inflicting on yourself."

Lioren did not acknowledge the other's apology because the guilty did not deserve one and said instead, "You are right, reimpressing your Educator tapes is not a good solution. My knowledge of Earth-human psychology is meager, but would it not be better if at this time your mind was your own, and not filled with others whose mind records were taken before they even knew of your existence, and whose apparent friendship for you was a self-delusion aimed at making their alien presence more bearable? At this time should you not be ordering the contents of your own mind, its thoughts, experiences, right or wrong decisions, and its considerable accomplishments during your own lifetime? This would help to pass your remaining time, and if your friends were no longer discouraged from visiting you, that would also shorten—"

"I have yet to meet an intelligent being," Mannen said, "who did not wish for a long life and an instantaneous death. But such wishes are rarely granted, are they, Lioren? My suffering does not compare with yours, but I will still have a long time to spend in a body deprived of all feeling and with a mind that is empty and alien and frightening because it is my own, a mind I can no longer fill."

The ex-Diagnostician's two recessed eyes were fixed on the one of Lioren's that was closest to it. He returned the patient's stare for several minutes, his mind recalling the words the other had spoken and searching everyone of them for unspoken meanings, but Mannen spoke before he did.

"I have not talked for so long in many weeks," it said, "and I am very tired. Go now, or I will be so discourteous as to fall asleep in the middle of a sentence."

"Please don't," Lioren said quickly, "because I have one more question to ask of you. It is possible that you are thinking that an entity who has already committed the monstrous and multiple crime of genocide would not suffer additional distress if he were to commit a single and, relatively, more venial offense as a favor to a colleague. Are you suggesting that I shorten your time of waiting?"

Mannen was silent for so long that Lioren checked the biosensors to be sure that it had not lost consciousness with its eyelids open; then it said, "If that was my suggestion, what would your answer be?"

Lioren did not wait as long before replying. "The answer would be no. If it is possible, I must try to reduce my guilt, not increase it by however small an amount. The ethical and moral aspects might be argued, but I could not justify such an act on medical grounds because there is no physical distress of any kind. Your distress is subjective, the product of a mind that is empty of all but one occupant, you, who is no longer happy there.

"But the experience is not new to you," Lioren went on, "because it was your normal condition before you became a Senior Physician and then a Diagnostician. I have already suggested that you fill your mind with old memories, experiences or professional decisions which brought you pleasure, or problems which you enjoyed solving. Or would you prefer to continue exercising it with new material?"

What he was about to say would sound callous and selfish and might well anger the patient into total noncooperation, but he said it anyway.

"For example," he added, "there is the mystery of Seldal's behavior."

"Go away," Mannen said in a weak voice, closing its eyes, "go now."

Lioren did not leave until the biosensor readings indicated the changes which told him that on this occasion the patient's sleep was not a pretense.

When he returned to the office next morning, Lioren deliberately concentrated on the routine work so as to avoid having to discuss Mannen with Cha Thrat. He did not think that the words of a terminal patient should be judged too harshly, nor be repeated to others, especially when they had no direct bearing on the Seldal investigation.

Of the other three Seldal post-op patients he questioned, two were willing to talk to him at length—about themselves, the hospital food, the nurses whose ministrations were at times as gentle as the hands of a parent or as insensitive as a kick from a Tralthan's rear leg, but about their Nallajim surgeon scarcely at all. During the little time Seldal spent with them, it listened more than it talked, which was a little unusual in a Senior but was not a character deviation serious enough to worry O'Mara. He was disappointed but not surprised when his general and necessarily vague questions brought no results.

The post-op care of the third patient was the responsibility of Tralthan and Hudlar nurses, who had been forbidden to discuss the case outside the ward. Seldal had likewise forbidden members of any physiological classification less massive than a Hudlar or Tralthan even to approach it. Lioren was curious about this mystery patient and decided to call up its medical record, only to find that the file was closed to him.

He was surprised and pleased when Charge Nurse Hredlichi contacted him to say that Mannen had left instructions that Lioren was to be allowed to visit it at any time. He was even more surprised at the patient's opening words.

"This time," it said, "we will talk about Senior Physician Seldal, your investigation and you yourself, and not about me."

Mannen's voice was slow, weak, and barely hovering above the limit of audibility, but there were no long pauses for breath, and its manner, Lioren thought, was that of an ailing Diagnostician rather than a terminal patient.

It had spoken to the Nallajim during its twice-daily ward round, and on both occasions Seldal had been pleased that the patient was talking to it again and showing interest in events and people other than itself. During the first talk it was obvious that Seldal was humoring its patient by answering Mannen's deliberately nonspecific questions about the latest hospital gossip and its other patients, and the Nallajim Senior had spent much longer with it than was clinically necessary.

"Naturally," Mannen continued, "that was simple professional courtesy extended to the person I once was. However, one of the people we discussed was the new Psychology Department trainee, Lioren, who seemed to be wandering about the hospital with no clear idea of what it was doing."

Lioren's medial limbs jerked outward instinctively into the Tarlan posture of defense, but the threat was removed by the patient's next words.

"Don't worry," Mannen went on, "we talked about you, not your interest in Seldal. Charge Nurse Hredlichi, who has four mouths and cannot keep any of them closed, told it of your frequent visits to me, and it was curious to know why I had allowed them and what we talked about. Not wishing to tell an outright lie this close to my end, I said that we talked about our troubles, and said that your problems made my own seem small by comparison."

Mannen closed its eyes for a moment, and Lioren wondered if the effort of that long, unbroken conversation had exhausted it, but then it opened them again and said, "During its second ward round I asked about its Educator tapes. Stop jerking your arms about like that, you'll knock over something. It is shortly to undergo the medical and psychological examinations for Diagnostician, and I know that any advice coming from an ex-Diagnostician with decades of experience would be welcomed. The questions regarding its methods of accommodating and adapting to its present mind-partners were expected and aroused no suspicion. Whether or not the information given so far will help your investigation I cannot say."

By the time Mannen had finished speaking, its voice was so low that Lioren had collapsed himself awkwardly onto his knees to bring his head close to the other's lips. He did not know if the information was helpful, but it had certainly given him a lot to think about.

"I am most grateful, Doctor," he said.

"I am doing you a favor, Surgeon-Captain," Mannen said. "Are you willing to do one in return?"

Without hesitation, Lioren replied, "Not that one."

"And if I was to . . . withdraw cooperation?" the other asked in a voice which carried only a few inches from its lips. "Or go back to pretending to be asleep? Or if I were to tell Seldal everything?"

Their heads were so close together that Lioren had to extend three of his eyes to cover the full length of the patient's incredibly emaciated body. "Then I would suffer embarrassment, distress, and perhaps punishment," he said. "It would be as nothing to the punishment I deserve. But you are suffering distress, of a kind that I can barely imagine, which is *not* deserved. You say that you find solace neither in the company of friends nor in preterminal contemplation of your past life. It may be that your empty mind is terrifying, not because it is empty but because its only occupant has become a stranger to you. But this mind is a valuable resource, the most valuable resource that was ever in your possession, and it should not be wasted by a premature termination, however accomplished. For as long as possible your mind should be used."

A long exhalation of the patient's breath pressed gently against Lioren's face, and then Mannen said weakly, "Lioren, you are . . . a cold fish."

Within a few minutes it was asleep and Lioren was on the way back to the office. Several times he collided with other life-forms, fortunately without injury on either side, because his mind was on the patient he had left rather than the ever-present problem of corridor navigation.

He was using the remaining hours or days of an emotionally distressed and terminal patient as a means of furthering a simple, unimportant, and nonurgent investigation, as he would use any suitable tool that came to hand which would enable him to complete a job. If in the process he altered or increased the efficiency of the tool, that was not an important consideration. Or was it?

He was remembering that on Cromsag he had been involved in solving a problem. On that occasion, too, he had considered the solution to be more important than any of the individuals involved, and his intellectual pride and his impatience had depopulated a planet. On his native Tarla that pride and high intelligence had been a barrier that none could penetrate, and he had had superiors and subordinates and family but no friends. Perhaps Mannen's singularly inaccurate physiological description, which he had put down to the mental confusion of fatigue, had been correct and Lioren was a cold fish. But it might not be entirely correct.

Lioren thought of the wasted and barely living entity he had just left, the pitiful and fragile tool that was performing exemplary work, and he wondered at the strange feelings of hurt and sadness that arose in him.

Was his first experience of friendship, like his first friend, to be short-lived?

As soon as Lioren entered the office he knew that something was wrong, because both Cha Thrat and Braithwaite swung round to face him. It was the Earth-human who spoke first.

"O'Mara is at a meeting and is not to be disturbed and, frankly, I have no idea how to advise you about this," Braithwaite said in a rapid, agitated voice. "Dammit, Lioren, you were told to be discreet in your enquiries. What have you been saying about your assignment, and to whom? We have just had a message from Senior Physician Seldal. It wants to see you in the Nallajim staff flocking lounge on Level Twenty-three."

Cha Thrat made the Sommaradvan gesture of deep concern, and added, "At once."

Chapter 12

SINCE the Nallajim LSVOs often entertained other-species colleagues, their lounge was spacious enough not to cause Lioren any physical inconvenience, but he wondered at the choice of meeting place. In spite of their fragile, low-gravity physiology, the birdlike species could be as abrasive in their conversational manner as any Kelgian, and if this one had found cause for complaint against Lioren, the expected course would have been for it to present itself in the Psychology Department and demand to see O'Mara.

Of one thing he felt very sure, Lioren thought as he moved between the nestlike couches filled with sleeping or quietly twittering occupants toward Seldal, this would not be a social occasion.

"Sit or stand, whichever is more comfortable for you," the

Senior Physician said, lifting a wing to indicate the couch's food dispenser. "Can I offer you anything."

It was wrong, Lioren told himself as he lowered his body into the downy softness of the couch, to feel sure about anything.

"I am curious about you," the Nallajim Senior said, the rapid twittering of its voice making an impatient background to the slower, translated words. "Not about the Cromsag Incident because that has become common knowledge. It is your behavior toward my patient Mannen that interests me. Exactly what did you say to him, and what did he say to you?"

If I told you that, Lioren thought, this meeting would not long remain a social occasion.

Lioren did not want to lie, and he was trying to decide whether it would be better to avoid telling all of the truth or simply remain silent when the Nallajim spoke again.

"Hredlichi tells me," it said, "and I use the Charge Nurse's words as clearly as I can recall them, that two of O'Mara's Psych types, Cha Thrat and yourself, approached it asking permission to interview its patients, including the terminal case, Mannen, regarding some planned improvements in ward environment. Hredlichi said that it was too busy to waste time arguing with you, and your physical masses were such that it could not evict you bodily, so it decided to accede where the patient Mannen was concerned knowing that the ex-Diagnostician would ignore you as it had done everyone else who tried to talk to it. But Hredlichi says that you spent two hours with the patient, who subsequently left instructions that you could visit it at any time.

"Ex-Diagnostician Mannen is highly regarded at Sector General," Seldal went on, "and its length of service on the staff is second only to that of O'Mara, who was and is its friend. When I joined the hospital it was in charge of training. It helped me then and on many occasions since so that I, too, consider it to be more than a medical colleague. But until yesterday, when it suddenly acknowledged my presence and began to ask questions which were lucid, general, but more often personal, it would not speak to anyone except you.

"I ask again, Lioren, what transpired between Mannen and yourself?"

"It is a terminal patient," Lioren said, choosing his words with care, "and some of the words and thoughts expressed might not have been those of the entity you knew when it was at the peak of its physical and mental powers. I would prefer not to discuss this material with others.''

"You would prefer not . . ." began Seldal, its angry, twittering speech rising in volume so that the sleeping Nallajims around them stirred restively in their nests. "Oh, keep your secrets if you must. Truly, you remind me of the departed Carmody, who was before your time. And you are correct, I would not want to know about it if a great entity like Mannen were to display weakness, even though I once shared my mind with an Earth-human DBDG who believed that feet of clay could sometimes form a most solid foundation.''

"Thank you for your forbearance, sir," Lioren said.

"I have learned forbearance," the Senior Physician said, "from a very close friend. I shall not explain that, but instead I shall tell you what I think went on between you.''

Lioren was greatly relieved that the other was no longer angry and, seemingly, did not suspect that it was the object of Lioren's investigation rather than Mannen. He was wondering whether the remark about learning from a very close friend was an important datum when the Nallajim resumed speaking.

"When Mannen discovered who you were during your first visit," Seldal went on, "it decided that you might have more problems than it had and became curious about you. This curiosity must have led to personal questions about your reactions to the Cromsag business that were distressing to you, but it was the first time in several weeks that Mannen showed curiosity about anything. Now it seems to be curious about everything. It has talked about you, and closely questioned me, and asked about my other patients, the latest gossip, everything. I am most grateful, Lioren, for the significant improvement your visits have brought about in its condition . . .''

"But the clinical picture—" Lioren began.

"Has not changed," it said, completing the sentence for him. "But the patient is *feeling* better.''

"Hredlichi also tells me," Seldal went on, "that you interviewed my other patients about a ward environment improvement scheme, with the exception of my isolation case who is forbidden visitors and all medical contacts not directly involved with its treatment. The case is a young and therefore relatively small member of a macrospecies, so there would be an element of risk involved to any life-form of more or less normal body mass approaching it closely. If you still want to do so, you now have my permission to visit it whenever you wish.''

"Thank you, Senior Physician," Lioren said, feeling grateful but even more confused by the way the conversation was going. "Naturally, I am curious about the secrecy surrounding that particular patient—"

"As is everyone else in the hospital," Seldal broke in, "who is not closely involved with its treatment, which, I must admit, is not going well. But I am not merely satisfying your curiosity, I have a favor to ask.

"My recent conversations with Mannen and the way it speaks of you," the Nallajim went on quickly, "make me wonder if the change you brought about in the ex-Diagnostician might be repeated with the young Groalterri patient, whose prognosis is being adversely affected for nonmedical reasons about which it will not speak. My idea is that it, too, may benefit from knowing that its problems are minor when compared with your own. But I will understand if you prefer not to assist me."

"I will be pleased to help you in whatever way I can," Lioren said, controlling his excitement and the volume of his voice with difficulty. "A—a Groalterri, here in the hospital? I have never seen one, and had doubts about their existence . . . Thank you."

"Lioren, you should take more time to consider," the Nallajim said. "As with Mannen, the process of recollection will be distressing for you. But it seems to me that you accept this distress willingly, as a just punishment that you must not avoid. I think this is wrong and unnecessary. At the same time I must accept these feelings, and use you and them as I would any other surgical tool, for the good of my patient. Nevertheless, I am sorry for inflicting this added punishment on you."

There was a little of the psychologist in every being, Lioren thought, and tried to change the subject. "May I also continue my visits to Doctor Mannen?"

"As often as you wish," Seldal replied.

"And discuss this new case with it?" Lioren asked.

"Could I stop you?" Seldal asked in return. "I will not discuss the case further lest my ideas influence your own. The Groalterri patient's medical file will be opened to you, including what little information there is on the species' home world."

It was very strange, Lioren thought as he left the Nallajim lounge, that the Senior Physician should be using him as a tool in the treatment of a difficult patient while he was using the other's patients as tools in his investigation of Seldal itself—not that he was making much progress with that.

He called briefly on Mannen to tell it about this new development and give its too-empty mind something more to think about before returning to the department. Chief Psychologist O'Mara was still absent, and Lieutenant Braithwaite and Cha Thrat were behaving as if they were about to perform a slightly premature Rite for the Dead over him. Lioren told them that he was not in any trouble, that Senior Physician Seldal had asked him for a favor which he was, of course, granting, and as a result of which he would have to copy some material for later study in his quarters.

"The *Groalterri* patient!" Braithwaite said suddenly, and Lioren turned to see that Cha Thrat and the lieutenant were standing behind him reading his display. "We aren't supposed to know that it is even in the hospital, and now you're involved with it. What is Major O'Mara going to think about this?"

Lioren decided that it was what Earth-humans called a rhetorical question and continued with his work.

Chapter 13

SINCE its formation by the original four star-traveling cultures of Traltha, Orligia, Nidia, and Earth, who had formed as its executive and law-enforcement arm the multispecies Monitor Corps, the Galactic Federation had expanded to include the members of sixty-five intelligent species and in population and area of influence had begun to live up to its original and somewhat grandiose name. But not all of the planetary cultures discovered by the Corps survey vessels were opened to full contact, because a few of them would not benefit from it.

These were the worlds whose technical and philosophical development were such that the sudden appearance among them of great ships from the sky, and the strange, all-powerful beings armed with wondrous devices that they contained, would have given the emerging cultures such a racial inferiority complex that their potential for future development would have been seriously inhibited. And there was one world on which the decision for making full contact was not the Galactic Federation's to make.

As befitted a culture that had been old and wise when the natives of Earth and Orligia and Traltha had still been wriggling through their primeval slime, the Groalterri had been very diplomatic about it. But they had let it be known without ambiguity that they would not tolerate the Federation's presence in their adult domain nor allow the maturity and delicacy of their thinking to be upset by a horde of chattering, moronic, other-species children. Both individually and as a race the Groalterri carried enough philosophical and physiological weight to make it so.

They did not have any objection to being observed from space, so the details of their physiological classification and living environment had been obtained by the long-range sensors of an orbiting survey vessel, and this was the only information available.

The Groalterri were the largest intelligent macro life-form so far discovered, a warm-blooded, oxygen-breathing, and amphibious species of physiological classification BLSU who, as individuals, continued to grow in size from their parthenogenetic birth to the end of their extremely long life spans. In common with other extravagantly massive life-forms, intelligent or otherwise, they found difficulty in moving about unaided, so that from the young-adult state onward they avoided potentially lethal gravitic distortion of their bodies by swimming or floating in their individual lakes or communal inland seas, many of which had been produced artificially and contained a level of biotechnology far beyond the understanding of the observers.

Another characteristic they shared with large creatures—the library computer cited the examples of the nonintelligent Tralthan yerrit and the Earth panda—was that the mass of the embryo was so small that often a pregnancy was not suspected until after the birth had taken place. In spite of the vast size and elevated intelligence levels of adult Groalterri, their offspring were relatively tiny and uncivilized in their behavior and remained so into early adolescence.

That was one of the reasons for the nursing attendants being chosen from the heavy-gravity Tralthan FGLI and Hudlar FROB classifications, Lioren thought as he prepared for his first sight of the patient. Another was that the Federation wanted to do the hitherto unapproachable Groalterri a favor, probably in the hope that it might one day be returned, and had dispatched a Monitor Corps transport vessel to move the seriously injured young one to Sector General for treatment. It was the Corps who had insisted on secrecy so as to minimize political and professional embarrassment should the patient terminate.

There were two unarmed but very large Earth-human Corpsmen guarding the entrance to the ward, a converted ambulance dock, to discourage unauthorized visitors and to advise those with authorization to don heavy-duty space suits. The ward atmosphere and pressure was suited to most warm-blooded oxygen-breathers, they explained to Lioren, but the protection might keep the patient from inadvertently killing him.

In his present mental state, the chance of having his life ended traumatically was a fate greatly to be desired, Lioren thought, but did as they advised without demur.

Even though Seldal's notes had prepared him for the young BLSU's body mass and dimensions, the sheer size of the patient came as a shock, and the thought that an adult Groalterri could grow to many hundreds of times as big was too incredible for his mind to accept as a reality. For the patient filled more than three-quarters the volume of the dock, and so large was it that the consequent distortion of perspective kept him from seeing more than a fraction of its surface features until he had used his suit thrusters to tour the vast body.

The dock was being maintained in the weightless condition with the patient lightly restrained by a net whose mesh was sufficiently open to allow medical examination and treatment to be carried out. On the dock's six inner surfaces, wide-focus pressor and tractor beams controlled from the Nurses' Station had been positioned so as to hold the creature suspended and out of contact with the walls.

The patient's overall body configuration, Lioren saw, was that of a squat octopoid with short, thick tentacular limbs and a central torso and head that seemed disproportionately large. The eight limbs terminated alternately in four sets of claws that would with maturity evolve into manipulatory digits while the remaining four ended in flat, sharp-edged, osseous blades that were larger than twice the spread of Lioren's medial arms.

In presapient times those four bone-tipped extremities would have been fearsome natural weapons, Seldal had warned him, and the very young of any species could sometimes revert to their savage past.

Lioren made another tour of the gigantic body, staying as far from the net that enclosed it as the dock walls and deck would allow. This time he studied the hundreds of tiny post-op scars and freshly dressed wounds as well as the areas of pustulating infection that covered half of the creature's upper body surface.

The condition had been caused by a deep penetration of the subdermal tissue by a nonintelligent, hard-shelled, and egg-laying insect life-form which did not appear to have the physical ability to achieve such depth, but the reason for the multiple traumatic penetration was unknown. In spite of the Groalterri language being held in the hospital's translation computer, so far the patient had refused to give any information about itself or the reason for its condition.

That was why Lioren ended his tour of the body by drifting to a weightless halt above the circular swelling that was the creature's head. There, centered above the four heavily lidded eyes that were equally spaced around the cranium, was the area of tightly stretched skin that served both as the creature's organ of speech and hearing.

Lioren made a quiet, untranslatable sound and said, "If this physical or verbal intrusion gives offense I apologize, for such is not my intention. May I speak with you?"

For a long moment there was no response; then the enormous flap of flesh that was the nearest eyelid opened slowly and Lioren found himself looking into the depths of a dark transparency that seemed to go on forever. Suddenly the tentacle just below him tensed, then curled upward and tore through the restraining net as if it had been the insubstantial structure of a web-spinning insect. The great, bony blade at its tip crashed against the wall behind him, leaving a deep, bright trench in the metal before continuing the swing past Lioren's head, so closely that the push of displaced air could be felt through his open visor.

"Another stupid, half-organic machine," the patient said, just as Lioren was caught by a tightly focused tractor beam and whisked back to the safety of the Nurses' Station.

Reassuringly the Hudlar duty nurse said, "The patient does not mind visual or tactile examinations or even surgery, but reacts in unsocial fashion to attempts at communication. The probability is that it meant to discourage rather than harm you."

"If it had wanted to harm me," Lioren said, remembering how that outsize, organic axe had whistled past his head, "my suit would not have been of much use."

"Nor would my own normally impenetrable Hudlar skin," the nurse said. "Doctor Seldal belongs to a fragile species in which cowardice is a prime survival characteristic but it, too, scorns the use of body armor. The few other visitors who come here are allowed to decide for themselves.

"I have found," the Hudlar went on, "that the patient is more likely to speak to an entity who is not encased in body armor, which it apparently regards as a being who is partly mechanical and of low intelligence. Its words to these uncovered visitors are few and never polite, but it does sometimes speak to them."

Lioren thought of the few words that the patient had spoken after nearly frightening him into premature termination with its pretended attack, and he began unfastening his nonprotective suit. "I am most grateful for your advice, Nurse. Please help me out of this thing and I shall try again. And, Nurse, if there is anything else you wish to say to me I will be pleased to listen."

As the FROB moved forward to assist him, its speaking membrane vibrated with the words, "You do not recognize me, Lioren. But I know you and I, too, am grateful for the helpful words that you spoke to my Kelgian friend, nurse-in-training Tarsedth, before and during our recent visit to your quarters. I am greatly surprised that Seldal allowed you to come here, but if there is anything further that I can do to assist you, you have only to ask."

"Thank you," Lioren said.

He was thinking that the assignment O'Mara had given him to investigate Seldal's behavior, and his unorthodox method of conducting it, was having unforeseen results. For reasons Lioren could not understand he seemed to be collecting friends.

The second time Lioren approached the patient's head he was wearing only his translator pack and a thruster unit to help him navigate in the weightless condition. Again he halted close to one of the enormous, closed eyes and spoke.

"I am not, in whole or in part, a machine," he said. "Again I ask with respect, can I speak to you?"

Once more the eyelid opened slowly like a great, fleshy portcullis, but this time the response was immediate.

"There is no doubt in either of our minds that you have the ability to speak to me," it replied in a voice that accompanied the translated words like a deep, modulated drumroll. "But if your question was carelessly phrased, as is much of the speech in this place, and you are asking whether I will listen and reply, I doubt it."

Below him one of the great tentacles stirred restively inside the torn netting, then became motionless again. "Your shape is new to me, but it is likely that your questions and behavior will be the same as all the others. You will ask questions whose answers should be already known through prior observation. Even the tiny Cutter called Seldal, who pecks at me and fills the wounds with strange chemicals, asks how I am. If it does not know, who does? And they all behave toward me as if they were the Parents with power and authority and I the tiny offspring needing consolation. It is as if insects were pretending to be wiser and larger than a Parent, which is ridiculous beyond belief.

"I speak to you very simply of these things," the BLSU went on, "in the hope that you have the authority to end this ridiculous pretense and that you will leave me undisturbed to die.

"Go," it ended, "at once."

The great eye closed as if to banish him from sight and mind, but Lioren did not move. "Your wishes in this matter will be passed without delay to the others concerned with your treatment, because the words that have passed between us are being recorded for later study by—"

Lioren broke off. All of the creature's tentacles were curling and writhing within the restraining net, which parted loudly in several places before they relaxed again.

"My words," it said, "are an expression of my thoughts that were given to you and earlier to those with whom I spoke. Without my express permission on each and every occasion, these thoughts are not to be shared with entities who are not present and whose minds are likely to misunderstand and distort my meaning. If this is being done, I shall speak no more. Go away."

Still, Lioren did not move. Instead he keyed his translator to the Nurses' Station frequency and prepared to speak once again in the manner of a Surgeon Captain.

"Nurse," he said, "please switch off all recording devices and erase the words spoken since my arrival. Do likewise with the earlier conversations between Doctor Seldal and the patient. Any personal words of the patient that you yourself have heard on this and previous occasions are to be treated as privileged communications and disclosed to no other person. From this moment on, and until the patient itself has given permission for you to do otherwise, you will cease listening in to any conversation that passes between the patient and anyone else, nor will you use your own organic sound sensors to do so. Do you fully understand your instructions, Nurse? Please speak."

"I understand," the Hudlar replied, "but will Senior Physician Seldal?"

"The Senior Physician will understand when I make it aware of the strong feelings of the patient regarding the unauthorized recording of its conversations. In the meantime I assume full responsibility."

"Breaking sound contact," the nurse said.

It was only the sound contact that had been broken, Lioren knew, because the nurse would be continuing to watch and record the proceedings on the clinical monitors as well as watching him even more intently on the visuals in case he had to be pulled out of trouble with the tractors again. He returned his attention to the eye of the patient, which was again closed.

"We may now speak," Lioren said, "without our words being overheard or recorded, and I shall not repeat anything you say without your express permission. Is this satisfactory?"

The patient's gargantuan body remained still, it did not speak, and its eye did not open. Lioren could not help remembering his first visit to ex-Diagnostician Mannen and thought that here, too, the clinical monitors were indicating that the patient was motionless but conscious. Perhaps the BLSU classification did not sleep, for there were several intelligent species in the Federation who had evolved in presapient conditions of extreme physical danger so that a part of their minds remained constantly on watch. Or it might be that the patient, being a member of a species said to be the most philosophically advanced yet discovered, had twice asked him to leave and was now ignoring him because it was too civilized to be capable of physically enforcing the request.

In Mannen's case it had been the patient's own curiosity that had caused it to break the silence.

"You have told me," Lioren said slowly and patiently, "that the attention and questions of the medical staff here are an irritation to you, because they swarm like tiny insects around a behemoth while behaving as if they had the authority of a parent. Have you considered that, in spite of their small size, they feel toward you the same concern and need to help you that is a parent's? The insect analogy is as distasteful to me as it is to the others, if you have told them of it, for we are not mindless insects.

"I much prefer," Lioren went on, "the analogy of the highly intelligent entity with one of lower intelligence of whom it has made a friend, or a pet, if that concept is understood by the Groalterri. Two such entities can often form a strong nonphysical bond with each other and, ridiculous though the idea might seem, should the one of greater intelligence become injured or in distress of some kind, the other will want to give solace and will grieve when it is helpless to do so.

"By comparison with yours," Lioren said, "the intelligence level of those around you is low. But we are not helpless and our purpose here is to relieve many different kinds of distress."

There was no response from the patient, and Lioren wondered if the other was treating his words as the buzzings of an irritating insect. But his pride would not allow him to accept that idea. He reminded himself that while this patient belonged to a superintelligent species, it was a very young member of that species, which should go a long way toward levelling the difference between them; one important characteristic in the young of any species was their curiosity about all things.

"If you do not wish to satisfy my curiosity about you, because of your earlier words being shared with others without your knowledge or consent," Lioren said, "you might be curious about one of the entities who are trying to help you, myself.

"My name is Lioren . . ."

He was there at Seldal's request because of an age-old and Galaxy-wide truism that in a place of healing there are always entities in worse condition than oneself, and that the one in lesser distress felt sympathy toward its less fortunate fellow and

seemed to benefit in the nonclinical area thereby. Plainly the
Nallajim Senior was hoping for a similar response from this
patient, but Lioren wondered whether an entity so massive in
size and intellect, and so tremendously long-lived as this one,
was capable of feeling sympathy for the stupid, ephemeral insect
hovering above its closed eye.

It took much longer than on the previous telling, because then
Mannen had known about the Federation and the Monitor Corps
and court-martial as well as the swarm of intelligent insects
called the Cromsaggar that Lioren had all but exterminated.
Many times his manner lost its clinical objectivity as the words
caused him to live again the terrible events on Cromsag, and he
had to remind himself several times that his memories were
being used as a psychological tool that caused pain to its user,
but finally it was over.

Lioren waited, glad of the patient's lack of response that was
enabling him to drive away those fearful images and regain control of his mind.

"Lioren," the Groalterri said suddenly, without opening its
eye, "I did not know that it was possible for a small entity to
bear such a great load of suffering. Only by not looking at you
can I continue to believe it, for in my mind I see an old and
greatly distressed Parent seeking help. But I cannot give you
that help just as you cannot help me because, Lioren, I, too, am
guilty."

Its voice had grown so quiet that the translator required full
amplification to resolve the word-sounds as it ended, "I am
guilty of a great and terrible sin."

Chapter 14

MORE than an hour passed before Lioren returned
to the Nurses' Station to find Seldal, its atrophied wings twitch-

ing and feathers ruffled in the Nallajim sign of anger, awaiting him.

"Nurse tells me that you ordered the voice recorders switched off," it said before Lioren could speak, "and the earlier conversations with the patient to be erased. You exceeded your authority, Lioren, which is a bad habit of yours that I thought you had given up after the Cromsag business. But you have spoken with the patient at greater length than all of the medical staff combined since its arrival. What did it say to you?"

Lioren was silent for a moment, then he said, "I cannot tell you exactly. Much of the information is personal and I have not yet decided what can and cannot be divulged."

Seldal gave a loud, incredulous cheep. "This patient must have given you information that will help me in its treatment. I cannot order a member of your department to reveal psychosensitive information about another entity, but I can request O'Mara to order you to do so."

"Senior Physician," Lioren said, "whether it was the Chief Psychologist or any other authority my response would have to be the same."

The Hudlar nurse had moved away so as to absent itself and avoid embarrassing its department head by overhearing an argument that entity was losing.

"May I assume that I still have your permission to continue visiting the patient?" Lioren asked quietly. "It is possible that I might be able to obtain information arrived at by observation and deduction and the detection of facts, material of nonpersonal nature about itself or its species which would assist you. But great care is needed if it is not to take offense, because it places great importance on the contents of its mind and the words used to reveal it."

Seldal's feathers were again lying like a bright and unruffled carpet around its body. "You have my permission to continue visiting. And now I presume you have no objection to me talking to my own patient?"

"If you tell it that the speech recorders will remain switched off," Lioren said, "it might talk to you."

As Seldal departed the Hudlar nurse returned to its position on the monitors. Quietly, it said, "With respect, Lioren, the Hudlar organ of hearing is extremely sensitive and cannot be turned off other than by swathing it in a bulky muffling device, the need for which was not foreseen in this ward and so it was not available to me.''

''Did you hear everything?'' Lioren asked, feeling a sudden anger that the patient's confidence had been breached and that Seldal, from whom he had been keeping the conversation a secret, would shortly be able to hear it all on the hospital grapevine. ''Including the crime it is supposed to have committed prior to its arrival here?''

''I was instructed not to hear,'' the Hudlar said, ''so I did not hear, and cannot discuss what I did not hear with anyone other than the entity who forbade me to hear.''

''Thank you, Nurse,'' Lioren said with great feeling. He stared for a moment at the other's identification patch, which bore only the hospital staff and department symbols because Hudlars used their names only among the members of the family or those whom they proposed to mate, and memorized it so that he would know the nurse again. Then he asked, ''Do you wish to discuss some aspect of that which you did not hear with me now?''

''With respect,'' the Hudlar said, ''I would prefer to make an observation. You appear to be gaining the patient's confidence with remarkable speed, by speaking freely about yourself and inviting an exchange in kind.''

''Go on,'' Lioren said.

''On my world and, I believe, among the majority of your own population on Tarla,'' the nurse said, ''it would not matter because we believe that our lives begin at birth and end with death, and we do not distinguish between the forms of wrongdoing which seem to be troubling the patient. But among the Groalterri, and in many other cultures throughout the Federation, you would be treading on dangerous philosophical ground.''

''I know,'' Lioren said as he turned to leave. ''This is no longer a purely medical problem, and I hope the library computer will give me some of the answers. At least I know what my first question will be.''

What is the difference between a crime and a sin?

When he returned to the department, Lioren was told that O'Mara was in the inner office but had left instructions not to be disturbed. Braithwaite and Cha Thrat were about to leave for the day, but the Sommaradvan held back, plainly wanting to question him. Lioren tried to ignore its nonverbal curiosity because he was not sure what, if anything, he could allow himself to say.

"I know that you are seriously troubled in the mind," Cha Thrat said, pointing suddenly at his screen. "Has your distress increased to the level where you are seeking solace in . . . Lioren, this is uncharacteristic and worrying behavior in a personality as well integrated as yours. Why are you requesting all that study material on the Federation's religions?"

Lioren had to pause for a moment to consider his answer, because it was suddenly borne in upon him that, since he had become involved with Seldal and its patients, he had spent much more time thinking about the troubles of Mannen and the Groalterri than his own. The realization came as a great surprise to him.

"I am grateful for your concern," he replied carefully, "but my distress has not increased since last we spoke. As you already know, I am investigating Seldal by talking to its patients, and the process has become ethically complicated, so much so that I am uncertain of how much I can tell you. Religion is a factor. But it is a subject about which I am totally ignorant, and I should not want to be embarrassed if I were to be asked questions about it."

"But who would ask questions about religion," Cha Thrat asked, "when it is a subject everyone is supposed to avoid? It causes arguments that nobody wins. Is it the terminal patient, Mannen, who might ask these questions? If it needs help of that kind, I wonder at it asking you rather than a member of its own species. But I understand your reticence."

Allowing another person to arrive at a wrong conclusion was not the same as lying, Lioren told himself.

Cha Thrat made a Sommaradvan gesture the significance of which Lioren did not know, and went on, "Speaking clinically, Lioren, I would say that you have been forgetting to eat as well as sleep. You can call up that stuff on your room console as well as from here. I cannot help you where Earth-human beliefs are concerned, but let us go to the dining hall and I will tell you all about the religions—there are five of them altogether—of Sommaradva. It is a subject about which I can speak with full knowledge if less than complete conviction."

During their meal and continued discussion in Lioren's quarters, Cha Thrat did not press him for information that he was unwilling to give, but he did not have such an easy time at his next visit to Mannen.

"Dammit, Lioren," the ex-Diagnostician said, who seemed no longer to be troubled by breathlessness, "Seldal tells me that you have been talking to the Groalterri, and it to you, for longer than anyone else in the hospital, and that you refuse to tell anyone about it. And now you want me to give you an ethical justification for your silence without telling me the reason why you won't speak.

"What the hell is going on, Lioren?" it ended. "Curiosity is killing me."

"Curiosity," Lioren said calmly, looking at the age-wasted body and face with its youthful eyes, "would only be a contributing factor."

The patient made an untranslatable sound. "Your problem, if I understand it correctly, is that during your second and much lengthier visit to the Groalterri you were given, presumably in exchange for personal data on yourself and information regarding the worlds and peoples of the Federation, a large amount of information about the patient, its people, and its culture. Much of this information is impersonal and clinical and extremely valuable both to the physician in charge of the Groalterri's treatment and to the cultural-contact specialists of the Monitor Corps. You, however, feel that you have sworn yourself to secrecy. But surely you know that neither you nor the patient have the right to conceal such information."

Lioren kept one eye directed toward the biosensors, watching for signs of respiratory distress following that long speech. He did not find any.

"The personal stuff, yes," Mannen went on. "My earlier attempt to get you to shorten my waiting time here was not to become general knowledge, for it affected only myself and had no bearing on the treatment of a patient of a new species or that culture's future relations with the Federation. The clinical or otherwise nonpersonal information you have been able to gather or deduce is pure knowledge that you have no right to keep to yourself. It should be available to everyone just as the operating principles of our scanners or the hyperdrive generators are available to those able to understand and use them without risk, although for a while in the bad old days the hyperdrive was considered to be a top secret, whatever that meant. But knowledge is, well, knowledge. You might just as well try to keep secret a natural law. Have you tried explaining all this to your patient?''

"Yes," Lioren said. "But when I suggested making the non-personal sections of our conversation public, and argued that it would not be breaking a confidence because it was clearly impractical to ask every single Groalterri in their population for their permission to reveal this information, it said that it would have to think carefully about its reply. I'm sure it would like to help us, but there may be a religious constraint, and I would not want to cause an adverse reaction through impatience. If it became angry, it is capable of tearing a hole through the structure and opening the ward to space.''

"Yes," Mannen said, showing its teeth. "Children, no matter how large they happen to be, can sometimes throw tantrums. Regarding the religious aspect, there are many Earth-humans who believe that—''

It stopped speaking because suddenly the small room was being invaded, first by Chief Psychologist O'Mara, followed by Senior Physicians Seldal and Prilicla, who flew in and attached itself with spidery, sucker-tipped legs to the ceiling, where its fragile body would be in less danger from unguarded movements by its more physically massive colleagues. O'Mara nodded in acknowledgment of Lioren's presence and bent over the patient. When it spoke its voice had a softness that Lioren had never heard before.

"I hear that you are talking to people again," O'Mara said, "and that you especially want to talk to me, to ask a favor. How do you feel, old friend?''

Mannen showed its teeth and inclined its head in Seldal's direction. "I feel fine, but why not ask the doctor?''

"There has been a minor remission of symptoms," Seldal responded before the question could be asked, "but the clinical picture has not changed substantially. The patient says that it is feeling better, but this must be a self-delusion and, whether it remains here or goes elsewhere in the hospital, it could still terminate at any time.''

O'Mara's mention of the patient wanting a favor worried Lioren. He thought that it was the same favor Mannen had asked

of him, except that now it would be a more public request for
early termination, and he felt both sorrow and shame that it
should be so. But the empath, Prilicla, was not reacting as Lioren
would have expected to such an emotionally charged situation.

"Friend Mannen's emotional radiation," Prilicla said, the
clicks and trillings of its voice like a musical background to the
words, "is such that it should not cause concern to a psychologist or anyone else. Friend O'Mara does not have to be reminded that a thinking entity is composed of a body and a mind,
and that a strongly motivated mind can greatly influence the
body concerned. In spite of the gloomy clinical picture, friend
Mannen is indeed feeling well."

"What did I tell you?" Mannen said. It showed its teeth again
to O'Mara. "I know that this is a fitness examination, with
Seldal insisting that I am dying, Prilicla equally insistent that I
am feeling well, and you trying to adjudicate between them. But
for the past few days I have been suffering from nonclinical,
terminal boredom in here, and I want out. Naturally, I would
not be able to perform surgery or undertake any but the mildest
physical exertion. But I am still capable of teaching, of taking
some of the load off Cresk-Sar, and the technical people could
devise a mobile cocoon for me with protective screens and gravity nullifiers. I would much prefer to terminate while doing
something than doing nothing, and I—"

"Old friend," O'Mara said, holding up one digit to indicate
the biosensor displays, "will you for God's sake stop for breath!"

"I am not entirely helpless," Mannen said after the briefest
of pauses. "I bet that I could arm-wrestle Prilicla."

One of the Cinrusskin's incredibly fragile forelimbs detached
itself from the ceiling and reached down so that its slender digits
rested for a moment on the patient's forehead. "Friend Mannen," Prilicla said, "you might not win."

Lioren had strong feelings of pleasure and relief that the favor
Mannen was asking would reflect neither shame nor dishonor
on the ex-Diagnostician's reputation. But there was also a selfish
feeling of impending loss, and for the first time since the others
had entered the room, Lioren spoke.

"Doctor Mannen," he said, "I would like . . . That is, may
I still go on talking to you?"

"Not," O'Mara said, turning to face Lioren, "until you damn
well talk to me first."

On the ceiling Prilicla's body had begun to tremble. It detached itself, made a neat half loop, and flew slowly toward the door as it said, "My empathic faculty tells me that shortly friends O'Mara and Lioren will be engaged in an argument, accompanied as it must surely be by emotional radiation of a kind I would find distressing, so let us leave them alone to settle it, friend Seldal."

"What about me?" Mannen said when the door had closed behind them.

"You, old friend," O'Mara said, "are the subject of this argument. You are supposed to be dying. What exactly did this . . . this trainee psychologist, do or say to you to bring about this insane urge to return to work?"

"Wild horses," Mannen said, showing its teeth again, "wouldn't drag it out of me."

Lioren wondered what relevance a nonintelligent species of Earth quadruped had to the conversation, and had decided that the words had a meaning other than that assigned by his translator.

O'Mara swung around to face him and said, "Lioren, I want an immediate verbal and later a more detailed written report of all the attendant circumstances and conversations that took place between this patient and yourself. Begin."

It was not Lioren's intention to be disobedient or insubordinate by refusing to speak, it was simply that he needed more time to separate the things he could say from those which should on no account be revealed. But O'Mara's yellow-pink face was deepening in color, and he was not to be given any time at all.

"Come, come," O'Mara said impatiently. "I knew that you were interviewing Mannen in connection with the Seldal investigation. That was an obvious move on your part even though, if Mannen did not ignore you as he had everyone else, it carried the risk of you revealing what you were doing to the patient—"

"That is what happened, sir," Lioren broke in, knowing that they were on a safe subject and hoping to stay there. "Doctor Mannen and I discussed the Seldal assignment at length, and while the investigation is not yet complete, the indications so far are that the subject is sane—"

"For a Senior Physician," Mannen said.

O'Mara made an angry sound and said, "Forget that investigation for the moment. What concerns me now is that Seldal noticed a marked, nonclinical change in its terminal patient which it ascribed to conversations with my trainee psychologist. Subsequently it asked that you talk to its Groalterri patient, who was stronger but being just as silent as Mannen, with the result that when it did speak you forbade the use of speech recorders.''

When the Chief Psychologist went on, his voice was quiet but very clear, in the way that Tarlans described as shouting in whispers, as it went on, ''Tell me, right now, what you said to these two patients, and they to you, that brought about the change in the Groalterri's behavior and caused this, this particular act of constructive insanity in a dying man.''

One of its hands moved to rest very gently on Mannen's shoulder and even more quietly it said, ''I have professional, and personal, reasons for wanting to know.''

Once again Lioren searched his mind in silence for the right words until he was ready to speak.

''With respect, Major O'Mara,'' Lioren said carefully, ''some of the words that passed between us contained nonpersonal information that may be revealed, but only if the patients give their agreement to my doing so. Regrettably the rest, which I expect is of primary interest to you as a psychologist, I cannot and will not divulge.''

O'Mara's face had again deepened in color while Lioren was speaking, but gradually it lightened again. Then suddenly the Chief Psychologist twitched its shoulders in the peculiarly Earth-human fashion and left the room.

Chapter 15

''YOU ask questions,'' the Groalterri said, ''endlessly.''

In such a massive creature it was impossible to detect changes of expression, even if the gargantuan features were capable of registering them, and the nonverbal signals he had been able to learn were few. Lioren had the feeling that this was not going to be a productive meeting.

"I also answer questions," Lioren said, "for as long as they are asked."

Around and below him the tightly curled tentacles stirred like great, organic mountain ranges caught in a seismic disturbance, and became still again. Lioren was not unduly worried, because the tantrum of his first visit had not been repeated.

"I have no questions," the patient said. "My curiosity is crushed by a great weight of guilt. Go away."

Lioren withdrew to indicate his willingness to obey, but only by a short distance to show that he still wanted to talk.

"Satisfying my curiosity," he said, "makes me forget my own guilt for a time, as does satisfying the curiosity of others. Perhaps I could help you to forget your guilt, for a while, by answering the questions you do not ask."

The patient did not move or speak, and Lioren, as he had done when previously faced with this form of negative reaction, took it as a reluctant acquiescence and went on talking.

The Groalterri was physiologically unsuited to travel in space, so he talked about one of the other species who were similarly hampered and others for whom star travel should have been impossible but was not. He spoke of the great strata creatures of Drambo, whose vast bodies could grow like a living carpet to cover the area of a subcontinent, who used as eyes the millions of flowers that made of their backs a light-sensitive skin, and who, in spite of the vegetable metabolism that made physical movement so slow, had minds that were quick and sharp and powerful.

He told of the vicious, incredibly violent and mindless Protectors of the Unborn, who neither slept nor ceased fighting from the moment they were born into their incredibly savage environment until they died because of the weakness of age and the inability to protect themselves from their lastborn. But within that organic fighting and killing machine there was an embryo whose telepathic mind was rich and full and gentle, taught as it was by the telepathy of its unborn brothers, and whose ability to think was tragically destroyed after its long gestation by the process of birth.

"Protectors of the Unborn have been brought to this hospital," Lioren went on, "where we are trying to devise ways of

birthing their offspring without the consequent mind destruction, and of training these newly born not to attack and kill
everyone on sight.''

While Lioren had been speaking, the Groalterri remained still
and silent. He resumed, but gradually his subject was changing
from descriptions of the physiological attributes of the beings
who made up the Federation to the philosophical viewpoints
which joined or sometimes separated them. He wanted to know
what was troubling the patient, so the change was deliberate.

Lioren went on. ''An act which is considered to be a great
wrong by one species because of an evolutionary imperative or,
less often, by a too-narrow philosophical education, can be
viewed by another as normal and blameless behavior. Often the
judge, who is never physically present but has others to speak
for it, is an immaterial entity who is believed to be the all-
knowing, all-powerful, and all-merciful Creator of All Things.''

Below and around him the tentacles stirred restively, the eye
that had been regarding him steadily closed, but there was no
other reaction. Lioren knew that he was taking a risk by continuing in this vein, but there was suddenly a need within him
to understand the mind of this great and greatly troubled being.

''My knowledge of this subject is incomplete,'' he continued,
''but among the majority of the intelligent species it is said that
this omnipotent and immaterial being has manifested itself in
physical form. The physiological classifications vary to suit the
environments of the planets concerned, but in all cases it man-
ifests itself as a teacher and lawgiver who suffers death at the
hands of those who cannot at first accept its teachings. But these
teachings, in a short time or long, form the philosophical foundation of mutual respect, understanding, and cooperation between individuals of that species which eventually lead to the
formation of a planetary and interstellar civilization.

''There are many beings who hold the belief that it is the
same being in every case who, whenever its creation is threatened and its teachings are most needed, manifested or will manifest itself on all worlds. But the common factors in all these
beliefs are sympathy, understanding, and forgiveness for past
wrongs, whatever form they have taken and no matter whether
they be venial or of the utmost gravity. The quality of this forgiveness is demonstrated by the manifestation's death, which is
reported in all cases to be shameful and physically distressing.

On Earth it is said that termination occurred after being attached with metal spikes to a wooden cross, and the Crepellian octopoids used what they called the Circle of Shame, in which the limbs are staked out at full extension on dry ground until death by dehydration occurs, while on Kelgia—''

"Small Lioren," the Groalterri said, suddenly opening its eye, "do you expect this omnipotent being to forgive your own grievous wrong?''

After the patient's long silence the question took Lioren by surprise. "I don't . . . What I mean is, there are others who believe that these teachers and lawgivers arise naturally in any intelligent culture which is in transition between barbarism and the beginnings of true civilization. On some worlds there have been many lawgivers, whose teachings vary in small details, not all of whose adherents believe them to be manifestations of an omnipotent being. All of these teachers advocated showing mercy and forgiveness to wrongdoers, and they usually died at the hands of their own people. Was there an entity of that kind, a great teacher and forgiver, in Groalterri history?''

The eye continued to regard him, but the patient's speaking membrane remained still. Perhaps the question had been offensive in some fashion, for it was plain that the Groalterri was not going to answer it. Sadly, Lioren ended, "I do not believe I can be forgiven because I cannot forgive myself.''

This time the response was immediate, and utterly surprising.

"Small Lioren," the Groalterri said, "my question has brought a great hurt to your mind, and for this I am sorry. You have been engaging my mind with stories of the worlds and peoples of your Federation, and of their strangely similar philosophies, and for a time my own great hurt was diminished. You deserve more of me, and shall be given more, than a hurt in return for a kindness.

"The information I shall now give you, and this information only, you may relay to and discuss with others. It concerns the origins and history of the Groalterri and contains nothing that is personal to myself. Any previous or subsequent conversations between us must remain private.''

"Of course!'' Lioren said, so loudly that in his excitement he overloaded his translator. "I am grateful; we will all be grateful. But—but our gratitude to you is impersonal. Can you at least tell me who and what you are?''

He stopped, wondering if asking the other's name had been a mistake, perhaps his last mistake.

One of the creature's tentacles uncurled suddenly and its bony tip whistled past Lioren's head to strike the metal wall, where it made deafening, intermittent contact for a few seconds before being as quickly withdrawn.

At the center of one of the few areas of plating left unscarred after its previous tantrum there was a perfect geometrical figure of an eight-pointed star. The lines making it up were straight and of equal depth and thickness, something between a deep, bright scratch and a fine, shallow trench in the metal, and the lines of the figure were accurately joined without gaps or overlapping.

"I am Small Hellishomar the Cutter," it said quietly. "You, Lioren, would call me a surgeon."

Chapter 16

HELLISHOMAR concentrated its attack on an area where the skin was thin and the underlying tissues soft, tearing into the flesh with all four blades until the bloody crater was large and deep enough to admit its body and equipment. Then it closed and sealed the flap of the entry wound behind it, switched on the lighting and eye-cover washers, checked the level of the flammables tank, and resumed burrowing.

This Parent was old, old enough to be the parent of Hellishomar's parent's parent, and the gray rot that afflicted the aged was already well established all over and deep within its gargantuan body. As was usual with Parents, it had concealed the early symptoms so as to avoid the days of severe pain and violence that surgery would entail until the visibly growing cancers had left it unable to move, and one of the passing Smalls had reported its condition to the Guild of Cutters.

Hellishomar was old for a Small as well as large for a Cutter, but its extensive knowledge and unrivaled experience more than made up for the damage caused by the size of the entry wounds it was forced to make; and here the deeper tissues were soft so that often he was able to squeeze through a single incision rather than hacking a bloody tunnel into perfectly healthy flesh.

Avoiding the larger blood vessels or heat-sealing those that could not be avoided, and ignoring the severed capilliaries which would close naturally, Hellishomar cut rapidly and accurately without waste of time. During deep work the compressed air tanks had to be small, otherwise the entry wound would have been larger, the damage greater, and the progress slower.

Then suddenly it was visible, the first internal evidence of the growth, and precisely in the predicted position.

Lying diagonally across the newly deepened incision there was a thin, yellow tube whose tough walls and oily surface had enabled it to slide away from the blade tentacle. It pulsed faintly as it drew nutrient from the gray, necrotic growth spreading over the Parent's surface tegument to the heart-root, or roots, deep inside the body. Hellishomar changed direction to follow it down.

Within a few moments there was another yellow tube visible on one side of the tunnel, then another and another, all converging towards a single point below him. Hellishomar cut and squeezed through them until the heart-root itself lay exposed like a veined, uneven globe that seemed to glow with its own sickly yellow light. In size it was only a little smaller than Hellishomar's head. Quickly he excised a clear space all around and above it, severing in the process more than twenty of the rootlets and two thicker tubes which were the connections to secondaries. Then, taking up a position which would allow the heat and bloody steam to escape and disperse along the entry wound rather than stewing the Cutter in his own body fluids, Hellishomar attacked the foul thing with his burner turned up to full intensity.

Hellishomar did not stop until the heart-root was converted to ash, and then he gathered the ashes into a small pile and flamed them again. He followed the connector to the secondary, burning it behind him as he went, until he found another heart-root and removed that. When the external Cutters had completed their work, the fine root connections to the surface growths, severed at both ends and starved of nutrient, would wither and shrink so that they could be withdrawn from the Parent's body with the minimum of discomfort.

In spite of the wipers that were laboring to keep the eye-covers clear, there was an increasing and irregular impairment of Hellishomar's vision. His movements were becoming slower, the strokes of his cutting blades less precise, and the quality of his surgery diabolical. He diagnosed the condition as a combination of heat exhaustion and asphyxiation and turned at once to begin cutting a path to the nearest breathing passage.

A sudden increase of resistance to the cutters indicated that he had encountered the tough outer membrane of a breathing passage. Carefully Hellishomar forced through an incision large enough to allow entrance to his head and upper body only so as to minimize bleeding from the wound, then stopped and uncovered his gills.

Water not yet warmed by the Parent's body heat washed past Hellishomar's overheated body, replacing the stale tanked air in his lungs and clearing both vision and mind. His pleasure was short-lived because a few moments later the flood of clear, gill-filtered water diminished to a trickle as the Parent changed to air-breathing mode. Quickly withdrawing the rest of his body from the wound, Hellishomar uncoiled his cutter-tipped tentacles to full extension, making the shallow, angled incisions in the breathing passage wall which would enable it to maintain position above the wound when the storm of inhaled air blew past.

The Parent's nerve network made it aware of everything that occurred in its vast body and the exact position of the events as they took place, and it also knew that wounds healed more readily in air than in water. As he expertly drew together the edges of the exit wound with sutures, Hellishomar wished that just once one of the great creatures would touch its mind, perhaps to thank him for the surgical intervention that would extend its life, or to criticize the Small selfishness which made it want thanks, or merely to acknowledge the fact of its existence.

Parents knew everything, but spoke of their knowledge to none but another Parent.

The wind of inhalation died and there was a moment of dead calm as the Parent prepared to exhale. Hellishomar made a final check on the wound sutures, released its grip on the wall, and dropped onto the soft floor of the breathing passage. There it rolled itself tightly into a ball of its own tentacles, and waited.

Suddenly its body was lifted and hurled along the breathing passage by a hurricane which coughed it onto the surface of the outside world . . .

"There Hellishomar had rested and replaced its consumables," Lioren went on, "because this Parent was old and large and there was still much work to do."

He paused so as to give O'Mara a chance to respond. When he had requested permission to make an immediate verbal report on his return from the Groalterri ward, the Chief Psychologist had expressed surprise in a tone which Lioren now recognized as sarcastic, but thereafter it had listened without interruption or physical movement.

"Continue," O'Mara said.

"I have been told," Lioren went on, "that the history of the Groalterri is composed entirely of memories handed down over the millennia. I have been assured of their accuracy, but archeological evidence to support them is not available. The culture has, therefore, no presapient history, and in this respect my report must be deductive rather than factual."

"Then by all means," O'Mara said, "deduce."

No early historical records had been kept on the mineral-starved swamp and ocean world of the Groalterri, because the life span of its people was longer and their memories clearer and more trustworthy than any marks placed upon animal skins or layers of woven vegetation that would fade and rot long before the lives of the writers would be ended. Groalter was a large world that orbited its small, hot sun once every two and one-quarter Standard Years, and one of its gigantic intelligent life-forms would have had to be unhealthy or unfortunate indeed not to have witnessed five hundred such rotations.

It was only with the recent advent—recent as the Groalterri measured the passage of time—of Small technology that permanent written records had been kept. These were concerned principally with the discoveries and observations made by the scientific bases that had been established, with great difficulty and loss of Small life, in the heavy-gravity conditions of the polar regions. Groalter's rapid rotation gave low levels of gravity only in a broad band above and below the equator, where the tidal effects of its large satellite kept the vast, inhabited oceans and swamps constantly in motion, and this continuing tidal action had long since eroded away its few equatorial landmasses.

In time—a long time even as the Groalterri measured it—their great, uninhabited moon would spin closer until it and the mother planet collided in mutual destruction.

The Small made such advances in technology as were possible in their impermanent environment. And every day of their young lives they tried to control the animal nature within them so that they might arrive more quickly at the mental maturity of the Parents, who spent their long lives thinking great thoughts while they controlled and conserved the resources of the only world that, because of their great size, they could ever know.

"There are two distinct cultures on Groalter," Lioren continued. "There are the Small, of which our overlarge patient is a member, and the Parents, of whom even their own children know little."

Within their first Groalter year the Small were forced to leave the Parents, to be cared for and educated by slightly more senior children. This seeming act of cruelty was necessary to the mental health and continued survival of the Parents because, during their years of immaturity, the Small were considered to be little more than savage animals whose quality of mentation and behavior made them utterly repellent to the adults.

In spite of being unable to bear their violent and unsettling presence, the Parents loved them dearly and watched over their welfare at a distance.

But the mind of a Small of the Groalterri, when compared with the level of intelligence and social behavior possessed by the average member species of the Federation, was neither savage nor stupid. For many thousands of Earth-standard years, during their long wait between birth and achieving adulthood, they had been solely responsible for the development of Groalterri physical science and technology. During that period they had no communication with their elders, and their physical contacts were incredibly violent and restricted to surgical interventions aimed at prolonging the Parents' lives.

"This behavior," Lioren continued, "is beyond my experience. Apparently the Small hold the Parents in high regard, and they respect and obey and try to help them as much as they are able, but the Parents do not respond in any way other than by passively and at times reluctantly submitting to their surgery.

"The Small use a spoken and written language, and the Parents are said to have great but unspecified mental powers which include wideband telepathy. They use them to exchange thoughts among themselves, and for the control and conservation of every nonintelligent living creature in Groalter's ocean. For some reason they will not use telepathy to talk to their own young or, for that matter, to the Monitor Corps contact specialists presently in orbit above their planet.

"Such behavior is totally without precedent," Lioren ended helplessly, "and beyond my understanding."

O'Mara showed its teeth. "It is beyond your present understanding. Nevertheless, your report is of great interest to me and of greater value to the contact specialists. Their ignorance of the Groalterri is no longer total, and the Corps will be grateful and pleased with their onetime Surgeon-Captain. I, however, am impressed but not pleased because the report of the lowest-ranking member of my department, Trainee Lioren, is far from complete. You are still trying to hide important information from me."

Clearly the the Chief Psychologist was better at reading Tarlan facial and tonal expressions than Lioren was at reading those of an Earth-human. It was Lioren's turn to remain silent.

"Let me remind you," O'Mara said in a louder voice, "that Hellishomar is a patient and this hospital, which includes Seldal and you and myself, is charged with the responsibility for solving its medical problem. Clearly Seldal suspected that there might be a psychological component to this clinical problem and, having observed the results of your talks with Mannen and knowing that it could not approach me officially because this department's responsibility lies only with the mental health of the staff, it asked you to talk to the patient. This may not be a psychiatric hospital, but Hellishomar is a special case. It is the first Groalterri ever to have spoken with us, or more accurately, with you. I want to help it as much as you do, and I have greater experience than you in tinkering with other-species mentalities. My interest in the case is entirely professional, as is my curiosity regarding any personal information it may have disclosed to you, information which will be used therapeutically and not discussed with anyone else. Do you understand my position?"

"Yes," Lioren said.

"Very well," O'Mara said when it was obvious that Lioren would say nothing more. "If you are too stupid and insubordinate to accede to a superior's request, perhaps you are intelligent enough to take suggestions. Ask the patient how it came by its injuries, if you haven't already done so and are hiding the answer from me. And ask whether it was Hellishomar or someone else who broke the Groalterri silence to request medical assistance. The contact specialists are puzzled by the circumstances of the distress call and wish clarification."

"I did try to ask those questions," Lioren said. "The patient became agitated and gave no answers other than to say that it personally had not requested assistance."

"What did it say?" O'Mara said quickly. "What were its exact words?"

Lioren remained silent.

The Chief Psychologist made a short, untranslatable sound and sat back in its chair. "The Seldal investigation you were given is not in itself important, but the constraints placed on you most certainly were. I knew that you would have to work through Seldal's patients to gather information, and that one of them was Mannen. I hoped that putting the two of you together, the patient suffering from preterminal emotional distress and refusing all contact with friends and colleagues, and a Tarlan whose problems made Mannen's look minor indeed, would cause him to open up to the stage where I might be able to help him. Without further intervention by me, you achieved results that were much better than I could have hoped for, and I am truly grateful. My gratitude and the minor nature of the affair allowed me to ignore your tiresome insubordination, but this is a different matter.

"It was Seldal's idea, not mine, that you should talk to the Groalterri," O'Mara continued, "and I did not learn of it until after the event. Until now I knew nothing of what passed between you, and now I want to know everything. This involves a first-contact situation with a species that is both highly intelligent and until now completely uncommunicative. But you have been able to talk to one of them, and for some reason have achieved more in a few days than the Monitor Corps in as many years. I am impressed and so will be the Corps. But surely you must see that withholding information, any information regardless of its nature, that might help widen contact is stupid and criminal.

"This is not the time for playing ethical games, dammit," O'Mara ended in a quieter voice. "It is much too important for that. Do you agree?"

"With respect—" Lioren began, when a sudden movement of O'Mara's hand silenced him.

"That means no," the Chief Psychologist said angrily. "Forget the verbal niceties. Why don't you agree?"

"Because," Lioren said promptly, "I was not given permission to pass on this kind of information, and I feel that it is important that I continue to do as the patient requests. Hellishomar is becoming more willing to give information about Groalter, at least, for general distribution. If I had not respected its confidence from the beginning, it is likely that we would have been given no information of any kind. Much more data on the Groalterri will be forthcoming, but only if you and the Corps are patient and I remain silent unless specifically directed otherwise by the patient. If I break confidence with Hellishomar, the flow of information will cease."

While he had been speaking, O'Mara's facial pigmentation had grown a dark shade of pink again. In an effort to avert what promised to be a major emotional outburst, Lioren went on. "I apologize for my insubordinate behavior, but the continuing insubordination is being forced on me by the patient rather than any lack of respect. It is grossly unfair to you, sir, because you wish only to help the patient. Even though it is not deserved, I would welcome any help or advice that you would be willing to give."

O'Mara's fixed, unblinking stare was making Lioren uneasy. He had the feeling that the other's eyes were looking directly into his mind and reading every thought in it, which was ridiculous because Earth-human DBDGs were not a telepathic species. Its face had lightened in color but there was no other reaction.

"Earlier," Lioren said, "when I said that the Groalterri behavior was beyond my understanding, you said that it was beyond my present understanding. Were you implying that the situation has a precedent?"

O'Mara's face had returned to its normal coloration. It showed its teeth briefly. "It has many precedents, almost as many as there are member species in the Federation, but you were too close to the situation to see them. I ask you to consider the sequence of events that occurs when an embryo is growing between the time of conception and birth, although for obvious reasons I shall discuss these events as they affect my own species."

The Chief Psychologist clasped its hands loosely together on the desktop and adopted the calm, clinical manner of a lecturer. "Growth changes in the embryo within the womb follow closely the evolutionary development of the species as a whole, although on a more compressed time scale. The unborn begins as a blind, limbless, and primitive water-dweller floating in an amniotic ocean, and ends as a small, physically helpless, and stupid replica of an adult person, but with a mind which will in a relatively short time equal or surpass that of its parents. On Earth the evolutionary path that led to the four-limbed land animal becoming the thinking creature Man was long, and with many unsuccessful side turnings which resulted in creatures that had Man's shape but not his intelligence."

"I understand," Lioren said. "It was the same on Tarla. But what is the significance in this case?"

"On Earth as on Tarla," O'Mara went on, ignoring the question, "there was an interim stage in the development of a fully intelligent, self-aware form of life. On Earth we called the early, less intelligent men Neanderthal and the form that violently replaced it Cro-Magnon. There were small physical variations between the two, but the important difference was unseen. Cro-Magnon man, although still little more than a savage animal, possessed what was called the New Mind, the type of mind which enables civilizations to grow and flourish and cover not one world but many. But should they have tried to teach their forebears beyond their ability to learn or left them alone? On Earth in the past there were many unhappy experiences between so-called civilized men and aboriginals."

At first Lioren did not understand the reason for O'Mara speaking in such oversimplified generalities, but suddenly he saw where the other was leading him.

"If we return to the analogy of prenatal and prehistoric evolution," the Chief Psychologist continued, "and assuming that the gestation period of the Groalterri is proportional to their life span, isn't it possible that they also experienced this preliminary stage of lesser intelligence? But let us also assume that their young experience it, not before but after they are born. This would mean that during the time from birth to prepuberty the Small belong temporarily to a different species from that of their elders, a species considered by the Parents to be cruel and savage and, relatively speaking, of low intelligence and diminished sensitivity. But these young savages are the well-beloved offspring of these Parents.''

O'Mara showed its teeth again. ''The highly intelligent and hypersensitive Parents would avoid the Small as much as possible, because it is likely that making telepathic contact with such young and primitive minds would be unpleasant in the extreme. It is also probable that the Parents do not make contact because of the risk of damaging their young minds, and retarding their later philosophical development by trying to instruct them before their immature brains are physiologically ready to accept adult teaching.

''That is the type of behavior we expect of a loving and responsible Parent.''

Lioren turned all of his eyes on the aging Earth-human, trying vainly to find the words of respect and admiration that were suited to the occasion. Finally, he said, ''Your words are not supposition. I believe them to describe the facts of the situation in every important respect. This information will greatly aid my understanding of Hellishomar's emotional distress. I am truly grateful, sir.''

''There is a way that you can show your gratitude,'' O'Mara said.

Lioren did not reply.

O'Mara shook its head and looked past Lioren at the office door. ''Before you leave,'' it said, ''there is information you should have and a question we would like you to ask the patient. Who requested medical assistance for it, and how? The usual communications channels were not used, and telepathy, originating as it does from an organic nondirectional transmitter of very low power, is supposed to be impossible at distances over a few hundred yards. There is also great mental discomfort when a telepath tries to force communication with a nontelepath.

''But the facts,'' the Chief Psychologist went on, ''are that Captain Stillson, the commander of the orbiting contact ship, reported having a strange feeling. He was the only member of the crew to have this feeling, which he likened to a strong hunch that something was wrong on the planetary surface. Until then nobody had even considered making a landing on Groalter without permission from the natives, but Stillson took his ship down to the precise spot where the injured Hellishomar was awaiting retrieval and arranged to transport the patient without delay to Sector General, all because he had a very strong feeling that he should do these things. The captain insists that at no time was there any outside influence and that his mind remained his own.''

Lioren was still trying to assimilate this new information, and wondering whether or not it should be given to the patient, when O'Mara spoke again.

''It makes me wonder about the mental capabilities of the adult Groalterri,'' it said in a voice so quiet that it might have been talking to itself. ''If they do not, as now seems evident, communicate with their own young because of the risk of stunting subsequent mental and philosophical development, that must also be the reason they refuse all contact with our supposedly advanced cultures of the Federation.''

Chapter 17

LIOREN'S next meeting with Hellishomar was very useful and intensely frustrating. It gave many interesting pieces of information about the life and behavior of the Small, and said that Lioren was free to discuss the material with others, but it seemed to be talking too much about a subject that was not on its mind. The Monitor Corps would be delighted with the details of Groalterri Small society that he was discovering, but Lioren had a strong feeling that the patient was talking to avoid talking about something else. After three hours of listening to information that was becoming repetitious, Lioren lost patience.

During the next pause he said quickly, ''Hellishomar, I am pleased and grateful, as will be my colleagues, for this information about your home world. But I would prefer to hear, and

I have the feeling that you would prefer to speak, about yourself."

The Groalterri stopped talking.

Lioren forced patience on himself and tried to find the right words of encouragement. Speaking slowly and with many pauses, so as to give Hellishomar every chance to interrupt his questions with an answer, he asked, "Are you concerned about your injuries? There is no need because Seldal assures me that the treatment, although delayed because of the size difference between surgeon and patient, is progressing well and your life is no longer threatened by the infection that has penetrated your body. Are you not a skilled Cutter and highly respected by the Small, who will soon welcome you back to continue the work of extending the lives of Parents? Surely these ailing Parents must also hold you in high regard because of the surgical skills that you can still—"

"I have grown too large to help the Parents," Hellishomar said suddenly, "or to continue as a Cutter. The Small will not want me, either. I am nothing but a failure and an embarrassment to all of them, and I am doubly ashamed because of the great wrong I have done."

Lioren wished that he had more time to think about the implications of this information, and his need to question Hellishomar more closely about it was like a great hunger in his mind. But he was moving into a sensitive area that had been approached before without success. It was likely that too many questions on this subject might seem to Hellishomar like an interrogation, might even imply a judgment and the apportioning of guilt on Lioren's part. His instincts told him that this was a time for further encouragement rather than questions.

"But surely you have grown in surgical experience as well as physical size," Lioren said. "You have said as much yourself. Among many of the peoples of the Federation, an entity who has amassed great knowledge, and who is no longer capable of the physical work involved, makes that knowledge available to the young and less experienced members of its profession. You could become a teacher, Hellishomar. Your knowledge could be passed on to others of the Small who are sure to be grateful to you for it, as would the Parents for the lives you will indirectly have saved. Is this not so?"

Hellishomar's enormous tentacles moved restively, heaving

like great, fleshy waves on an organic ocean. "It is not so, Lioren. The Small will pretend that I do not exist, so that my shame will drive me to the loneliest and most inhospitable part of the swamp that I can find, and the Parents . . . The Parents will ignore and never speak with their minds to me. There are precedents, thankfully a very few, in Groalterri history for what will happen to me. I will be an outcast for the whole of my very long life, with only my thoughts and my guilt for company, for that is the punishment I deserve."

The words, thought Lioren with a sudden rush of remembered pain and guilt, were an echo of those he had used so often to himself, and for a moment he could think of nothing but the Cromsaggar. Frantically he tried to return his mind to Hellishomar's sin, which could not possibly be as grievous as that of wiping out a planetary population. Perhaps one of the Small, or even a Parent, had died because of something Hellishomar had or had not done. With Lioren's crime there could be no real comparison.

In an unsteady voice Lioren said, "I cannot know whether or not your punishment is deserved unless you tell me of the crime, or the sin, you have committed. I know nothing of Groalterri philosophy or theology, and I would be pleased to learn of these matters from you if you are allowed to discuss them. But from my recent studies I know that there is one factor common to all the religions practiced throughout the Federation, and that is forgiveness for sins. Are you sure the Parents will not forgive you?"

"The Parents did not touch my mind," Hellishomar replied. "If they did not do so before I left Groalter, they never will."

"Are you sure?" Lioren said again. "Did you know that the Parents touched the mind of the officer commanding the ship orbiting your planet? The touch was gentle and almost without trace, and it was the first and only time that a Groalterri made direct contact with an off-worlder, but nevertheless the captain was directed accurately to the place where you were dying."

Without giving Hellishomar time to respond, Lioren continued. "You have already told me that the Parents are philosophically incapable of inflicting physical damage or pain, and that even the most skilled Cutters among the Small are too crude and awkward in their methods to undertake surgery on one of their own kind; only the oldest and largest Parents become sick, the Small never. It is certain that your Small colleagues could never equal the delicacy and precision of the work performed by Seldal. You know this to be so, and you know also that if you had not been taken to this hospital you would be dead.

"That being so," Lioren went on quickly, "is it not possible, indeed is it not a certainty that the Parents responsible for your presence here have already forgiven you? By their willingness to break with Groalterri tradition to ask help from an off-planet species, have they not given proof that they have forgiven you, that they value you and are doing all that they can to help you return to full health?"

While he had been speaking, the patient's great body had remained absolutely motionless, but it was the stillness of extreme muscular tension rather than repose. Lioren hoped that the Hudlar nurse on the tractor beam was alert to the situation and ready to pull him out.

"They spoke to a strange, Small-minded off-worlder," Hellishomar said, "but not to me."

Be careful, Lioren told himself warningly, *this might be a very hurt and angry Groalterri*. "I had assumed from what you told me earlier that the Parents did not touch the minds of the Small for any reason. Was I mistaken? What do they say to you?"

Hellishomar's great muscles were still fighting each other, and so evenly matched were they that its body remained motionless. "Are you less intelligent than I assumed, Lioren? Don't you realize that the Small do not remain the Small forever? In preparation for the transition into adulthood of the most senior among us, the Parents touch our minds gently and instruct us in the great laws that guide and bind the long lives of the Parents. We are given the reasons why they seek to live for as long as possible in spite of sickness and physical pain—so that they may be adequately prepared to Go Out. All of these laws are passed on in simplified form to the very young among us by Small teachers who are on the verge of maturity.

"I have waited with patience for the Parents to speak to me," Hellishomar went on, "because I have grown old and large and should rightly have been a young Parent by now. But they do not speak to me. In Groalterri history there are precedents for my situation, a very few of them, fortunately, so I knew that a long, lonely, unhappy and uneventful mental life lay ahead of me. Then in my great despair I committed the most grievous sin of all, and now the Parents will never speak to me.''

As the implications of what the other had been saying became clear to Lioren, a great wave of sympathy washed over his mind, and with it the growing excitement of being on the verge of a full understanding of Hellishomar's problem. He was remembering Seldal's description of the patient's clinical condition and Hellishomar's insistence that the Small were impervious to illness. Now he knew the nature of the great sin that Hellishomar had committed, because Lioren had come very close to committing it himself.

He wished that there was some way that he could bring consolation to this gravely troubled being, or relieve the inner distress of knowing that among its own highly intelligent kind it was mentally retarded. That had been the reason Hellishomar had tried to end its own life.

He said gently, ''If the Parents touch the minds and speak to the Small who are nearing maturity, and for the first time to an off-worlder ship captain in the hope that your injuries could be successfully treated, then they must have a high regard, perhaps a great affection, for you. The reason they do not speak and tell you so is because you cannot hear them. Am I right, Hellishomar?''

''To my shame,'' Hellishomar replied, ''you are right.''

''It is possible,'' Lioren said, carefully avoiding all mention of Hellishomar's other shame, ''that your future life will not be lonely. If embarrassment or other reasons keep the Small from talking to you, and you cannot hear the words of the Parents, there are others who would gladly speak and listen and learn from you. The off-worlders would be pleased to set up a base on the polar hard ground and make it as comfortable as possible for you. If the Parents do not allow this, you could be provided with communications devices which would enable two-way contact to be maintained from orbit. Admittedly, this would not be as satisfactory as full telepathic contact with the Parents, but many questions would be asked and answered by the off-worlders and yourself. Their curiosity about the Groalterri is as great as is yours about the Federation, and will require a long time to satisfy. It is said by many of our foremost thinkers that, to a truly intelligent entity, the satisfaction of curiosity is the greatest

and most lasting of pleasures. You would not be lonely, Hellishomar, nor would there be little to occupy your mind.''

Around and below Lioren the patient's body was stirring although muscular tension was still evident.

''You would not be exchanging mere words,'' Lioren went
on quickly, ''or the verbal questions and answers and descriptions that have passed between us here. When you are well again,
large-screen viewing facilities will be made available to you.
The visuals will be three-dimensional and in full color. Not only
will they show you the physical structure of the galaxy in which
we live and the tiny fraction of it that is populated by the Federation, but display to you in as much detail as you desire the
science and cultures and philosophies of the many and widely
varied intelligent life-forms who are its members. Arrange-
ments could be made that would enable you to question these
life-forms and, visually and aurally, to live among many of
them. Your life would be long, Hellishomar, but full and
interesting so that the absence of Parent mental contact would
not be so—''

''No!''

Once again the razor-edged, bony tip of a cutting tentacle
whistled past Lioren's head to crash against the wall plating.
Surprise and fear paralyzed both his body and mind, but only
for an instant. Before the metallic reverberations had died away
he was talking urgently to the Hudlar in the Nurses' Station,
telling it not to pull him out. If Hellishomar had wanted that
cutting blade to strike him, he would have been a bloody, dis-
membered corpse by now. With a great effort he forced himself
to speak calmly.

''Have I offended you?'' Lioren asked. ''I do not understand.
If nobody else is willing to speak to you, why do you refuse
contact with the Fed—''

''Stop talking about it!'' Hellishomar broke in, its voice loud
and unmodulated as that of a person who could not hear itself
speak. ''I am unworthy, and you tempt me to an even greater
sin.''

Lioren was deeply puzzled by this sudden change in the other's behavior, but decided to give the words and circumstances
that had led up to it more serious thought at another time. He
hoped that the ban on conversation referred to the one hyper-

sensitive topic, whatever that was. But now he had to apologize without knowing what he was apologizing for.

"If I have given offense," Lioren said, "such was not my intention and I am truly sorry. What is it that I've said that offends you? We can discuss a subject of your choosing. The work of this hospital, for example, or the Monitor Corps's continuing search for inhabited worlds in the unexplored reaches of our galaxy, or scientific disciplines practiced throughout the Federation that are unknown to a water world like Groalter—"

Lioren broke off, his body and tongue alike paralyzed with fear. The razor edge of a cutting blade had swept up to within a fraction of an inch of his forebody and face. Any higher and it would have lopped off two of his eyestalks. Suddenly the flat of the blade pressed hard against his chin, chest, and abdomen, pushing him away. Hellishomar's tentacle continued to uncurl to full extension, and the blade was not withdrawn until Lioren had been deposited back at the entrance to the Nurses' Station.

"Officially I have heard nothing," said the Hudlar nurse on duty, after it had satisfied itself that Lioren was uninjured, "but unofficially I would say that the patient does not want to speak to you."

"The patient needs help . . ." Lioren began.

He fell silent then because his thoughts were rushing far ahead of his words. The recent conversation with Hellishomar, together with the information he had already gathered or deduced about the Groalterri culture, was forming a picture in his mind that grew clearer with every moment that passed. Suddenly he knew what had to be done to and for Hellishomar and the entities who were capable of doing it, but there were serious moral and ethical considerations that worried him. He was sure, or as sure as it was possible to be before the event, that he was right. But he had been right on a previous occasion, right and proud and impatient in his self-confidence, and the population of a world had all but died. He did not want to take on the responsibility for destroying another planetary culture, not alone.

"And so do I," he finished.

Chapter 18

H E found Senior Physician Prilicla in the dining hall, its four sets of slowly beating, iridescent wings maintaining a stable hover above the tabletop while it ingested a yellow, stringy substance which the menu screen identified as Earth-human spaghetti. The process by which the little empath drew the strands from the platter and used its delicate forward manipulators to weave them into a fine, continuous rope which disappeared slowly into its eating mouth was one of the most fascinating sights that Lioren had ever seen.

As he was about to apologize for interrupting the other's meal, Lioren discovered that the musical trills and clicks of the Cinrusskin's speech came from a different orifice.

"Friend Lioren," Prilicla said. "I can sense that you are not feeling hunger, or even repugnance at my unusual in-flight method of eating, and that your predominant feeling and probable reason for approaching me is curiosity. How may I satisfy it?"

Cinrusskin GLNOs were empaths, emotion-sensitives who were forced to do everything in their power to insure that the emotional radiation of those around them was as pleasant as possible because to do otherwise would have caused them to suffer the identical feelings that they had caused. In their words and deeds Cinrusskins were invariably pleasant and helpful, but Lioren was nonetheless relieved and grateful for the reminder that it was unnecessary to waste time on verbal politeness.

"I am curious about your empathic faculty and in particular its similarities to full telepathy," he said. "My special interest is in the organic structures, the nerve connections, blood supply, and operating mechanism of an organic transmitter-receiver, and the clinical signs and subjective effects on the possessor should the faculty malfunction. If permitted, I would like to interview any telepaths among the hospital staff or patients, or entities like yourself who do not depend solely on aural channels of communication. This is a private project and I am finding great difficulty obtaining information on the subject."

"That is because the information available is sparse," Prilicla said, "and too speculative as yet to be given to the clinical library. But please, friend Lioren, rest your mind. The growing anxiety you are feeling indicates a fear that news of your private project will be passed to others. I assure you that this will not happen without your prior permission . . . Ah, already you are feeling better and, naturally, so am I. Now I will tell you what little is known."

The seemingly endless rope of spaghetti disappeared, and the platter had been consigned to the disposal slot when the Cinrusskin made a feather-light landing on the table.

"Flying aids the digestion," it said. "Telepathy and empathy are two vastly different faculties, friend Lioren, although it is sometimes possible for an empath to appear telepathic when words and behavior and knowledge of the background support the emotional radiation. Unlike telepathy, empathy is not a rare faculty. Most intelligent beings possess it to a certain extent, otherwise they could never have progressed to civilization. There are many who believe that the telepathic faculty was present in all species, and that it became dormant or atrophied when the more accurate verbal and visually reproducible language evolved. Full telepathy is rare and telepathic contact between different species is rare indeed. Have you had any previous experience of mind contact?"

"Not that I was aware of," Lioren said.

"If it had happened, friend Lioren," the empath said, "you would have been aware of it."

Full telepathy was normally possible only between members of the same species, Prilicla went on to explain. When a telepath tried to make contact with a nontelepath, the stimulation of a faculty long dormant in the latter had been described as an attempted exchange of signals between two mismatched organic transmitter-receivers. Initially the subjective effects on the nontelepath were far from pleasant.

At present there were three telepathic species in the hospital, all of whom were patients. The Telfi life-forms were physiological classification VTXM, a group-mind species whose small, beetlelike bodies lived by the direct conversion of hard radiation. Although individually the beings were quite stupid, the gestalt entities were highly intelligent. Investigating their ultra-hot metabolism closely was to risk death by radiation poisoning.

Access to the remaining telepathic life-forms was restricted. They were the Gogleskan healer Khone and its recent offspring and two Protectors of the Unborn, all of whom were at Sector General for clinical and psychological investigation by Diagnostician Conway, Chief Psychologist O'Mara, and Prilicla itself.

"Conway has had successful contact as well as surgical experience with both of these life-forms," the empath went on, "although it is still too recent and radical to have found its way into the literature. Your colleague Cha Thrat has also had extended contact with the Gogleskan, Khone, and helped deliver its child. It would save time and effort if you simply talked to these entities, or asked that the relevant clinical notes be made available to you . . . I am sorry, friend Lioren. From the intensity of your emotional radiation it is clear that my suggestion was not helpful."

Prilicla was trembling as though its fragile body and pipestem limbs were being shaken by a great wind that only it could feel. But it was an emotional gale whose origin was Lioren himself, so he strove to control his feelings until the empath's body was again at rest.

"It is I who should apologize for distressing you," Lioren said. "You are correct. I have strong, personal reasons for not involving other members of my department, at least until I know enough to speak without wasting their time. But I would dearly like to read the Diagnostician's clinical notes and visit the patients you mentioned."

"I can feel your curiosity, friend Lioren," Prilicla said, "but not, of course, the reasons for it. My guess is that it has something to do with the Groalterri patient."

It paused and once again its body trembled, but only for a moment. "Your control of your emotional radiation is improving, friend Lioren, and I compliment and thank you for it. But there is no cause for the fear in your mind. I know that you are hiding something from me, but not being a telepath I do not know what it is. I would not relay my suspicions to others in case I caused emotional distress in you that would rebound on myself.''

Lioren relaxed, feeling grateful and reassured, and knowing that with this entity he did not have to vocalize his feelings. But the empath was still speaking.

''It is common knowledge,'' Prilicla said, ''that you are the only being within the hospital who has talked freely with Hellishomar. Because my empathic faculty is bound by the inverse square law, it increases in sensitivity with proximity to the radiating mind. I have deliberately avoided approaching the Groalterri because Hellishomar is a deeply distressed and desperately unhappy entity, full of guilt and grief and pain, and it has a mind so powerful that there is nowhere within the hospital that I can escape completely from these terrible and continuing feelings. However, since you began to visit Hellishomar there has been a marked decrease in the intensity of this distressing emotional radiation and for that, friend Lioren, I am truly grateful.

''When Hellishomar's name is mentioned,'' the empath went on before Lioren could speak, ''I detected from you an emotion that is closer to a strong hope than an expectation. It was strongest when telepathy was mentioned. That is why you will be allowed to visit the telepathic patients. Copies of the relevant clinical files will be made available to you for study. If now is a convenient time, we will begin by visiting the Protectors of the Unborn.''

The Cinrusskin's six iridescent wings began to beat slowly and it rose gracefully into the air above the table.

''You are radiating an intense feeling of gratitude,'' Prilicla went on as it flew above Lioren toward the dining-hall entrance, ''but it is not strong enough to conceal an underlying anxiety and suspicion. What troubles you, friend Lioren?''

His first impulse was to deny that anything was troubling him, but that would have been like two Kelgians trying to lie to each other—his deepest feelings were as visible to Prilicla as a Kelgian's mobile fur. ''I am anxious because these are Conway's patients, and if you are allowing me to visit them without permission you might find yourself in trouble. My suspicions are that Conway has already given its permission and for some reason you are not telling me why.''

''Your anxiety is unfounded,'' Prilicla said, ''and your suspicions are accurate. Conway was about to ask you to visit these patients. They are here for close observation and investigation which, to them, is the clinical equivalent of a prison sentence of unknown duration. They are cooperative but not happy and are missing their home planets. We know of two patients, Mannen and Hellishomar, who have benefited from talking to you and, with apologies for any hurt to your feelings, friend Conway thought that visits from you would do no harm even if they did no good.

"I don't know what it is that you say to them," the empath went on, "and according to the grapevine you won't even tell O'Mara precisely how you achieve your results. My own theory is that you use the reversal technique, so that instead of the doctor extending sympathy to the patient the opposite occurs, and proceed from there. I have used this technique myself on occasions. Being fragile and emotionally hypersensitive myself, people are inclined to feel sorry for me and allow me, as Conway describes it, to get away with murder. But for you, friend Lioren, they can really feel sorry because—"

For a moment Prilicla's hovering flight became less than stable as the terrible memories of a depopulated planet came flooding back into his mind. Of course they all felt sorry for him, but no less sorry than he felt for himself. Desperately he fought to push those memories back to the safe place he had made for them, where they could trouble only his sleep, and he must have succeeded because the Cinrusskin was flying straight and level again.

"You have good control, friend Lioren," Prilicla said. "Your close-range emotional radiation is uncomfortable to me but no longer as distressing as it was during and after the court-martial. I am glad for both our sakes. On the way there I will tell you about the first two patients."

The Protector of the Unborn belonged to physiological classification FSOJ, a large, immensely strong life-form with a heavy, slitted carapace from which protruded four thick tentacles, a heavy, serrated tail, and its head. The tentacles terminated in a cluster of sharp, bony projections which made them resemble spiked clubs. The main features of the head were the well-protected, recessed eyes, the large upper and lower mandibles, and teeth which were capable of deforming all but the strongest metal alloys.

They had evolved on a world of shallow seas and steaming jungle swamps where the line of demarcation between animal and vegetable life, so far as physical mobility and aggression were concerned, was unclear. To survive at all, a life-form had to be immensely strong, highly mobile, and unsleeping, and the dominant species on that planet had earned its place by fighting and moving faster and reproducing its kind with a greater potential for survival than any of the others.

The utter savagery of their environment had forced them to evolve a physical form that gave maximum protection to the vital organs. Brain, heart, lungs, and greatly enlarged womb, all were housed deep inside the organic fighting machine that was the Protector's body. Their gestation period was abnormally extended because the embryo had to grow virtually to maturity before parturition, and it was rare for an adult to survive the reproduction of more than three offspring. An aging parent was usually too weak to defend itself against attack by its lastborn.

The principal reason for the Protectors' rise to dominance on their world was that their young were already fully educated in the techniques of survival long before they were born. In the dawn of their evolution the process had begun as a complex set of survival characteristics at the genetic level, but the small physical separation of the brains of the parent and its developing fetus had led to an effect analogous to induction of the electro-chemical activity associated with thought. The result was that the embryos became short-range telepaths receiving everything the parent saw or felt.

And before the fetus was half-grown there was taking form within it another embryo that was also increasingly aware of the violent world outside its self-fertilizing grandparent, until gradually the telepathic range increased until communication became possible between embryos whose parents came close enough to see each other.

To minimize damage to a parent's internal organs, the growing fetus was paralyzed within the womb, and the prebirth deparalysis also caused loss of both sentience and the telepathic faculty. A newborn Protector would not survive for long in its incredibly savage environment if it was hampered by the ability to think.

With nothing to do but receive impressions from the outside world, exchange thoughts with the other Unborn, and try to extend their telepathic range by making contact with various forms of nonsentient life around them, the embryos developed minds of great power and intelligence. But they could not build anything, or engage in any form of technical research, or do anything at all that would influence the activities of their parents and protectors, who had to fight and kill and eat continually to maintain their unsleeping bodies and the unborn within them.

"That was the situation," Prilicla went on, "before friend Conway was successful in delivering an Unborn without loss of sentience. Now there are the original Protector and its offspring, who is itself a young Protector, and the embryos growing within both of them, all but the original parent in telepathic contact. Their ward, which was built to reproduce the FSOJs' home environment, is the next opening on the left. You may find the sight disturbing, friend Lioren, and the noise is certainly horrendous."

The ward was more than half-filled by a hollow, endless cylinder of immensely strong metal latticework. The diameter of the structure was just wide enough to allow continuous, unrestricted movement in one direction to the FSOJ patients it contained, and which curved and twisted back on itself so that the occupants could use all of the available floor area that was not required for access by the medical attendants or environmental support equipment. The cylinder floor reproduced the uneven ground and natural obstacles like the mobile and voracious triproots found on the Protectors' home planet, while the open sections gave the occupants a continuous view of the screens positioned around the outer surface of the cylinder. Onto the screens were projected moving, tri-d pictures of the indigenous plant and animal life which they would normally encounter.

The open lattice structure also helped the medical attendants to bring to bear on the patients the more positive aspects of the life-support system. Positioned between the projected screen images were the mechanisms whose sole purpose was to beat, tear, or jab at the occupants' rapidly moving bodies with any required degree of frequency or force.

Everything possible was being done, Lioren noted, to make the Protectors feel at home.

"Will they be able to hear us?" Lioren shouted above the din. "Or we them?"

"No, friend Lioren," the empath replied. "The screaming

and grunting sounds they are making do not carry intelligence, but are solely a means of frightening natural enemies. Until the recent successful birthing the intelligent Unborn remained within the nonsentient Protector and heard only the internal organic sounds of the parent. Speech was impossible and unnecessary for them. The only communication channel open to us is telepathy.''

"I am not a telepath," Lioren said.

"Nor are Conway, Thornnastor, and the others who have been contacted by the Unborn," Prilicla said. "The few known species with the telepathic faculty evolved organic transmitter-receivers that are automatically in tune for that particular race, and for this reason contact between members of different telepathic species is not always possible. When mental contact occurs between one of these entities and a nontelepath, it usually means that the faculty in the latter is dormant or atrophied rather than nonexistent. When such contact occurs the experience for the nontelepath can be very uncomfortable, but there are no physical changes in the brain affected nor is there any lasting psychological damage.

"Move closer to the exercise cage, friend Lioren," Prilicla went on. "Can you feel the Protector touching your mind?"

"No," Lioren said.

"I feel your disappointment," the empath said. A faint tremor shook its body and it went on, "But I also feel the young Protector generating the emotional radiation characteristic of intense curiosity and concentrated effort. It is trying very hard to contact you."

"I'm sorry, nothing," Lioren said.

Prilicla spoke briefly into its communicator, then said, "I have stepped up the violence of the attack mechanisms. The patient will suffer no injury, but we have found that the effect of increased activity and apparent danger on the endocrine system aids the process of mentation. Try to make your mind receptive."

"Still nothing," Lioren said, touching the side of his head with one hand, "except for some mild discomfort in the inter-cranial area that is becoming very . . ." The rest was an untranslatable sound which rivaled in volume the noise coming from the Protectors' life-support system.

The sensation was like a deep, raging itch inside his brain

combined with a discordant, unheard noise that mounted steadily in intensity. This must be what it is like, Lioren thought helplessly, when a faculty which is dormant is awakened and forced to perform. As in the case of a muscle long unused, there was pain and stiffness and protest against the change in the old, comfortable order of things.

Suddenly the discomfort was gone, the unheard storm of sound in his mind faded to become a deep, still pool of mental silence on which the external din of the ward had no effect. Then out of the stillness there came words that were unspoken from a being who did not have a name but whose mind and unique personality were an identification that could never be mistaken for any other.

"You are feeling seriously disturbed, friend Lioren," Prilicla said. "Has the Protector touched your mind?"

Rather, Lioren answered silently, *it has almost swamped my mind.* "Yes, contact was established and quickly broken. I tried to help it by suggesting . . . It asked for another visit at a later time. Can we leave now?"

Prilicla led the way into the corridor without speaking, but Lioren did not need an empathic faculty to be aware of the Cinrusskin's intense curiosity. "I did not realize that so much knowledge could be exchanged in such a short time," he said. "Words convey meaning in a trickle, thoughts in a great tidal wave, and problems explained instantly and in the fullest detail. I will need time alone to think about everything it has told me so that my answers will not be confused and half-formed. It is impossible to lie to a telepath."

"Or an empath," Prilicla said. "Do you wish to delay your visit to the Gogleskan?"

"No," Lioren replied. "My lonely thinking can wait until this evening. Will Khone use telepathy on me?"

Prilicla had a moment of unstable flight for some reason, then recovered. "I certainly hope not."

The empath explained that adult Gogleskans used a form of telepathy which required close physical contact, but, except when their lives were threatened, they did everything possible to avoid such contact. It was not simple xenophobia that ailed them, but a pathological fear of the close approach of any large creature, including nonfamily members of their own species. They possessed a well-developed spoken and written language which had allowed the individual and group cooperation necessary for growth of civilization, but their verbal contacts were rare and conducted over the greatest practicable distance and in the most impersonal terms. It was not surprising that their level of technology had remained low.

The reason for their abnormally fearful behavior was a racial psychosis implanted far back in their prehistoric past. It was a subject which Lioren was strongly advised to approach with caution.

"Otherwise," Prilicla said as it checked its flight above the entrance to the side ward reserved for the Gogleskans, "you risk distressing the patient and endangering the trust that has gradually been built up between Khone and those responsible for its treatment. I am unwilling to subject it to the emotional strain of a visit from two strangers, so I shall leave you now. Healer Khone is a frightened, timid, but intensely curious being. Try to converse impersonally as I have suggested, friend Lioren, and think well before you speak."

A wall of heavy, transparent plastic stretching from floor to ceiling divided the room into equal halves. Hatches for the introduction of food and remote handling devices hung apparently unsupported like empty white picture frames. The treatment half of the ward contained the usual tools of medical investigation modified for use at a distance and three viewscreens. Only two of them were visible to the adult Gogleskan, the third being a repeater for the patient monitor in the main ward's nursing station. Not wishing to risk giving offense by staring at Khone directly, Lioren concentrated his attention on the picture on the repeater screen.

The Gogleskan healer, Lioren saw at once, was classification FOKT. Its erect, ovoid body was covered by a mass of long, brightly colored hair and flexible spikes, some of which were tipped by small, bulbous pads and grouped into digital clusters so as to enable eating utensils, tools, or medical instruments to be grasped and manipulated. He was able to identify the four long, pale tendrils that were used during contact telepathy lying amid the multicolored cranial hair. The head was encircled by a narrow metal band that supported a corrective lens for one of the four, equally spaced and recessed eyes. Around the lower body was a thick skirt of muscle on which the creature rested, and whenever it changed position four stubby legs were extended below the edge of the muscular skirt. It was making untranslatable moaning sounds, which Lioren thought might be wordless music, to its offspring, who was almost hairless but otherwise a scaled-down copy of its parent. The sound seemed to be coming from a number of small, vertical breathing orifices encircling its waist.

Beyond the transparent wall, the metal plating had been covered with a layer of something that resembled dark, unpolished wood, and several pieces of low furniture and shelves of the same material were placed around the inner three walls. Clumps of aromatic vegetation decorated the room, and the lighting reproduced the subdued orange glow of Gogleskan sunlight that had been filtered through overhead branches. Khone's accommodation was as homelike as the hospital's environment technicians could make it, but Khone was too timid to complain about anything except a sudden and close approach of strangers.

A timid entity, Prilicla had described it, who was perpetually fearful and intensely curious.

"Is it permitted," he asked in the prescribed impersonal manner, "for the trainee Lioren to examine the medical notes of the patient and healer, Khone? The purpose is the satisfaction of curiosity, not to conduct a medical examination."

A personal name could be given only once, at the Time of First Meeting, Prilicla had told him, for the purpose of identification and introduction, and never mentioned again except during written communication. Khone's body hair stirred restively and for a moment it stood out straight from the body, making the little entity appear twice its real size and revealing the long, sharply pointed stings that lay twitching close against the curvature of the lower torso. The stings were the Gogleskans' only natural weapon, but the poison they delivered was instantly lethal to the metabolism of any warm-blooded oxygenbreather.

The moaning sound died away. "Relief is felt that clinical examination by another fearsome but well-intentioned monster is not imminent," Khone said. "It is permitted and, since access to the medical notes cannot be forbidden, gratitude is felt for the polite wording of the request. May suggestions be made?"

"They would be welcomed," Lioren said, thinking that the

Gogleskan's forthright manner was not what he had expected. Perhaps the timidity was not evident during verbal exchanges.

"The entities who visit this ward are invariably polite," Khone said, "and frequently politeness retards conversation. If the curiosity of the trainee is specific rather than general, there would be an advantage if the patient rather than the medical notes were consulted."

"Yes, indeed," Lioren said. "Thank you . . . That is, helpfulness has been shown and gratitude is felt. The trainee's primary interest lies in the—"

"It is presumed," the Gogleskan went on, "that the trainee will answer as well as ask questions. The patient is an experienced healer, by Gogleskan standards, and knows that both parent and firstborn are healthy and are protected from physical danger or disease. The firstborn is too young to feel anything other than contentment, but the parent is prey to many different feelings, the strongest of which is boredom. Does the trainee understand?"

"The trainee understands," Lioren replied, gesturing toward the inward-facing display screens, "and will try to relieve the condition. There is interesting visual material available on the worlds and peoples of the Federation—"

"Which shows monstrous creatures inhabiting crowded cities," Khone broke in. "Or packed tightly together in close, nonsexual contact inside air or ground vehicles, or similar terrifying sights. Terror is not the indicated cure for boredom. If knowledge is to be obtained about the visually horrifying peoples and practices of the Federation, it must be slowly and of one person at a time."

Even a Groalterri, Lioren thought, would not live long enough to do that. "As the uninvited guest is it not proper for the trainee to give answers before asking questions of the host?"

"Another unnecessary politeness," Khone replied, "but appreciation is felt nonetheless. What is the trainee's first question?"

This was going to be much easier than he had expected, Lioren thought. "The trainee desires information on Gogleskan telepathy, specifically on the organic mechanisms which enable it to function and the physical causes, including both the clinical and subjective symptomology present if the faculty should malfunction. This information might prove helpful with another patient whose species is also tele—''

''*No!*'' Khone said, so loudly that the young one began making agitated, whistling sounds that did not translate. A large patch of the Gogleskan's body hair rose stiffly outward and, in a manner that Lioren could not see clearly, wove the strands into the shorter growth of its offspring and held it close to the parent's body until the young one became quiet again.

''I'm very sorry,'' Lioren began, in his self-anger and disappointment forgetting to be impersonal. He rephrased quickly. ''Extreme sorrow is felt, and apologies tendered. It was not the intention to cause offense. Would it be better if the offensive trainee withdrew?''

''No,'' Khone said again, in a quieter voice. ''Telepathy and Gogleskan prehistory are most sensitive subjects. They have been discussed in the past with the entities Conway, Prilicla, and O'Mara, all of whom are strange and visually threatening but well-trusted beings. But the trainee is strange and frightening and not known to the patient.

''The telepathic function is instinctive rather than under conscious control. It is triggered by the presence of strangers, or anything else that the Gogleskan subconscious mind considers a threat that, in a species so lacking in physical strength, is practically everything. Can the trainee understand the Gogleskan's problem, and be patient?''

''There is understanding—'' Lioren began.

''Then the subject can be discussed,'' Khone broke in. ''But only when enough is known about the trainee for the patient to be able to close its eyes and see the person enclosed in that visually horrendous shape, and so override the instinctive panic reaction that would otherwise occur.''

''There is understanding,'' Lioren said again. ''The trainee will be pleased to answer the patient's questions.''

The Gogleskan rose a few inches onto its short legs and moved to the side, apparently to have a better view of Lioren's lower body, which had been hidden by one of the display screens, before it spoke.

''The first question is,'' it said, ''what is the trainee training to be?''

''A Healer of the Mind,'' Lioren replied.

''No surprise is felt,'' Khone said.

Chapter 19

THE questions were many and searching, but so polite and impersonal was the interrogation that no offense could be taken. By the time it was over, the Gogleskan healer knew almost as much about Lioren as he did himself. Even then it was obvious that Khone wanted to know more.

The young one had been transferred to a tiny bed at the back of the compartment, and Khone had overcome its timidity to the extent of moving forward until its body touched the transparent dividing wall.

"The Tarlan trainee and onetime respected healer," it said, "has answered many questions about itself and its past and present life. All of the information is of great interest, although plainly much of it is distressing to the listener as well as the speaker. Sympathy is felt regarding the terrible events on Cromsag and there is sorrow and helplessness that the Gogleskan healer is unable to give relief in this matter.

"At the same time," Khone went on, "there is a feeling that the Tarlan, who has spoken openly and in detail of many things normally kept secret from others, is concealing information. Are there events in the past more terrible than those already revealed, and why does the trainee not speak of them?"

"There is nothing," Lioren said, more loudly than he had intended, "more terrible than Cromsag."

"The Gogleskan is relieved to hear it," Khone said. "Is it that the Tarlan is afraid lest its words be passed on to others and cause embarrassment? It should be informed that a healer on Gogplesk does not speak of such matters to others unless given permission to do so. The trainee should not feel concern."

Lioren was silent for a moment, thinking that his utter and impersonal dedication to the healing art and the self-imposed discipline that had ruled his past life had left him neither the time nor the inclination to form emotional ties. It was only after the court-martial, when any thought of career advancement was ridiculous and the continuation of his life was the cruelest of all punishments, that he had become interested in people for reasons other than their clinical condition. In spite of their strange shapes and even stranger thought processes, he had begun to think of some of them as friends.

Perhaps this creature was another.

"A similar rule binds the healers of many worlds," he said, "but gratitude is expressed nonetheless. The reason other information has been concealed is that the beings concerned do not wish it to be revealed."

"There is understanding," Khone said, "and additional curiosity about the trainee. Has the repeated telling reduced the emotional distress caused by the Cromsag Incident?"

Lioren was silent for a moment; then he said, "It is impossible to be objective in this matter. Many other matters occupy the trainee's mind so that the memory returns with less frequency, but it still causes distress. Now the trainee is wondering whether it is the Gogleskan or the Tarlan who is better trained in other-species psychology."

Khone gave a short, whistling sound which did not translate. "The trainee has provided information that will enable a troubled mind to escape for a time from its own troubles because this healer, too, has thoughts which it would prefer not to think. Now the Tarlan visitor no longer seems strange or threatening, even to the dark undermind that feels and reacts but does not think, and there is an unpaid debt. Now the trainee's questions will be answered."

Lioren expressed impersonal thanks and once again sought information on the functioning, and especially the symptoms of malfunctioning, of the Gogleskan telepathic faculty. But to learn about their telepathy was to learn everything about them.

The situation on the primitive world of Goglesk was the direct opposite of that on Groalter. Federation policy had always been that full contact with a technologically backward culture could be dangerous because, when the Monitor Corps ships and contact specialists dropped out of their skies, they could never be certain whether they were giving the natives evidence of a technological goal at which to aim or a destructive inferiority complex. But the Gogleskans, in spite of their backwardness in the physical sciences and the devastating racial psychosis that forced them to remain so, were psychologically stable as individuals, and their planet had not known war for many centuries.

The easiest course would have been for the Corps to withdraw and write the Gogleskan problem off as insoluble. Instead they had compromised by setting up a small base for the purposes of observation, long-range investigation, and limited contact.

Progress for any intelligent species depended on increasing levels of cooperation between individuals and family or tribal groups. On Goglesk, however, any attempt at close cooperation brought a period of drastically reduced intelligence, a mindless urge to destruction, and serious physical injury in its wake, so that the Gogleskans had been forced into becoming a race of individualists who had close physical contact only during the periods when reproduction was possible or while caring for their young.

The situation had been forced on them in presapient times, when they had been the principal food source of every predator infesting Goglesk's oceans. Although physically puny, they had been able to evolve weapons of offense and defense—stings that paralyzed or killed the smaller life-forms, and long, cranial tendrils that gave them the faculty of telepathy by contact. When threatened by large predators they linked bodies and minds together in the numbers required to englobe and neutralize with their combined stings any attacker regardless of its size.

There was fossil evidence that a bitter struggle for survival had been waged between them and a gigantic and particularly ferocious species of ocean predator for millions of years. The presapient Gogleskans had won in the end, but they had paid a terrible price.

In order to englobe and sting to death one of those giant predators, physical and telepathic linkages between hundreds of presapient FOKTs were required. A great many of them had perished, been torn apart and eaten during every such encounter, and the consequent and often repeated death agonies of the victims had been shared telepathically by every member of the group. A natural mechanism had evolved that had fractionally reduced this suffering, diluting the pain of group telepathy by generating a mindless urge to destroy indiscriminately everything within reach that was not an FOKT. But even though the Gogleskans had become intelligent and civilized far beyond the level expected of a primitive fishing and farming culture, the mental wounds inflicted during their prehistory would not heal.

The high-pitched audible signal emitted by Gogleskans in distress that triggered the joining process could not be ignored at either the conscious or unconscious levels. That call to join represented only one thing, the threat of ultimate danger. And even in present times, when the danger was insignificant or imaginary, it made no difference. A joining led inevitably to the mindless destruction of everything in their immediate vicinity—housing, vehicles, crops, farm animals, mechanisms, book and art objects—that they had been able to build or grow as individuals.

That was why the present-day Gogleskans would not allow, except in the circumstances Khone had already mentioned, anyone to touch or come close to them or even address them in anything but the most impersonal terms while they fought helplessly and, until the recent visit of Diagnostician Conway to Gogleskans, hopelessly against the condition that evolution had imposed on them.

"It is Conway's intention to break the Gogleskan racial conditioning," Khone went on, "by allowing the parent and offspring to experience gradually increasing exposure to a variety of other life-forms who were intelligent, civilized, and obviously not a threat. It was thought that the young one, in particular, might become so accustomed to the process that its subconscious as well as its conscious mind would be able to control the blind urge that previously caused a panic reaction leading to a joining. Mechanisms have also been devised by the hospital which distort the audible distress signal so that it becomes unrecognizable. The triggering stimulus and subsequent urge to mindless destruction would then be limited to the capabilities of one rather than a large group of persons acting in concert. Another solution which has doubtless already occurred to the trainee would be to excise the tendrils which allow contact telepathy and make it impossible for a joining to occur. But that solution is not possible because the tendrils are needed to give comfort and later to educate the very young, as well as to intensify the pleasures of mating, and the Gogleskans suffer privations enough without becoming voluntary emotional cripples.

"It is Conway's expectation and our hope," Khone concluded, "that this two-pronged attack on the problem will enable the Gogleskans to build with permanence and advance to a level of civilization commensurate with their intelligence.''

Normally Lioren found it difficult to detect emotional overtones in translated speech, but this time he felt sure that there was a deep uncertainty within the other's mind that had not been verbalized.

''This trainee may be in error,'' Lioren said, ''but it senses that the Gogleskan healer patient is troubled. Is there dissatisfaction with the treatment it is receiving? Are there doubts regarding the abilities or expectations of Conway—?''

''No!'' Khone broke in. ''There was one brief and accidental sharing of minds with the Diagnostician when it visited Goglesk. Its abilities and intentions are known and are beyond criticism. But its mind was crowded with other minds full of strange experiences and thoughts so alien that the Gogleskan wanted to call for a joining. Much was learned from the mind of Conway and much more remains incomprehensible, but it was plain that the proportion of the Diagnostician's mind available for the Goglesk project was small. When doubts were first expressed, the Diagnostician listened and its words were confident, reassuring, and dismissive, and it may be that Conway does not fully understand the nonmedical problem. It cannot or will not believe that, out of all the intelligent races that make up the Federation, the Gogleskan species alone is accursed and doomed forever to self-inflicted barbarism by the Authority which Orders All Things.''

Lioren was silent for a moment, wondering if he was about to become involved once again in a problem that was philosophical rather than clinical, and unsure of his right or ability as a Tarlan unbeliever to engage in a debate on other-species theology. ''If there was a telepathic touching,'' he said, ''then the Diagnostician must have seen and understood what is in the healer's mind, so that the doubts may be groundless. But the trainee is completely ignorant in this matter. If the healer wishes it, the trainee will listen to these doubts and not be dismissive. A fear was mentioned that the situation on Goglesk would never change. Can the reason for this fear be explained more fully?''

''Yes,'' Khone said in a quieter voice. ''It is a fear that one entity cannot change the course of evolution. It was evident from Conway's mind, and from the thoughts and beliefs of those entities who shared that mind when the touching occurred, that the situation on Goglesk is abnormal. On the other worlds of the Federation there is a struggle between the destructive forces of environment and instinctive, animal behavior on one side and the efforts of thinking and cooperating beings on the other. By some entities it is called the continuing battle to impose order upon chaos, and by many the struggle between good and bad, or God against the Evil One. On all of these worlds it is the former, at times with great difficulty, who is gaining ascendancy over the latter. But on Goglesk there is no God; only the pre-historic but still all-powerful Devil rules there . . .''

The Gogleskan's erect, ovoid body was trembling, its hair was raised like clumps of long, many-colored grass, and the four yellow spikes that were its stings were beaded with venom at the tips. For it was seeing again the images that had been indelibly printed into its racial memory, the terrible pictures complete with their telepathically shared death agonies as the gigantic predators had torn its joined forebears into bloody tat-ters. Lioren suspected that the signal of ultimate distress, the Call for Joining, would have already gone out if Khone had not controlled its instinctive terror with the reminder that the only other Gogleskan capable of linking telepathically with it was its own sleeping offspring.

Gradually Khone's trembling diminished, and when the erect hair and stings were again lying flat against its body, it went on. ''There is great fear and even greater despair. The Gogleskan feels that the help of the Earth-human Diagnostician, with good-will and the resources of this great hospital at its disposal, are not enough to alter the destiny of a world. It is a stupid self-delusion on the part of this healer to think otherwise, and a gross act of ingratitude to tell Conway of these feelings. Everywhere in the Federation there is a balance between order and chaos, or good and evil, but it is inconceivable that a Gogleskan and its child could alter the destiny, the habits and thinking and feelings of an entire planetary population.''

Lioren made the sign of negation, then realized that the ges-ture would be meaningless to Khone. ''The healer is wrong. There are many precedents on many different worlds where one person was able to do just that. Admittedly, the person con-cerned was an entity with special qualities, a great teacher or lawgiver or philosopher, and many of its followers believed that it was the manifestation of their God. It is not certain that the healer and its child, with Conway's assistance, will change the course of Gogleskan history, but it is possible.''

Khone made a short, wheezing sound which did not translate. ''Such wildly inaccurate and extravagant compliments have not been received since the prelude to first mating. Surely the Tarlan is aware that the Gogleskan healer is neither a teacher nor a leader nor a person with any special qualities. That which the trainee suggests is ridiculous!''

''The trainee is aware,'' Lioren said, ''that the healer is the only member of its species to have faced its Devil, to have broken its racial conditioning to the extent of coming to a place like Sector General, a place filled with monstrous but well-intentioned beings the majority of whom are visually more terrifying than the Dark One that haunts the Gogleskan racial memory. And the trainee disagrees because it is self-evident that the healer possesses special qualities.

''For it has demonstrated beyond doubt,'' Lioren went on before Khone could react, ''that it is possible for one Gogleskan who was continually in fear of the close approach of its own kind to overcome and, with practice and great strength of will, to understand and even befriend many of the creatures out of nightmare who live here. This being so, is it not possible, even probable, that it will be able to find and teach this quality to others of its kind, who will in time spread its teachings throughout their world until gradually the Dark One loses all power over the Gogleskan mind?''

''That is what Conway believes,'' Khone said. ''But is it not also probable that the followers will say that the teacher is damaged in the brain, and be fearful of the great changes that they would have to make in their customs and habits of mind? If it persisted in its attempts to make them think in new and uncomfortable ways, they might drive the teacher from them and inflict serious injury or worse.''

''Regrettably,'' Lioren said, ''there are precedents for such behavior, but if the teaching is good it outlives the teacher. And the Gogleskans are a gentle race. This teacher should feel neither fear nor despair.''

Khone made no response and Lioren went on. ''It is a truism that in any place of healing a patient will invariably find others in a more distressed condition than itself, and derive some small comfort from the discovery. The same holds true among the distressed worlds. The healer is also wrong, therefore, in thinking that Goglesk is uniquely accursed by fate or whichever other agency it feels is responsible.

"There are the Cromsaggar," Lioren went on, maintaining a quiet tone within the sudden clamor of memories the word aroused, "whose curse was that they were constantly ill and constantly at war because fighting each other was the only cure for their disease. And there are the Protectors, who fight and hunt and kill mindlessly for every moment of their adult lives, and who would make the long-extinct Dark Ones of Goglesk seem tame by comparison. Yet within these terrible organic killing machines live, all too briefly, the telepathic Unborn whose minds are gentle and sensitive and in all respects civilized. Diagnostician Thornnastor has solved the Cromsag problem, which was basically one of endocrinology, so that the few surviving natives of that planet will no longer be condemned to unending, reluctant warfare. Diagnostician Conway has made itself responsible for freeing the Protectors of the Unborn from their evolutionary trap, but everyone feels that it is the Gogleskan problem which will be more easily solved—"

"These problems have already been discussed," Khone broke in, its whistling speech increasing in pitch as it spoke. "The solutions, although complex, involve medical or surgical conditions that are susceptible to physical treatment. It is not so on Goglesk. There the problem is not susceptible to physical solution. It is the most important part of the genetic inheritance that enabled the species to survive since presapient times and cannot be destroyed. The evil that drives the race to self-destruction and self-enforced solitude was, is, and always will be. On Goglesk there has never been a God, only the Devil."

"Again," Lioren said, "it is possible that the healer is incorrect. The trainee hesitates lest offense is given through ignorance of Gogleskan religious beliefs that may be held by the—"

"Impatience is felt," Khone said, "but offense will not be taken."

For a moment Lioren tried desperately to remember and organize the information he had recently abstracted from the library computer. "It is widely taught and believed throughout the Federation that where there is evil there is also good, and that there cannot be a devil without God. This God is believed to be the all-knowing, all-powerful but compassionate supreme being and maker of all things, and is also held to be ever-present but invisible. If only the Devil is evident on Goglesk it does not necessarily mean that God is not there because all of the beliefs, regardless of species, are in agreement that the first place to look for God is within one's self.

"The Gogleskans have been struggling against their Devil since they first developed intelligence," Lioren went on. "Sometimes they have lost but more often of late they have made small gains. It could be that there is one Devil and many who unknowingly carry their God within them."

"These are like the words spoken by Conway," Khone said. "But the Diagnostician encourages with advanced medical science and advises more rigorous training in the mental disciplines. Is Goglesk's benefactor unable to believe in God or our Devil or any other form of nonphysical presence?"

"Perhaps," Lioren said. "But regardless of its beliefs the quality of its assistance remains unaltered."

Khone was silent for so long that Lioren wondered if the interview was over. He had a strong feeling that the other wanted to speak, but when they eventually came the words were a complete surprise.

"Additional reassurance might be felt," Khone said, "if the Tarlan spoke of its own beliefs."

"The Tarlan," Lioren said carefully, "knows of many different beliefs held by its own people as well as those on other worlds, but the knowledge is recently acquired, incomplete, and probably inaccurate. It has also discovered in the histories of the subject that such beliefs, if they are strongly held, are matters of faith which are not susceptible to change through logical argument. If the beliefs are very strongly held, the discussion of alternative beliefs can give offense. The Tarlan does not wish to offend, and it does not have the right to influence the beliefs of others in any fashion. For these reasons it would prefer that the Gogleskan takes the lead by describing its own beliefs."

It had been obvious from the beginning that Khone was deeply troubled, even though the precise nature of the problem had been unclear. This was not an area where advice could be given in total ignorance.

"The Tarlan is being evasive," Khone said, "and cautious."

"The Gogleskan," Lioren said, "is correct."

There was a short silence, then Khone said, "Very well. The Gogleskan is frightened, and despairing, and angry about the Devil that lives within the minds of its people and constantly tortures and binds them in chains of near-barbarism. It is preferred that nothing be spoken of the nonmaterial supports its people use to solace and encourage themselves because this Gogleskan, as a healer, doubts the efficacy of nonmaterial medication. It asks again, what kind of God does the Tarlan believe in?

"Is it a great, omniscient, and all-powerful creator," Khone went on before Lioren could reply, "who allows or ignores pain and injustice? Is it a god who heaps undeserved misfortune on a few species while blessing the majority with peace and contentment? Does it have good or even godly reasons for permitting such terrible events as the destruction of the Cromsaggar population, or for the evolutionary trap which imprisons the Protectors of the Unborn and for the dreadful scourge it has inflicted on the Gogleskans? Can there be any sin committed in the past so grievous that it warrants such punishment? Does this God have intelligence and ethical reasons for such apparently stupid and immoral behavior, and will the Tarlan please explain them?"

The Tarlan has no explanations, thought Lioren, because he is an unbeliever like yourself. But he knew instinctively that that was not the answer Khone wanted, because if it was truly an unbeliever it would not be so angry with the God it did not believe in. This was a time for soft answers.

Chapter 20

"As has already been stated," Lioren said quietly, "the Tarlan will give information but will not try to influence the beliefs or disbeliefs of others. The religions on the majority of the Federation planets, and the god worshiped by their followers, have much in common. Their god is the omniscient, omnipotent, and omnipresent Creator of All Things, as has already been stated, and is in addition believed to be just, merciful, compassionate, deeply concerned for the well-being of all of the intelligent entities it has created, and forgiving of the wrongs committed by them. It is generally believed that where there is God there is also the Devil, or some evil and less well defined entity or influence which constantly seeks to undo God's work among its thinking creatures by trying to make them behave in the instinctive manner of the animals, which they know they are not. Within every thinking creature there is this constant struggle between good and evil, right and wrong. Sometimes it seems that the Devil, or the tendency to animal behavior that is in all thinking beings, is winning and that God does not care. But even on Goglesk good has begun to make gains, minor though they may be, over evil. Had this not been so the Gogleskan healer would not be here and undergoing instruction in the use of the anti-joining sound distorters. Because it is also said that God helps even those who do not believe in its existence—''

''And punishes those who do,'' Khone broke in. ''The questions remain. How does the Tarlan explain a compassionate God who allows such massive cruelty?''

Lioren did not have an answer, so he ignored the question. ''It is often said that belief in God is a matter of faith rather than physical proof, that it does not depend on the level of intelligence possessed by the believer and that when the quality of mentation is weak the faith is stronger and more certain. The implication is that only the relatively stupid believe in the metaphysical or the supernatural or a life after physical death, while the more intelligent entities know better and believe only in themselves, the physical reality they experience around them and their ability to change it for the better.

''The complexities of this external reality, from the galaxies that stretch out to infinity and the equally complex microuniverses of which it is made, are given scientific explanations which are little more than intelligent guesses that are subject to continual modification. Most unconvincing of all are the explanations for the presence of creatures who have evolved in the area between the macro- and microcosm, creatures who think and know, and know that they know, and who try to understand the whole of which they are but the tiniest part while striving to change it for the better. To the enlightened few among these thinkers it is considered right to behave well toward each other and cooperate individually and as peoples and other-planet species so that peace, contentment, and scientific and philosophical achievement is attained for the greatest number of beings. Any person or group or system of thinking which retards this process is considered wrong. But to the majority of these thinkers good and evil are abstractions, and God and the Devil but the superstitions of less intelligent minds.''

Lioren paused, trying to find the right words of certainty and reassurance about a subject of which he felt very uncertain. ''For the first time in its history, the Galactic Federation has been contacted by a superintelligent, philosophically advanced, but technologically backward race called the Groalterri. The contact was indirect because this species believes that direct mental contact would result in irreversible philosophical damage to those races which hitherto considered themselves to be highly intelligent. One of their young sustained injuries which they were unable to treat, and they requested the hospital to accept it as a patient and gave reassurances that the young one was not yet intelligent enough for contact with it to be psychologically damaging. During conversations with it the Tarlan discovered, among other things, that it and the hyperintelligent adult members of its race are not unbelievers.''

Tufts of stiff, bristling fur were standing out from Khone's body, but the Gogleskan did not speak.

''The Tarlan feels no certainty about this,'' Lioren said, ''and wishes only to make an observation. It may be that all intelligent species pass through a stage when they think that they know the answers to everything, only to progress further to a truer realization of the depth of their ignorance. If the most highly intelligent and philosophically advanced species yet discovered believes in God and an afterlife then—''

''Enough!'' Khone broke in sharply. ''The existence of God is not the question. The question, which the Tarlan is trying to avoid by providing other and more interesting material for debate, remains the same. Why does this all-powerful, just, and compassionate God act so cruelly and unjustly where some of its creatures are concerned? To the Gogleskan the answer is important. Great distress and uncertainty is felt.''

But what exactly do you believe or disbelive, Lioren wondered helplessly, *so that I can try to relieve your distress*? Because he did not believe in prayer he wished desperately for
inspiration, but all that he could find to talk about were the
recently learned beliefs of others.

"The Tarlan does not know or understand the purposes and
behavior of God," he said, "It is the creator of all things and
must therefore possess a mind infinitely superior and more complex than that possessed by any of its creations. But certain facts
are generally accepted about this being which may assist in understanding behavior that, as the healer has noted, is very often
at variance with what is believed to be its intentions.

"For example: It is believed to be the omniscient creator of
all things," Lioren continued, "who has the deep concern of a
parent for the welfare of each and every one of its creations,
although the more general belief is that this love is reserved
principally for its thinking creations. Yet all too often it appears
to behave as an angry, irrational, or uncaring parent than a loving one. It is also widely believed that the creator works its
purpose within all of its thinking creatures, whether or not they
believe in its existence.

"Another belief held by most species is that God created
them in its own image and that they will one day live forever in
happiness with their creator in an afterlife which has as many
names as there are inhabited planets. This belief is particularly
troublesome to many thinkers for the reason that the variety of
physiological classifications among intelligent life-forms encountered within the known Galaxy makes this a logical and
physical impossibility—"

"The Tarlan is restating the question," Khone said suddenly,
"not providing an answer."

Lioren ignored the interruption. "But there are others who
have come to share a different belief and think that they know a
different god. These beings are not as intelligent as the Groalterri, whose thoughts on this subject are and will probably always
remain unknown to us. They were unhappy with the idea that
such a complex but perfectly ordered structure as the universe
around them is without purpose and came into being by accident. It troubled them that there were probably more stars in
their sky than individual grains of sand on the beaches surrounding Goglesk's island continent. It troubled them that the more

they discovered about the subatomic unreality that is the foundation of the real world, the more hints there were of a vast and complex macrostructure at the limits of resolution of their most sensitive telescopes. It also troubled them that intelligent, self-aware creatures had come into being with a growing curiosity and need to explain the universe they inhabit. They refused to believe that such a vast, complex, and well-ordered structure could occur by accident, which meant that it had to have had a creator. But they were a part of that creation, the only part composed of self-aware entities, creatures who knew and were aware that they knew, so they believed all intelligent life to be the most important part of the creation so far as the creator was concerned.

"This was not a new idea," Lioren continued, "because many others believed in a God who had made them and loves them and watches over them, and who would take them to itself in the fullness of time. But they were troubled by the uncharacteristic actions of this loving god, so they modified their idea of God's purpose so that its behavior might be more easily explained.

"They believe that God created all things including themselves," Lioren said slowly, "but that the work of creation is not yet complete."

Khone had become so still and silent that Lioren could not hear its normally loud respiration. He went on. "The work is not complete, they say, because it began with the creation of a universe that is still young and may never die. Exactly how it began is unknown, but at present it contains many species who have evolved to high intelligence who are spreading in peace among the stars. But the rise from animal to thinking being, the process of continuing creation, or evolution if one is an unbeliever, is not a pleasant process. It is long and slow and often many necessary cruelties and injustices occur among those who are part of it.

"They also believe," Lioren continued, "that the present differences in physiology and enviromental requirements are unimportant since evolution, or creation, is leading toward increased sentience and a reduced dependence on specialized appendages. The result, in the greatly distant future, will be that thinking creatures will have evolved beyond their present need for the physical bodies that house their minds. They will become immortal and join together to achieve goals that cannot be envisaged by the near-animals of the present. They will become Godlike and a true image, as they were and are promised, of the being who created them. It is held that the spirits or souls of the mentally and philosophically immature entities who have and will inhabit this universe for many eons to come will also share in this future immortality and be one with their God, because it is believed to be a philosophical absurdity that the creator of all things would discard the most important, if presently incomplete, parts of its own creation.''

Lioren paused to await Khone's reaction; then another thought occurred to him. ''The Groalterri possess very high intelligence and they are believers, but will not talk about their beliefs or anything else with those of lower intelligence levels lest they damage immature minds. It may be that every intelligent species must find its own way to God, and the Groalterri are further along the path than the rest of us.''

There was another long silence; then Khone asked very quietly, ''Is this, then, the God in which the Tarlan believes?''

From the other's tone Lioren knew that his answer should be ''Yes,'' because he felt sure now that the Gogleskan was a doubter who desperately wanted its doubts dispelled, and that he should take advantage of the situation by quickly reassuring the patient if he wished to obtain the telepathy information he wanted. But an unbeliever telling a lie in the hope of making a doubter believe was dishonorable and dishonest. It was his duty to give what reassurance he could, but he would not lie.

Lioren thought for a long moment, and when he replied he was surprised to discover that he meant every word.

''No,'' he said, ''but there is uncertainty.''

''Yes,'' Khone said, ''there is always uncertainty.''

.... It is noll ....
....
....
....
....
....
....

Chapter 21

LIOREN'S answer had satisfied the Gogleskan, or perhaps had satisfactorily reinforced its doubts, because Khone did not ask any more questions about God.

Instead, it said, "Earlier the Tarlan expressed curiosity regarding the organic structures associated with the Gogleskan telepathic faculty and reasons why a loss or a diminution of function takes place. As is already known by the Tarlan, the solitary nature of the Gogleskan life-form precluded the development of sophisticated surgical techniques, and only a very few healers could force themselves to investigate internally a Gogleskan cadaver. The information available is sparse and regret is felt for any disappointment caused. But a debt is owed and it is now encumbent upon the Gogleskan to answer rather than ask questions."

"There is gratitude," Lioren said.

Khone's fur twitched, rose and stood out in long, uneven tufts all over its body—a clear indication of the mental effort required to discuss personal matters. But the reaction, Lioren discovered quickly, was also intended as a demonstration.

"Contact telepathy is used only on two occasions," Khone said, "in response to a tribal Call for Joining when a real but more often an imaginary danger threatens, or for the purpose of reproduction. As has already been explained, the emotional trigger of the signal is highly sensitive. A minor injury, a sudden surprise or change in normal conditions, or an unexpected meeting with a stranger can cause it to operate unintentionally, whereupon a group forms by intertwining the body fur and telepathic tendrils. This fear-maddened group entity reacts to the real or imagined threat by destroying everything that is not a Gogleskan in the immediate vicinity as well as causing self-inflicted injuries to individual members. At such times the mental state makes it impossible to be objective or qualitative about the functioning or malfunctioning of the telepathic faculty, since the ability to make clinical observations, or even to think coherently, is submerged in the panic reaction.

"Doubtless the Tarlan will know from experience that a similar but much more pleasant emotional upheaval occurs between partners during the process of sexual conjugation. But here the Gogleskan telepathic linkage insures that the sensations of both are shared, and doubled. Small variations or diminution of sensation, if present, would be difficult to detect or remember afterward."

"The Tarlan is without experience in this area," Lioren said. "Healers on Tarla expecting advancement to high positions in the profession are required to forgo such emotional distractions."

"There is deep sympathy," Khone said. It paused for a moment, then went on, "But an attempt will be made to describe in detail the physical preliminaries and telepathically reinforced emotional responses associated with the Gogleskan sex act—"

It broke off because another person had entered the room. It was a DBDG female wearing the insignia of a Charge Nurse and pushing a food-dispenser float before it.

"Apologies are tendered for this interruption," the nurse said, "which has been delayed for as long as possible in the expectation that this discussion would soon be concluded. But the patient's principal meal is long overdue and harsh words will be directed toward the medical entity charged with its care should a convalescent patient be allowed to starve to death. If hunger is also felt by the visitor and it wishes to remain with the patient, food can be provided that is metabolically acceptable, although perhaps not entirely palatable, to the Tarlan life-form."

"Kindness is shown," Lioren said, realizing for the first time how long Khone and himself had been talking and how hungry he was, "and gratitude is felt."

"Then please defer further discussion until the food has been served," the Charge Nurse said, making the soft, barking sound that its species called laughter, "and spare my maidenly, Earth-human blushes."

As soon as the Charge Nurse left them, Khone reminded him that it had more than one mouth and was therefore capable of eating and answering questions at the same time. By then Lioren had reconsidered and decided that the Gogleskan's information, interesting though it might be in itself, would not enlarge his knowledge of possible dysfunction in the organic transmitter-receiver mechanism of Groalterri telepathy. Apologetically and impersonally, he told the other that the information was no longer required.

"Great relief is felt," Khone said, "and offense is not taken. But a debt remains. Are there other questions whose answers might be helpful?"

Lioren stared at Khone for a long time, contrasting the tiny, upright, ovoid body of an adult Gogleskan with that of Small Hellishomar the Cutter, who completely filled a ward large enough to accommodate an ambulance ship, and tried to frame another polite refusal. But suddenly he felt so angry and disappointed and helpless that it required a great effort to make the proper, impersonal words come.

"There are no more questions," he said.

"There should always be more questions," Khone said. The spikes of fur drooped and the body slumped onto its apron of muscle so that Lioren could almost feel its disappointment. "Is it that the ignorant Gogleskan lacks the intelligence to answer them, and now the Tarlan wishes to leave without further waste of time?"

"No," Lioren said firmly. "Do not confuse intelligence with education. The Tarlan requires specialist information that the Gogleskan has had no chance to learn, so it is not intelligence that is lacking. To the contrary. Has the healer more questions?"

"No," Khone said promptly. "The healer has an observation to make, but hesitates lest it give offense."

"Offense will not be taken," Lioren said.

Khone rose to its full height again. "The Tarlan has demonstrated, as have many entities before it, that a suffering shared is a suffering diminished, but in this case it appears that the sharing is not equal. The Cromsag Incident, which makes the problem with the Dark Devil of Goglesk seem insignificant by comparison, has been described in detail, but its full effect upon the entity responsible for it has not. Much has been said about the beliefs and Gods, or perhaps the one God, of others, but nothing about its own God. Perhaps the God of Tarla is special, or different, and does not possess the qualities of understanding and justice with compassion where the most important parts of its creation are concerned. Does it expect its creatures to do no wrong at all, even by accident? The excuse given for the Tarlan's silence, that it does not wish to influence unfairly the beliefs of another with its more extensive knowledge, is laudable. But the excuse is weak indeed, for even an ignorant Gogleskan knows that a belief, even one that is often weakened by self-doubt, is not susceptible to change by logical argument. And yet the Tarlan speaks freely about the beliefs of others while remaining silent about its own.

"It is assumed," Khone went on before Lioren could reply, "that the Tarlan is deeply troubled by guilt over the Cromsaggar deaths, a guilt that is increased because the punishment it considers due for this monstrous crime has been unjustly withheld. Perhaps it seeks both punishment and forgiveness and believes that both are being withheld."

It was obvious that Khone was trying to find a way of helping him, but so far its lengthy observation had been neither offensive nor helpful, for the good reason that Lioren was beyond help.

"If the Creator of All Things is unforgiving," Khone went on, "or if the Tarlan does not believe in the existence of this Creator, there can be no forgiveness there. Or if that small part of God, or if there is disbelief and a nonreligious word is preferred, the good that struggles constantly with the evil in all intelligent creatures, then the Tarlan will not be able to forgive itself. The Cromsag Incident cannot be wholly forgotten or its psychological scars entirely healed, but the wrong must be forgiven if the Tarlan's distress is to be relieved.

"It is the Gogleskan's advice and strong recommendation," Khone ended, "that the Tarlan should seek forgiveness from others."

Not only was Khone's observation lengthy and inoffensive, it was a complete waste of time. Lioren had difficulty controlling his impatience as he said, "From other, less morally demanding Gods? From whom, specifically?"

"Is it not obvious?" Khone said in a tone no less impatient than his own. "From the beings who have been so grievously wronged—from the surviving Cromsaggar."

For a moment Lioren was so deeply shocked and insulted by the suggestion that he could not speak. He had to remind himself that an insult required knowledge of the target to give it force, and this one was based on complete ignorance.

"Impossible," he said. "Tarlans do not apologize. It is utterly demeaning, the act of a misbehaving young child trying to reduce or turn away the displeasure of a parent. The small wrongs of children can be forgiven by the wronged, but Tarlans, adult Tarlans, fully accept the responsibility and the punishment for any crime they have committed, and would never shame themselves or the person they have wronged with an apology. Besides, the patients in the Cromsaggar ward are cured and under observation rather than treatment. They would probably become demented with hate and terminate my life on sight."

"Was not that the fate which the Tarlan desired?" Khone asked. "Has there been a change of mind?"

"No," Lioren replied. "Accidental termination would resolve all problems. But to, to *apologize* is unthinkable!"

Khone was silent for a moment; then it said, "The Gogleskan is expected to break its evolutionary conditioning and to think and behave in new ways. Perhaps in its ignorance it considers that the effort needed to best the Dark Devil in its mind is small compared with that required to apologize to another thinking entity for a well-intentioned mistake."

You are trying to compare subjective devils, Lioren thought. Suddenly his mind was filled with the sight and sound and touch of Cromsaggar warring or mating or dying amid the filthy ruins of a culture they themselves had destroyed. He saw them lying helpless in the aseptic beds of the medical stations and in tumbled, lifeless heaps after the orgy of self-destruction that had come about as the result of his premature cure. Remembrance of the sight and strength and close touch of them came rushing into his mind like a bursting wave of sensation that included the feeling of a wardful of them tearing him apart as they tried to exact vengeance for the death of their race. He felt a strange satisfaction and peace in the knowledge that his life would soon be over and his terrible guilt discharged. And then came the images of probability, of the nurses on duty, heavy-gravity Tralthans or Hudlars, restraining them and rescuing him before lethal damage could be inflicted; and he imagined the long, lonely convalescence with nothing to occupy his mind but the dreadful, inescapable memories of what he had done to the Cromsaggar.

Khone's suggestion was ridiculous. It was not the behavior expected of an honorable Tarlan of a society in which few indeed lacked honor. To admit to a mistake that was already obvious to

all was unnecessary. To apologize for that mistake in the hope
of reducing the punishment due was shameful and cowardly and
the mark of a morally damaged mind. And to lay bare the inner
thoughts and emotions before others was unthinkable. It was
not the Tarlan way.

Neither, as Khone had just reminded him, was it the Gogleskan way to fight the Dark Devil in their minds; or to make
physical contact other than for the purposes of reproduction or
comforting the young, or to address another entity who was not
a mate, parent, or offspring in anything but the briefest and most
impersonal terms, but Khone was trying to do all those things.

Khone was changing its ways, gradually, as were the Protectors of the Unborn. The changes both species had to make were
extraordinarily difficult for them and called for a mighty and
continuing effort of will, but they were not in themselves cowardly and morally reprehensible acts, as was the one that Khone
had suggested that Lioren commit. And suddenly he was thinking about Hellishomar, whose condition was the reason for his
present investigation into other-species telepathy as well as the
cause of his present mental turmoil.

The young Groalterri, too, was struggling with itself. Against
all its natural instincts, its training as a Cutter and the teachings
of its near-immortal Parents, it had changed and forced itself to
do something reprehensible indeed.

Hellishomar had tried to kill itself.

"I need help," Lioren said.

"The need for help," Khone said, "is an admission of personal inadequacy. In an entity with pride and authority it might
be considered the first step toward an apology. Regrettably, I
am unable to give it. Do you know where or from whom this
help is available?"

"I know who to ask," Lioren replied, then stopped as the
realization came to him that during the last exchange Khone and
he had omitted the Gogleskan impersonal manner of address,
and that they had spoken to each other as would close members
of a family. He did not know what this signified and did not
want to risk asking for clarification because Khone had misunderstood him.

From the other's words it was clear that Khone had assumed
that the help he wanted was with his own Cromsaggar problem,
whereas the truth was that he badly needed specialist assistance

with Hellishomar's case. Initially the person he must ask for it was O'Mara, then Conway, Thornnastor, Seldal, and whoever else was qualified to give it. He admitted to himself that he was not qualified, and that interviewing telepathic life-forms in an attempt to solve the problem by himself had been a sop to his vanity as well as being an inexcusable waste of time.

Asking help from others, which would of necessity reveal the lack of knowledge and ability within himself, was not the Tarlan way. But he had been receiving help from many entities in the hospital, often without asking for it, and he did not expect that repeating the shameful process would cause any severe emotional trauma.

As he was leaving Khone's ward a few minutes later, Lioren wondered if his own habits of thought were beginning to change.

Very slightly, of course.

Chapter 22

SENIOR Physician Seldal was present because Hellishomar had been its responsibility from the beginning and it had more clinical experience with the patient than any of the others, although that situation was expected to change very soon. The Tralthan Diagnostician-in-Charge of Pathology, Thornnastor, and the equally eminent Earth-human Conway, who had been recently appointed Diagnostician-in-Charge of Surgery, were there to discover why Chief Psychologist O'Mara, who was the only entity with sufficient authority to call such a high-level meeting at short notice, had thought it necessary to bring them together to discuss a patient who was supposedly well on the way to a full recovery.

It reminded Lioren of his recent court-martial, and even though the arguments would be clinical rather than legal, he thought that when it came the cross-examination would be much less polite. Seldal spoke first.

Indicating the big clinical viewscreen, it said, "As you can see, the Groalterri patient presented with a very large number, close on three hundred, punctured wounds that were equally divided over the dorsal and lateral areas and in the anterior region between the tentacles, where the tegument is thin and affords minimum natural protection. The punctures were apparently caused by a fast-flying and burrowing insect species which laid eggs and introduced infection to the wound sites. The Nallajim operational procedure was judged to be best suited to the treatment of the condition, and I was assigned. Because of the patient's unusually large body mass, progress has been slow, but the prognosis is good except for an unfortunate lack of—"

"Doctor Seldal," Thornnastor broke in, its voice sounding like an impatient, modulated foghorn. "Surely you asked the patient how its wounds were sustained?"

"The patient did not give this information," Seldal said, the rapid, background twittering of its natural voice reflecting its irritation at the interruption. "I had been about to say that it rarely spoke to me, and never about itself or its condition."

"The distribution of the punctures," Diagnostician Conway said, speaking for the first time, "is too localized to suggest a random attack by an insect swarm. To my mind, the angles of penetration and the concentration on one clearly defined area indicates a common point of origin, as in an explosion, although I suppose it is possible that Hellishomar disturbed a hive and the insects attacked the parts of its body that were closest to them. From what little we know of the Groalterri species, they have refused to speak to everyone, so the reticence of the patient may be irritating but not unusual. In the past we have all treated our share of uncooperative patients."

"Hellishomar was cooperative during treatment," Seldal said, "and when it spoke it did so with politeness and respect, but without saying anything about itself. I suspected that the clinical picture might have psychological implications, and I asked Surgeon-Captain Lioren to speak to the patient in the hope that—"

"Surely this is a matter for the Chief Psychologist," Thornnastor said impatiently. "What are a couple of busy Diagnosticians doing here?"

"I," O'Mara said in a quiet voice, "was not consulted."

Thornnastor's four eyes and Conway's two stared at O'Mara for a moment; then all six were directed at Lioren. It was probably fortunate that he could not read Tralthan or Earth-human expressions.

"In the hope," Seldal went on, "that Lioren would have a similar degree of success in making a reticent patient talk as it had achieved with another of my patients, the former-Diagnostician Mannen. At the time I was not sure whether the matter was important enough to ask for the help of the Chief Psychologist. Now Lioren believes that it is, and, after consultation with the Surgeon-Captain, I am in total agreement."

Seldal settled back into its perch, and Lioren placed two of his medial limbs on the table and tried to order his thoughts.

Thornnastor's six elephantine feet thumped restively against the floor in a manner which could have indicated impatience or curiosity. Conway made an untranslatable sound and said, "Surgeon-Captain, for the nonmedical improvement you have brought about in Doctor Mannen, who was my tutor and is my friend, I am most grateful. But how can we help you with what appears to be a psychiatric problem?"

"Before I begin," Lioren said, "I would prefer that you do not use my former title. You know that I am forbidden and have forsworn the practice of medicine, and the reason for it. However, I cannot change the way my mind works, and my past training leads me to the conclusion that Hellishomar's problem is not entirely psychiatric. But first I must discuss briefly the patient's evolutionary and philosophical background."

Thornnastor's feet remained at rest and there were no other interruptions while Lioren described the strangely divided cultures of the telepathic Parents and the more technologically oriented Small, and how strongly the latter were affected by the teachings of the former and by the uncertainties of approaching maturity. He told them how O'Mara had explained that the division was due to an uncompleted stage of their evolution, that the Small were subintelligent by Groalterri standards until they reached maturity, although the concern of the Parents for their Small was very strong. The intelligent macrospecies inhabiting Groalter were so physically massive and extremely long-lived that their numbers had to be strictly controlled if their planet and their race was not to become extinct. Orbital observations had shown that the total Groalterri population of both Parents and Small numbered less than three thousand, so that the birthing of a Small was an extremely rare event and the parental regard for the newborn proportionately large.

Lioren was careful to speak in the most general terms, and he was particularly careful to give only information that Hellishomar had given him permission to pass on, or material that he had been able to deduce for himself.

"Doubtless you will discover for yourselves that the information I am about to give you regarding the patient is incomplete," Lioren went on. "This is a deliberate omission on my part, and I have told the Chief Psychologist O'Mara why he and yourselves must be kept in partial ignorance—"

"You told O'Mara that," Conway broke in, showing its teeth, "and you are still alive?"

"Because Hellishomar is the first and only source of data on the Groalterri culture," Lioren continued, deciding that it was not a serious question. "This information is of great value to the Federation and the hospital, but I have been told that a small proportion of it is not for general distribution. Were I to break confidence with the patient there is a risk, virtually a certainty, that the source of this valuable knowledge would dry up. My observations of the patient's behavior and clinical condition, however, are as complete and accurate as I can make them."

Lioren paused briefly so as to select words that would combine maximum information with complete confidentiality. "Patient Hellishomar came here at the unconscious direction, or suggestion or whatever means was used on the captain of the orbiting vessel, of the Parents because they hoped that it could be treated. They themselves are physically and temperamentally incapable of inflicting pain or injury on another intelligent life-form, and the treatment was not available on Groalter because the surgical procedures of the Small, while precise enough, are too crude for the fine work of removing large numbers of deeply embedded insects. Senior Physician Seldal has been performing this work as only it can, but with the minimum of verbal contact with the patient. I had nothing but verbal contact with Hellishomar and had many opportunities to observe its behavior while we were speaking. These observations led me to the conclusion, a conclusion with which Seldal and O'Mara now agree, that the infected insect punctures were not the only reason for Hellishomar being sent here."

They were all watching him and so still were they that the whole office with its living contents might have been a holograph.

"From our conversations together," Lioren went on, "it has become obvious that Hellishomar has grown much too old and large to live and practice as a Cutter among the Small, and that by now it should be undergoing the psychological as well as the physical changes that precede full maturity. But the Parents have not touched minds with it, as is customary at this time, or if they have tried to do so it has not been aware of it because the patient is telepathically deaf, and the possibility exists that Hellishomar is mentally retarded."

There was a short silence that was broken by Thornnastor. "Judging by the evidence you have given us so far, Surgeon-Captain, I would say it is a strong probability."

"Please do not use my former title," Lioren said.

The Earth-human, Conway, made a dismissive gesture with one hand. "You still retain the manner of a Surgeon-Captain if not the rank, so the mistake is excusable. But if you are convinced that Hellishomar is mentally defective, that is not the concern of Pathology or Surgery, so what are Thornnastor and myself doing here?"

"I am not fully convinced," Lioren replied, "that the condition is due to a congenital defect. Rather, I favor the theory that there might be a structural abnormality which has temporarily affected the proper development of the patient's telepathic faculty without, however, impairing the other brain functions. This theory is based on behavioral observations by myself as well as those reported by Seldal, and on conversations with the patient which I will not repeat in detail."

O'Mara made an untranslatable sound but did not speak. Lioren ignored the interruption and went on. "Hellishomar is a Cutter, the Groalterri equivalent of a surgeon, and, although the gross differences in its body mass and ours mean that its work seems crude by our standards, it has displayed to me and to the ward's vision recorders a high degree of muscular coordination and precision of control. There was no evidence of the uncoordinated movements or the mental confusion normally expected of a damaged or otherwise abnormal brain. Even though it is only an immature member of a species whose adult minds are immeasurably more advanced than our own, in conversation it displays a mind that is flexible, lucid in its thinking, and well able to debate the finer points of philosophy, theology, and ethics that have arisen between us. This is not, I submit, the physical behavior or the quality of thinking expected of a congenitally defective brain. I believe that the deficiency lies only with the telepathic faculty and that there is a high probability that the abnormality causing it is localized and may be operable.''

The Chief Psychologist's office became a still picture once again. "Go on," Conway said.

"For the first time," Lioren resumed, "the Groalterri have contacted the Federation so that we at Sector General might cure one of their ailing Small. Perhaps they are hoping that Hellishomar's cure will be complete. We should do our best not to disappoint them.''

"We should do our best," Conway said, "not to kill the patient. Do you realize what you are asking?''

Thornnastor answered the question before Lioren could reply. "It will require the investigation of a living and conscious brain about which we know nothing, because there are no Small cadavers available for prior investigation. We will be looking for structural abnormalities when we do not even know what is normal. Microbiopsies and sensor implants will not give data of the precision required for a cerebral procedure. Our deep scanners cannot be used because the level of radiation needed to penetrate a cranial structure of that size would almost certainly interfere with the locomotor muscle networks, and we cannot risk a patient of Hellishomar's mass making involuntary muscle movements during an op. To a greater or lesser degree, depending on the findings of the nonsurgical investigation, we will be trusting to luck and instinct. Has the patient been informed of the risks?''

"Not yet," Lioren replied. "As the result of a recent conversation with the patient there was an emotional upset of some kind. Hellishomar broke off verbal contact and physically evicted me from the ward, but I am hoping to resume communication soon. I will inform it of the situation and try to obtain its permission and cooperation during the operation.''

"Thankfully," Conway said, showing its teeth again, "that is your problem." It turned toward O'Mara. "Chief Psychologist, in matters pertaining to Patient Hellishomar and until further notice I want Trainee Lioren placed under my authority. I shall take overall surgical responsibility for this one, and move it to the top of my operating schedule. Thornnastor, Seldal, and Lioren will assist. And now, if there is nothing further to detain us—"

"With respect, Diagnostician Conway," Lioren said urgently, "I am forbidden to practice—"

"So you have said," Conway broke in as it rose to its feet. "You will not be required to cut, simply to observe and advise and give nonsurgical support to the patient. You are the only one among us who may have sufficient knowledge of the patient's mind and thought processes—and it is Hellishomar's mind that we will be tinkering with—to keep it from ending up a worse mental cripple than you say it already is.

"You *will* assist."

Lioren was still trying to think of a reply when the office had emptied except for O'Mara and himself. The Chief Psychologist had risen to its feet, which was a clear nonverbal signal that Lioren should also leave. He remained where he was.

Hesitantly, he said, "If I had sought personal interviews with Diagnosticians Conway and Thornnastor individually, the result would have been the same, but much time would have been wasted because they are busy entities and appointments with them are difficult to obtain for a trainee. I am grateful for your help in expediting this matter, especially as you and they could not be given full information about the patient. You remained silent so as not to embarrass me by calling attention to my deliberate omission.

"But it is a new and more serious problem," Lioren went on, "which was my prime reason for asking for your help. Again I may only discuss it in general terms—"

The Chief Psychologist seemed to be in respiratory distress for a moment, but it recovered quickly and held up one hand for silence.

"Lioren," O'Mara asked in a very quiet voice, "do you think we are all mentally defective?"

Chapter 23

L IOREN knew that an answer was not expected because the questioner was about to provide its own.

"Thornnastor and Conway and Seldal are not stupid," O'Mara continued. "My latest records show that their three minds are currently in possession of a total of seventeen Educator tapes, and the donor entities who made those recordings were not stupid, and I, making due allowance for the subjective nature of the assessment, would place my own level of intelligence as well above average."

Lioren was about to agree, but O'Mara gestured for silence.

"Seldal's description of the clinical picture," the Chief Psychologist went on, "together with the knowledge you have already obtained regarding the Groalterri society as a whole, and your new information that the patient is by its race's standards a mental defective, indicates a very high probability that Hellishomar's injuries were the result of a failed suicide attempt. Thornnastor, Conway, Seldal, and myself know this, but we would certainly not embarrass the patient or risk worsening its emotional distress by telling it that we knew or by making the knowledge public. If the circumstances are as you describe, the patient had every reason to destroy itself.

"But now," O'Mara said, raising its voice slightly as if to emphasize the point, "we have to give it an even stronger reason to live whether or not the cranial surgery is successful. You and, if the situation was normal and you were not such a pig-headed, self-righteous trainee, I as your superior should be trying to discover such a reason. You are the sole channel of communication to the patient, and it is better that no other person, myself included, tries to usurp that position. But must I remind you that I am the Chief Psychologist of this weird and wonderful establishment, that I have much experience in prying into the minds of its even weirder staff, and that it is my right and your duty to keep me fully informed so that you can make full use of my experience while talking to this Groalterri. I shall be disappointed and seriously irritated with you if you pretend that the patient did not attempt suicide.

"And now," he ended, "what exactly is this new and more serious problem with Hellishomar?"

For a moment Lioren sat in the quiet desperation of hope, afraid to answer the question in case there was no hope—or worse, that he would have to find the answer for himself. The Chief Psychologist's face had grown pink with irritation at the delay when he spoke.

"The problem," Lioren said, "is with me. I have to make a difficult decision."

O'Mara sat back into its chair, features no longer discolored. "Go on. Is it difficult for you because it may involve breaking the patient's confidence?"

"No!" Lioren said sharply. "I told you this is my problem. Maybe I should not ask your advice and risk making it yours."

The Chief Psychologist showed no sign of irritation at Lioren's insubordinate tone as it said, "And maybe I should not allow you any further contact with Hellishomar, once we have its permission for the operation. Placing together two beings who are so guilt-ridden that both would like nothing better than to end their own lives is a greater risk, to my mind, because the chances are even that the results could be beneficial or disastrous. So far you have managed to avoid a disaster. Please begin by telling me why you think that it is not my problem, and allow me to assess the risks."

"But that would require a long explanation of the problem itself," Lioren protested. "I would also have to include background information, much of which is speculative and probably inaccurate."

O'Mara raised one hand from the desk and allowed it to fall again. "Take your time," it said.

Lioren began by describing again the strange, age-segregated Groalterri culture, but he did not take much time because in the beginning he was repeating information that was already known, and O'Mara was not an Earth-human noted for its patience. He said that by virtue of their great size and unguessable abilities, the Parents controlled their population nondestructively and maintained their planet, its nonintelligent animal and vegetable and mineral resources in optimum condition, because they were an extremely long-lived species and this was the only world that they would ever have. On Groalter all life was of value and intelligent life was precious indeed. The control mechanisms, the laws that were to govern every day of a Groalterri's incredibly long life, were taught by the Parents to the pre-adults, who passed them on to the younger Small down to the age when they first began to think and speak. These laws, which governed all future behavior on Groalter, were not physically enforced because the evidence pointed to this being a philosophically advanced and nonviolent race. The Small were taught, verbally when they were very young and telepathically as they approached adulthood, so thoroughly that the process more closely resembled deep conditioning. The guilt felt by a lawbreaker, and the punishment that it inflicted on itself, was of a degree of severity possible only to the recipient of the strictest and most comprehensive form of religious indoctrination.

"Which is a theory supported by the fact," Lioren continued, "that Hellishomar has made several references to committing not a serious crime or an offense but a grievous sin. To the Groalterri the most grievous of all sins is the deliberate and premature destruction of a life. It matters not whether the sin is of commission or omission, or if the life concerned was close to its beginning or near its end. And if the Small and their Parents are deeply religious, that faced me with other questions.

"What kind of god would a life-form that is well-nigh immortal believe in? And what is their hope or expectation of an afterlife?"

"My own hope," O'Mara said, lowering the lines of fur above its eyes, "is that you will eventually get to the point. This could become an interesting religious debate if I could allow myself the time for it, but so far I do not see a problem where you are concerned."

"But there is a problem," Lioren said, "and their religious beliefs are very much involved. And so, to my shame, am I."

"Explain," O'Mara said, "and try to take less time about it."

"In all of the religions that I have recently been studying, I found that their adherents have many beliefs in common. Apart from a few who are fractionally more long- or short-lived than us, all enjoy what we consider to be an average life span . . ."

In precivilized times, when many religions were originating and beginning to shape the thinking of their adherents toward a respect for the person and property of others that formed the basis of civilized behavior, the hopes and needs of these people were simple. Apart from a few individuals who had seized power, the lives of these beings were unhappy, filled with un-remitting toil, plagued by hunger and disease, or under the con-stant threat of violent and premature death, and their life expectancy was far below the present average.

It was natural that they should hope and dream and finally believe in teachings which gave the promise of another life, a Heaven, in which they would not toil or hunger or feel pain or suffer separation from their friends, and where they would live forever.

"In contrast," Lioren went on, "the Groalterri already pos-sess virtual immortality, so their lives are already long enough for a further physical extension not to be high on their list of priorities. Because of their vast size and lack of mobility, they telepathically control or otherwise cause their food supply to come to them, so they do not have to toil. They are too large to suffer injury, and disease and pain are unknown among them until they are approaching termination, when they call on the Small Cutters to help them further extend their lives before what Hellishomar calls the Escape or the Time of Going Out.

"At first, I assumed this to be the case of a long-lived entity wanting to live even longer in spite of the increasing pain suf-fered during the terminal decades, but this would be the type of behavior expected of small-minded, selfish entities, which the Parents were not. It came to me that their terminal years, which the Small are sworn to extend for as long as possible, are needed so that they would have the maximum time possible in which to prepare their minds and make themselves worthy of what they expect to find in the afterlife.

"To the tremendous minds and gigantic bodies of the Groal-terri," Lioren said, "it may be that Heaven is the place and condition where they can seek and ultimately discover the se-crets of all creation, and while doing so, the condition they most desire is mobility. They need it so that they can escape from the great, organic prisons that are their bodies, and from their planet, and Go Out. Perhaps they long to travel freely through a universe that is infinitely large and provides their great minds with an intellectual challenge that is also infinite.''

O'Mara raised one hand from the desk, but the interruption seemed to be polite rather than impatient. It said, ''An ingenious theory, Lioren, and, I think, very close to the truth. But I still do not see where you have a problem.''

''The problem,'' Lioren said, ''lies in the intention of the Parents in sending Hellishomar to us, and my subsequent behavior toward the patient. Did they influence us into bringing it to Sector General in the hope that we might effect a complete cure for their Small Cutter, as would any parents deeply concerned for the welfare of one of their young? Or do they believe that we might not be able to treat the infected wounds that were then threatening its life, much less recognize the patient as a mental defective? Are they hoping that the treatment it receives here, and the people it meets during that treatment, will give a mind that is incapable of further intellectual and spiritual progression an experience that it will find strange and stimulating and enjoyable before it passes into the substandard Heaven or Limbo that is reserved for the few mentally flawed Groalterri?

''Hellishomar is telepathically deaf and dumb,'' Lioren continued, ''so the Parents cannot tell it what their intentions are, or that they have forgiven it for the sin it tried to commit, or that they feel compassion for its distress and are simply doing their best to relieve the suffering of a mental cripple by giving it the memories of what, to a living Groalterri, is a unique experience of leaving its planet. But I believe that the patient is more intelligent, and much stricter in its religious self-discipline, than the Parents realize.

''Hellishomar is trying to refuse their gift.

''When it was brought here,'' he went on quickly, ''Hellishomar offered no resistance and obeyed only the simple requests of Seldal and the nurses during initial examination and treatment. It would not ask or answer questions about itself, and for long periods it kept its eyes closed. Only when I told the patient about myself and it discovered that I, too, had committed a grievous sin and was still suffering from guilt and distress over it, did Hellishomar begin to talk freely about itself. Even then it made me promise not to pass on certain personal information, and it showed great agitation when I tried to talk about the member species and planets of the Federation. When I offered to show supporting visual material it became very agitated and distressed.

"I insist," Lioren said, "or rather I suggest most strongly that its contacts with other species be kept to a minimum, and that information on all subjects other than its forthcoming treatment be withheld, if necessary by switching off the translator and covering its eyes if life-forms new to its present experience are operating—"

"Why?" O'Mara asked sharply.

"Because Hellishomar is a sinner," Lioren replied, "and believes itself unworthy of being given even this tiny glimpse of Heaven. To the highly intelligent and questing minds trapped within the physically massive Groalterri body, Going Out, escaping at death from the imprisonment of their planet, is Heaven. Sector General and all the varied life-forms it contains is a part of that much deserved afterlife."

O'Mara showed its teeth. "This place has been called many things, but never Heaven. I can see that Hellishomar faces a theological problem which we must try to help it resolve, but I still cannot see that you have a problem. What exactly is troubling you?"

"Uncertainty, and fear," Lioren replied. "I don't know what the Parents' intentions were when they touched the mind of the orbiting ship's captain. That touching must have revealed much about the Federation, but they seem to have ignored the religious implications because they caused Hellishomar to be brought here. Perhaps their adult theology is more sophisticated and liberal than the form they have to teach to the less able minds of the Small, or they simply did not realize what they were doing. Maybe, as I have already said, they believed that Hellishomar was about to die of its self-inflicted injuries and they wanted to give it this small experience of Heaven because they were unsure of the fate of a mental cripple in their afterlife and they are a compassionate race. Or perhaps they are expecting us to cure the patient of all its defects and return Hellishomar to take its place among the Parents. But what will happen if we cure only its physical injuries?

"It is the answer to that question which frightens me," Lioren ended, "and that is the problem that so terrifies me that I am afraid to solve it without help."

"Terrifies you, how?" O'Mara asked, in the quiet, absent-minded manner of a questioner who is already working out the answer for itself.

"There are precedents on many worlds," Lioren replied, "for prophets and teachers coming out of the wilderness to spread beliefs which attack the old order. On Groalter there is no violence, and no way of silencing a religious heretic who is deaf to the words of its elders. The mental cripple, Hellishomar, might be so filled with its new knowledge that it could not subject itself to the voluntary seclusion expected of it. Instead it might bring to the immature minds of the younger Small the knowledge that Heaven contains great machines for traveling between the stars, as well as other technological wonders, and that it is peopled with a great variety of short-lived creatures who are in many cases less intelligent and certainly less moral in their behavior than the Groalterri. As a result the Small might try using their limited technology and planetary resources to build machines so that a few of them could Go Out before reaching Parenthood, much less waiting until the end of their lives, and the many who could not go would cause disaffection and destabilization among the Small. Worse, they might take Hellishomar's teachings with them into adulthood, and the delicate physical and philosophical balance that has maintained the Groalterri planet and culture for many thousands of years would be destroyed.

"I have already destroyed the Cromsaggar," Lioren ended miserably, "and I fear that I am bringing about an even greater philosophical destruction in the minds of the most advanced culture to be discovered since the Federation came into being."

O'Mara placed its hands together and looked down at them for a moment before it spoke. There was a heavy emphasis on the first word as it said, "We do indeed have a problem, Lioren. The simple answer would be to lose the patient, allow Hellishomar to terminate here, for the greater good of its people, naturally. But that is a solution which we would find ethically unsound, a relic of our presapient past. Our rejection of it would have the agreement of the entire hospital staff, the Monitor Corps, the Federation, and the Groalterri Parents. We must therefore do the best that we possibly can do for the patient, in the hope that the Parents also knew what they were doing when they sent it to us. Agreed?"

Without waiting for a reply, the Chief Psychologist went on. "The suggestion that you should be the only contact with the patient is a valid one. Hellishomar will be isolated from all other visual and verbal contact during surgery, and I shall certainly not contact it. At least, not directly.

"You have been doing very well," O'Mara continued. "But you lack my professional experience or, as Cha Thrat insists on describing it, my knowledge of the subtler spells. You do not know everything, Lioren, even though you often act as if you do. For example, there are several well-tried methods of reestablishing communication and friendly relations with an other-species patient who has broken off contact for emotional reasons—"

O'Mara stopped and, with its eyes still directed toward Lioren, one hand moved to the desk communicator. "Braithwaite, reschedule today's appointments for this evening or tomorrow. Be diplomatic; Edanelt, Cresk-Sar, and Nestrommli are Seniors, after all. For the next three hours I am not here.

"And now, Lioren," it went on, "you will listen and I shall talk . . ."

Chapter 24

"THE modifications to the ward structure necessary for the performance of this operation will be completed within the hour," Diagnostician Conway said, loudly enough to be heard above the din of shouting voices and the metallic clangor of massive equipment being moved into position and given its final operational checks, "and the surgical team is already standing by. But any cranial investigation involving a newly discovered intelligent species, especially of a macro life-form like yourself, must of necessity be exploratory and with a high element of risk. For anatomical and clinical reasons, the sheer body mass combined with our present ignorance regarding the metabolism involved makes any estimate of the quantity of medication required sheer guesswork, so that the procedure will have to be carried out without benefit of anesthetic.

"Such a procedure is completely contrary to normal practice," Conway went on, in a voice which was less than steady, "so that it is the psychological rather than the clinical preparations which Chief Psychologist O'Mara and I must satisfy ourselves are complete."

Hellishomar did not speak. It was probable, thought Lioren, that the Groalterri knew nothing of the tiresome Earth-human habit of asking questions in the form of statements.

Conway looked quickly at the large openings that had been cut in the deck, walls, and ceiling all around them, and at the heavily braced structural supports for the tractor- and pressor-beam installations projecting from them before going on. "It is imperative that you do not move during the procedure, and you have told us several times that you will remain still. But, with respect, that is too much to expect from a fully-conscious patient when the degree of pain being inflicted is unknown, and there is a risk of our instruments stimulating the locomotor network and causing involuntary body movements. Total restraint and immobility will therefore be imposed by use of wide-focus tractor and pressor beams even though we may not, as you have assured us, require them."

Hellishomar remained silent for a moment; then it said, "Surgery under anesthesia is not practiced by Groalterri Cutters, so I would not consider your procedure abnormal or the discomfort associated with the entry wound of major importance. As well, you will remember that Seldal, Lioren, and yourself have assured me that, in the majority of life-forms of your clinical experience, deep cranial surgery can be undertaken without discomfort since the protection afforded by the thickness of the cranium obviates the necessity for pain sensors within the brain itself."

"That is true," Conway said. "But the Groalterri life-form is like no other in the hospital's experience, so it is not a certainty.

"Another and more important reason for the absence of anesthesia," the Diagnostician continued before Hellishomar could reply, "is that we will be forced to call on you from time to time for a report on the subjective effects of our surgery while the operation is in progress. The high intensity of scanner radiation required to penetrate and chart the cranial contents, although harmless in itself, would almost certainly affect the local nerve networks and cause—''

"All this has been explained to me," Hellishomar said suddenly, "by Lioren."

"And it is being explained again by me," Conway said, "because I am performing the operation and must be absolutely sure that the patient is fully aware of the risks. Are you?"

"I am," Hellishomar said.

"Very well," Conway said. "Is there anything else you would like to know about the procedure? Or anything that you would like to do or say, up to and including changing your mind and canceling the operation entirely? This can still be done without any loss of self-respect. In fact I, personally, would consider it to be an intelligent decision."

"I have two requests," Hellishomar said promptly. "Shortly I will be experiencing the first cranial surgery to be performed on a member of my species. As a Cutter as well as the patient I am deeply interested in the procedure and would appreciate a translated description of, and the reasons for, your actions while the operation is in progress. During the operation I might need to talk with the entity Lioren on another channel, but privately. If this conversation becomes necessary, no other entity in the hospital is to overhear our words. That is my second and more important requirement."

Both the Diagnostician and the Chief Psychologist turned to look at Lioren. He had already warned them that Hellishomar would make such a request and that it would not accept a negative answer.

Reassuringly, Conway said, "My intention is to talk through the procedure and record it in sound and vision for staff-training purposes, so there is no reason why you should not overhear the original. We can also arrange for a second communications channel, but you will not be able to operate it yourself because your manipulatory appendages are too massive for the control mechanism. I suggest that both channels be controlled by Lioren, and any private words you have for Lioren be prefixed by its name so that all others can be switched out of the conversation. Would that be satisfactory?"

Hellishomar did not reply.

"We understand that privacy at such times is of great importance to you," O'Mara said suddenly, staring at one of the patient's enormous, closed eyes. "As Chief Psychologist of this establishment I possess the authority of a Parent. I can assure you, Hellishomar, that your second communication channel will be private and secure."

The Chief Psychologist's curiosity regarding the words that had and would pass between Hellishomar and Lioren was personal, professional, and intense. But if there was disappointment in O'Mara's voice, it was lost in translation.

"Then I would like you to proceed with minimum delay," Hellishomar said, "lest I take Diagnostician Conway's good advice and change my mind."

"Doctor Prilicla?" Conway said quietly.

"Friend Hellishomar's emotional radiation fully supports its decision to proceed," the empath said, joining the conversation for the first time. "The feeling of impatience is natural in the circumstances, and the expression of self-doubt may be considered as an oblique verbal pleasantry rather than indecision. The patient is ready."

A great wave of relief, so intense that he could see Prilicla shaking with it as well, burst over Lioren's mind. But the empath's trembling was slow and regular, like the movements of a stately dance, and indicated the presence of emotional radiation that was pleasant rather than painful. Even with O'Mara advising him at every stage, it had taken five days and nearly as many nights of argument, closely reasoned at times but at others purely emotional, to obtain Hellishomar's agreement to the operation. It was only now that he knew they had succeeded.

"Very well," Conway said. "If the team is ready we will go in. Doctor Seldal, I'd be obliged if you would open."

The instruments required for the macroprocedure, the drills and cutters and suction tubes so massive that some of them had to be individually manned, hung in position all around them. The preparations, Lioren had thought, more closely resembled those for a mining operation than a surgical procedure. But the Diagnostician's words were another example of an oblique verbal pleasantry, because the operating team was ready and waiting, and Seldal had already been thoroughly briefed on its part at every stage of the operation.

Politeness was a lubricant, Lioren thought, that reduced friction but wasted time.

Even though Hellishomar was a member of a macrospecies with a head that was large in proportion to its enormous body, the sheer size of the operative field came as a shock to Lioren. The area of the flap of tegument that was excised and drawn back to reveal the underlying bone structure was larger than any of the decorative rugs scattered around his living quarters.

"Doctor Seldal is controlling the subdermal bleeding by clamping off the incised capilliaries," Conway was saying, "which in this patient more closely resemble major blood vessels, while I drill vertically through the cranium to the upper surface of the meningeal layer. The drill is tipped with a vision sensor linked to the main monitor, which will show us when it reaches the surface of the membrane . . . We're there.

"The drill has been withdrawn and replaced by a high-speed saw of identical length," the Diagnostician continued a few minutes later. "This is being used to extend the original borehole laterally until a circular opening has been made in the cranium of sufficient diameter so that, when the resulting plug of osseous material is removed, the surgeons will be able to enter the wound and work freely. That's it. The plug is being removed now and will be kept under moderate refrigeration pending its replacement. How is the patient?"

"Friend Hellishomar's emotional radiation," Prilicla said quickly, "suggests feelings of mild discomfort, or more severe discomfort that is under firm control. Feelings of uncertainty and anxiety normal to the situation are also present."

"A reply from me," Hellishomar said, opening the eye nearest to the display screen, "seems unnecessary."

"For the moment, yes," Conway said. "But later I will need the kind of help which only you will be able to give. Try not to worry, Hellishomar, you are doing fine. Seldal, climb aboard."

Lioren wished suddenly that he could find something reassuring to say to the patient, because he, having convinced O'Mara and Conway and finally Hellishomar itself of the necessity for the operation, bore the responsibility for what was to happen here. But he could not excuse breaking into the operating team's conversation without invitation, and the private communication channel was closed to him until or unless Hellishomar spoke his name, so he remained silent and watchful.

Looking like a pink-flecked, shaven log of a large tree, the bony plug was lifted clear while Seldal, its three spindly legs strapped together so as to minimize bodily projections, was being lifted into Conway's backpack so that only its long, flexible neck, head, and beak were uncovered. A similar pack containing the instruments and inflatable equipment that both surgeons would use was strapped tightly to Conway's chest and abdomen. The Diagnostician's legs were not strapped together, but the sharp contours of its feet were encased in thick padding, and a white, frictionless overgarment was drawn over the limbs and fastened at the shoulders so that only the arms and head were uncovered. A transparent helmet that was free of external projections and large enough to accommodate the necessary lighting and communications equipment was added. Seldal, whose upper body was naturally streamlined, kept its head and beak pressed firmly against the back of Conway's helmet. The Nallajim wore only eye protection and an attachment for the thin air line running into the corner of its mouth.

"Zero gravity in the operative field," Conway said. "Ready, Seldal? We will now enter the wound."

A tractor beam seized their weightless bodies in its immaterial grasp, deftly upended them, and lowered them heads first into the narrow opening. The thick cable loom comprising their air supply, suction and specimen extraction hoses, and the emergency rescue line unreeled like a multicolored tail behind them. Conway's helmet lighting showed the smooth, gray walls of the organic well they had created moving past them, and an enlarged and enhanced image was reproduced on the external display.

"We are at the base of the entry well," Conway said, "level with the internal surface of the cranium, and have encountered what is probably the equivalent of the protective meningeal sheath. The membrane responds to firm hand pressure, in a way which suggests the presence of underlying fluid, and what appears to be the outer surface of the brain itself lies just beyond. A precise estimate of the distance is difficult because either the membrane or the fluid, or perhaps both, are not completely transparent. A small test incision is being made through the membrane. That's strange."

A moment later the Diagnostician went on, "The incision

has been extended and opened, but there is still no apparent loss of fluid. Oh, so that's it . . . ."

Conway's voice sounded pleased and excited as it went on to explain that, unlike in other species of its experience, the cerebrospinal fluid, which helped protect the brain structure from shocks by acting as a lubricant between the inner cranium and brain, was not in the Groalterri species a fluid. It was instead a transparent, semisolid lubricant with the consistency of a thin jelly. When a small piece of the jelly was cut away for closer examination and then replaced, it immediately rejoined the main body without any trace of the earlier incision. This was fortunate since it enabled them to go through the meninges without having to worry about controlling fluid losses, and they could move laterally with minimal resistance and loss of time between the brain surface and the meningeal layer to the first objective, a deep fissure between two convolutions in the area suspected of housing the Groalterri telepathic faculty.

"Before we proceed," Conway said, "is the patient aware of any unusual physical sensations or psychological effects?"

"No," Hellishomar said.

For a few moments the main screen gave glimpses of Conway's hands and Seldal's beak, brightly lit by the helmet lamp, as they pushed themselves carefully through the clear jelly between the smooth inner meninges and the massively wrinkled outer surface of the cortex and into the narrow crevice.

"As closely as we can estimate," Conway went on, "this fissure extends about twenty yards on each side of our entry point and the average depth is three yards. On the upper brain surface the division between adjoining convolutions is clearly evident, but with depth the walls begin to press together. The pressure is not sufficient to be life-threatening, and the effort required to push the surfaces apart is minimal and does not reduce our mobility, but it would seriously hamper any surgical procedure that may become necessary and quickly cause disabling levels of fatigue. Soon we will have to deploy the rings."

Hellishomar had not spoken directly to Lioren, even on the open channel, so that he had no way of knowing what was going through the patient's mind. But Prilicla's gauzy wings were beating slowly, and the stability of its hovering flight made it plain that there was no source of unpleasant emotional radiation in the area.

"Ease your mind, friend Lioren," the empath said quietly. "At this time your anxiety is greater than friend Hellishomar's."

Greatly reassured, Lioren returned his attention on the main screen.

"This is the lobe where the highest concentration of trace metals occurs," Conway said. "It has been chosen because similar traces have been associated with the telepathic function of the few other species known to possess the faculty, and although the operating mechanism remains unclear, the higher concentration of metal indicates the presence of an organic transmitter-receiver. It is the possible impairment of the patient's higher brain functions, including the telepathic faculty, that we are trying to investigate and correct.

"Regrettably our charting of this area is imprecise," it continued. "This is because the volume and density of the cranial contents would make it necessary to use very high power levels on our deep scanners, which would cause interference with neural activity.

"For this reason the portable, low-powered scanner will be used briefly and only in an emergency.

"The patient's earlier cooperation in making voluntary muscle movements at our direction and submitting to external touch, pressure, and temperature stimuli has enabled us, by observing the local increases in neural activity, to identify those areas and eliminate them from the investigation. This information was obtained by sensor only, a detection system which produces no troublesome radiation, but which lacks the precision of the scanner."

Lioren could not believe that there was anyone in the hospital, either presently on the staff or future trainees, who did not know the difference between a scanner and a sensor, and assumed that the explanation was for the patient's benefit.

"It was expected," Conway went on, "that the brain of a macro life-form would be more open and coarse-structured to correspond with its large body mass. As we can now see, the blood supply network is on the expected large scale, but the neural structure appears to be as highly condensed and finely structured as that of a being of smaller mass. I cannot . . . it is completely beyond my ability to estimate the level of mentation possible to a brain of this size and complexity."

Lioren stared at the enlarged image of Conway's hands as

they stretched slowly forward, pushed palms outward to each side, and then moved back out of sight, as if the Diagnostician was swimming endlessly through a fleshy ocean. For a moment he tried to put himself in Hellishomar's place, but the thought of a white, slippery, two-headed insect crawling about in his brain was so repulsive that he had to control a sudden feeling of nausea.

Conway's voice became uneven and its respiration more audible as it went on. "While we cannot be completely certain of what is or is not normal in this situation, it seems that the investigation so far has uncovered no evidence of structural abnormality or dysfunction. Our progress is being gradually impeded by increasing pressure from the fissure walls. At first this was ascribed to increasing fatigue in my arm muscles, but Seldal, who has no arms to tire, notes a similar increase in pressure against the outer surface of its carrying pouch. It is not thought to be a psychosomatic effect caused by claustrophobia.

"Mobility and the field of view are seriously reduced," it added. "We are deploying the rings."

Lioren watched as Conway struggled to pull the first ring over their heads and, with the help of Seldal's incredibly flexible neck and beak, position it at waist level before breaking the compressed-air seal and inflating it around them. Two more rings were inflated at knee and shoulder level and joined into a hollow, rigid cylinder by longitudinal spacers. When the initial triple-ring deployment was complete, they added another ring and spacers to extend the structure forward. By deflating and withdrawing the rearmost ring and attaching it in front, and varying the lengths of the spacers, they were able to move the hollow cylinder and travel within it in any required direction. The open structure provided all-around visibility and ready access to perform surgery.

They were no longer swimmers in a near-solid ocean, Lioren thought, but miners boring through a tunnel that they carried with them.

"We are encountering increasing resistance and pressure from one wall of the fissure," Conway said. "The tissues on that side appear to be both stretched and compressed. You can see there, and over there, where the blood supply has been interrupted. Some of the vessels are distended where the blood has pooled and others deflated and all but empty. This does not appear to be a naturally occurring condition, and the absence of necrosis in the area suggests that the circulation is seriously impeded but so far not completely blocked. The structural adaptation that has taken place also suggests that the condition has been present for a long time.

"Scanning is needed to find its cause and source," Conway went on. "I will use the hand scanner briefly, at minimum penetration, now. How does the patient feel?"

"Fascinated," Hellishomar said.

The Earth-human barked softly. "No emotional or cerebral effects are reported by the patient. I will try again with a little more penetration."

For a few seconds Conway's scanner image appeared on the main screen, then dissolved. The recording was projected onto an adjacent screen and frozen for study.

"The scanner shows the presence of another membrane at a depth of approximately seven inches," the Diagnostician continued. "It is no more than half an inch thick, and has a dense, fibrous structure and a degree of convex curvature which, if continued uniformly, would enclose a spherical body of approximately ten feet in diameter. The underlying tissue structure is still unclear but shows a marked difference to that encountered so far. It may be that this is the site of the lobe responsible for the telepathic faculty. But there are other possibilities which can only be eliminated by surgical investigation and tissue analysis. Doctor Seldal will make the incision and obtain tissue samples while I control the bleeding."

The main screen was filled with a picture of Conway's hands, looking enormous and distorted because of the proximity of the helmet's vision pickup, as they fitted a cutter to the Nallajim Senior's beak. Then an index finger moved forward to outline the position and extent of the required incision.

There was a sudden blur of motion as the back of Seldal's head and neck briefly obscured the operative field.

"You can see that the initial incision has not uncovered the membrane," Conway went on, "but the underlying pressure has forced apart the edges of the wound to a degree that, if we don't relieve the situation by extending the incision at once, there is a serious risk of it tearing open at each end. Seldal, would you go a little deeper and extend . . . Oh, *damn*!"

It was as Conway had foreseen. The incision had torn apart

at each end and weightless globules of blood were drifting out of it and totally obscuring the operative field. Seldal had discarded the cutter because its beak came into view gripping the suction unit, which it moved expertly along and inside the wound so that Conway could find and seal off the bleeders. Within a very few minutes the wound, now with torn, uneven edges and fully three times its original length, was clear and gaping open to reveal at its base a long, narrow ellipse of utter blackness.

"We have uncovered a strong, flexible, and light-absorbent membrane," the Diagnostician resumed, "and two tissue samples have been taken. One is being sent out to you through the suction unit for more detailed study, but my analyzer reading indicates an organic material that is totally foreign to the surrounding tissues. Its cell structure is more characteristic of a vegetable than an—What the blazes is happening? We can feel the patient moving. It *must* remain absolutely still! We are not supposed to be in an area where accidental stimulation of the motor muscles is possible. Hellishomar, what is wrong?"

The Diagnostician's words were lost in the bedlam of the outer ward, where the tractor and pressor units were emitting audible and visible signals of overload as their operators struggled to keep Hellishomar's heaving body motionless. The Groalterri's enormous head was jerking from side to side against its immaterial restraints, and the ends of the incision were tearing and bleeding again. Prilicla's body was being shaken by an emotional gale, and everyone seemed to be shouting questions, instruction, or warnings at each other.

But it was Hellishomar who succeeded in making itself heard above the din, suddenly and with one word.

"*Lioren!*"

Chapter 25

"**I** am here," Lioren said, switching quickly to the secure channel, but the sounds that the patient was making did not translate.

"Hellishomar, please stop moving," Lioren said urgently. "You could seriously injure, perhaps kill yourself. And others. What is troubling you? Please tell me. Is there pain?"

"No," Hellishomar said.

Telling the patient that it might kill itself would be a waste of time, Lioren thought, because the Groalterri's presence in the hospital was due to it trying to do just that. But the reminder that it was endangering others must have penetrated the frenzy in its mind, because the violence of its struggles was gradually diminishing.

"Please," Lioren asked again. "What is troubling you?"

The reply came slowly at first, as if each and every word had to break through a great, individual wall of fear, shame and self-loathing; then suddenly the words rushed out in a near-incoherent flood that swept away all such barriers. As he listened to Hellishomar pouring out everything that was in its mind, Lioren's confusion changed slowly to anger and then to sadness. This was utterly ridiculous, he told himself. Had he been an Earth-human he might have been barking with laughter by now at this display of ignorance from a member of a species that was the most highly intelligent of any race known to the Federation. But if Lioren had learned anything since joining O'Mara's department it was that emotional distress was the most subjective of all phenomena, and the most difficult to relieve.

But this was an entity trained in the Groalterri concepts of healing. It was a young and perhaps mentally retarded Cutter whose experience was restricted to peripheral surgery performed on aged members of its own race, and it was viewing an intercranial procedure, on itself, for the first time. In those circumstances ignorance was excusable, he told himself, provided it remained a temporary condition.

"Listen," Lioren said quickly into the first, brief pause in the tirade. "Please listen carefully to what I am saying, ease your mind, and above all, be still. The blackness inside your head is *not* the physical manifestation of your guilt, nor did it grow because of evil thoughts or any sin committed by you. It is likely that it is a bad and a dangerous thing, but it is not your spirit or soul or any part of—"

"It is," Hellishomar broke in. "It is the place where I am. The thinking, feeling, and grievously sinning me who tried to destroy myself lives in that place, and it has a blackness that is beyond hope."

"No," Lioren said firmly. "Every intelligent entity I know of believes that its personality, its soul lives in the brain, usually a short distance behind the visual receptors. They believe this because, even when there has been gross trauma and physical dismemberment, it remains intact. Sometimes there is physical damage or disease that causes the personality to change. But this change does not come about because of an act of will, so the entity concerned cannot be held responsible for subsequent behavior."

Hellishomar remained silent and its body movements had reduced to the point where the overload lights were no longer showing on the tractor-beam installations.

Lioren went on quickly. "It is possible that the inability of your brain to mature to the stage where direct mind-to-mind contact can be achieved with the Parents is due to a genetic defect. But it is also possible that the crimes you blame yourself for committing were the result of a disease or injury to the brain, and the reason for these wrongful thoughts and actions may now have been found. You must know that the black mass that Conway and Seldal have uncovered is not your personality, because you have told me yourself that the soul is immaterial, that when the Parents die and their bodies decay and return their substance to the world, their souls leave Groalterri to begin their never-ending exploration of the universe—"

"While my own soul," Hellishomar said, beginning to struggle against the restraints again, "sinks like a stone into the mud of the ocean floor, to fester in darkness forever."

Lioren felt that he would lose what little control he had gained over the situation if he did not speak quickly, and move the argument from metaphysics to medicine. Focusing one of his eyes on the side screen where the results of Conway's analysis were being displayed, he went on. "It may well rot at the bottom of your ocean if that is where you want it placed, but more likely it will end in a waste-disposal furnace at Sector General. I do not know what it is exactly, but it is not your soul or, for that matter, any other part of you. It is completely foreign material, a vegetable form of life, an invader of some kind. I ask you to be calm and to think, to think as a Groalterri Cutter and healer, and to remember if there was anything in your past experience that resembles this black growth. Please think carefully."

For several moments Hellishomar was silent and absolutely still. The ward was quiet again and he could hear the voice of Conway saying that it was about to resume the operation.

"Please wait, Doctors," Lioren said, switching briefly to the public channel. "I may have important clinical data for you." On the main screen one of the Diagnostician's hands waved acknowledgment, and he returned to the private channel.

"Hellishomar," Lioren said again, "please try to recall anything resembling this black growth, whether the memory is from recent experience, the less certain recollections of infancy, or even the hearsay experiences of others. Can you remember having contact with such a growth, or having suffered an injury, not necessarily to the cranium, which would have allowed it to enter the bloodstream?"

"No," Hellishomar said.

Lioren thought for a moment. "If you do not remember, is it possible that you contracted the disease as a very small infant, before you were capable of forming memories? Can you recall any later reference to something like this happening to you by an older Small charged with your care? This person may not have considered it important at the time, or mentioned it until you were grown and—"

"No, Lioren," Hellishomar broke in. "You are trying to make me believe that this foul thing in my brain is not the result of wrong thinking, and what you are doing is a great kindness. But I have already told you, it is only the very aged Parents who are afflicted with diseases, the Small never. We are strong and healthy and immune. The invisible attackers you have told me about are ignored, and those large enough to be visible are treated as a nuisance and simply brushed away.''

Lioren had been hoping that he would discover something useful to Conway and Seldal by questioning the patient, but he was making no progress at all. He was about to signal them to proceed when another thought occurred to him.

"These pests that you brush away," he said. "Please tell me all that you can remember about them."

Hellishomar's replies sounded polite but very impatient, as if it had guessed that the other's only intention was to keep its mind on other things and the answers were unimportant. But gradually its answers became very important indeed and Lioren's questions more precise. Slowly his earlier feeling of hopelessness was changing to one of excitement and mounting anxiety.

"From all that you have told me," Lioren said urgently, "I am convinced that the pest you call a skinsticker is the original cause of your trouble, but I do not want to waste time giving my reasons to you and then again to the operating team. A final question. Will you give me permission to speak of this to the others? Not all that has passed between us, and nothing about your thoughts and fears, only the details of the description and behavior of the skinstickers."

Subjectively it seemed that a very long time elapsed without any response from Hellishomar. Lioren could hear Conway, Seldal, and the support staff in the ward talking together, their words muffled by his earpads but their impatience plain. He tried again.

"Hellishomar," Lioren said, "if my theory is correct, your life may be at risk, and the cerebral damage will certainly render you incapable of future coherent thought. Please, your answer is needed quickly."

"The Cutters inside my skull are also at risk," Hellishomar said. "Tell them."

Without taking time to reply Lioren switched to the public channel and began to speak.

Although he could not be absolutely certain because of the small amount of information that the patient had been able to give him, Lioren said that he felt sure the original cause of the black intercranial growth was due to infestation by a species of parasitic vegetable vermin known to the Groalterri as a skinsticker, which was considered to be a periodic nuisance rather than a threat to life. Nothing was known about the life cycle or reproduction mechanism of the skinsticker because they could be easily removed, brushed away with the manipulatory tentacles or by rubbing the affected area of tegument against a tree, and a life-form with the enormous physical mass and limited dexterity of the Groalterri had neither the desire nor the ability to investigate the habits of a near-microscopic form of plant life.

Skinstickers were black, spherical, and covered with a vegetable adhesive which enabled them to attach themselves to the host's body and extend their single feeder root while they were still too small to be seen. They required only an organic food source and the presence of light and air to grow very quickly to the size when they became a nuisance and were removed. They could be destroyed by crushing between hard surfaces or by burning, and after removal the root, which had a high liquid content, withered quickly and fell out of the wound it had made.

Lioren went on, "My theory is that this case was the result of infestation by a single skinsticker which gained entry via a small abrasion which the patient no longer remembers or through the puncture wound left by the root of an earlier and unsuccessful skinsticker, and was carried through the circulatory system until it lodged in the cranium. Once there it had a virtually limitless food supply but not, apart from the tiny amount of oxygen it was able to absorb from the local blood supply, the light and air its metabolism required for optimum growth. The growth rate was inhibited but it has had a great many years, a young Groalterri's very long lifetime, in which to grow to its present size."

Except for the slow and near-silent beating of Prilicla's wings, the ward might have been a still picture as Lioren finished speaking. It was Conway who reacted first.

"An ingenious theory, Lioren," the Diagnostician said, "and while obtaining this information and discussing it between you, you have succeeded in pacifying our patient. That was well done. But whether or not your theory is correct, and I believe that it is, our procedure must continue as originally planned."

Imperceptibly Conway's manner changed from one of person-to-person conversation to that of lecturer-student instruction as it went on. "This foreign tissue, tentatively identified as a massively overgrown Groalter skinsticker, will be excised in very small pieces whose size will be dictated by the maximum orifice setting of our suction unit. Many hours of patient, careful work will be required to accomplish this, particularly in the later stages if there are adhesions to healthy brain tissue, and rest periods or relays of surgeons may be necessary. However, since the patient has shown no impairment or deterioration in mentation since its arrival here, and the growth has been present for a very long time, its removal may be considered necessary but non-urgent. We will be able to take all the time we need to insure that—"

"No," Lioren said harshly.

"No?" Conway sounded too surprised to be angry, but Lioren knew that the anger would not be long in coming. "Why not, dammit?"

"With respect," Lioren said, "the screen shows that your original incision is widening and extending in length. Let me remind you that the skinsticker grows rapidly in the presence of light and air and, after a great many years in the airless dark, light and air are again present."

For a few moments Conway directed angry and self-abusive words at itself, then suddenly the main screen turned black as it switched off its helmet lighting and said, "This will slow the rate of growth a little. I need time to think . . ."

"You need more surgical assistance," Thornnastor said. "I will—"

"No!" Seldal broke in. "Another set of enormous, awkward feet in here is what we don't need! There isn't enough space as it is to—"

"My feet aren't that big—" Conway began.

"Not yours," said Seldal. "I'm sorry, for a moment I was thinking of—"

"Doctors!" Thornnastor said, speaking suddenly with the voice and authority of the hospital's senior Diagnostician. "This is not the time for arguments about the relative sizes of your ambulatory appendages. Please desist. I was about to say that the Nidian Senior, Lesk-Murog, is available and anxious to assist. Its surgical experience is as large as its feet are small. Conway, what are your instructions?"

The main screen brightened again as Conway switched on its helmet light. "We need a much wider suction unit, a flexible pipe of six inches' diameter or as large as Lesk-Murog can handle, linked to one of the air circulation pumps, so that large pieces of the growth can be excised and withdrawn quickly. We cannot work without light, but we should be able to reduce the air that has leaked from the edges of our breathing masks by withdrawing it with the operative debris and replacing it with an inert gas pumped through the existing suction line. The inert should inhibit the skinsticker's rate of growth as effectively as a complete absence of air, but that is a hope rather than an expectation.''

"I understand, Doctor," Thornnastor said. "Maintenance technicians, you know what is required. Lesk-Murog, prepare yourself. Quickly, everyone.''

A subjective eternity passed before the equipment was set up and the diminutive Lesk-Murog, looking like a plastic-encased, long-tailed rodent with one end of the new suction pipeline attached to its backpack, disappeared headfirst into the entry wound. Conway and Seldal had already cut through the skinsticker's outer membrane and were excising small pieces and feeding them into the original suction unit, although it was obvious that the black growth was increasing in size in spite of their efforts because the incision continued to widen and tear in both directions. But with the Nidian Senior's arrival the situation changed at once.

"This is much better," said Conway. "We are beginning to make progress now and are excising deeply into the growth. As soon as we have hollowed it out sufficiently, Seldal and Lesk-Murog will go inside and pass the excised material out to me for disposal. Don't cut such large pieces, doctors, please. If this suction unit blocks we'll be in real trouble. And watch where you're swinging that blade, Lesk-Murog, I have no wish to become an amputee. How is the patient?''

"It is radiating anxiety, friend Conway," Prilicla said, "with secondary but still strong feelings of excitement. Neither are at levels to cause distress.''

Since a further reply was unnecessary, Hellishomar and Lioren did not speak.

The main screen showed glimpses of rapidly moving Earth-human and Nidian hands and a furiously pecking Nallajim beak plying instruments that glittered brightly against the light-absorbent blackness of the growth. While describing the procedure Conway broke off to say that they were feeling more like miners digging for fossil fuel than surgeons engaged on a brain operation. The Diagnostician's words were complaining but its voice sounded pleased because the environment of inert gas was seriously inhibiting further growth and the work was going well.

"The cavity has been enlarged sufficiently so that all three of us are now able to work inside and attack the growth independently," Conway said. "Doctors Seldal and Lesk-Murog are able to stand upright while I am forced to kneel. It is becoming very warm in here. We would be obliged if the inert gas you are pumping was reduced in temperature so as to avoid the risk of heat prostration. The inner surface of the growth's enclosing membrane has been exposed over several large areas and it is beginning to sag under the weight of the surrounding brain structure. Please increase the internal gas pressure immediately to keep it from collapsing all over us. How is the patient?"

"No change, friend Conway," Prilicla said.

For a time the operation proceeded in silence. It was clear what the surgeons were doing and there was nothing new for Conway to describe, until suddenly he said, "We have discovered the location of the feeder root and are evacuating its liquid content. The root has shrunk to less than half its original circumference and is being withdrawn with negligible resistance. It is very long but appears to be complete. Seldal is making a deep probe to insure that none of it has been left behind. No other roots have been discovered, nor anything resembling connective pathways to a secondary growth.

"The inner surface of the membrane is now totally exposed," the Diagnostician went on. "We are excising it in narrow strips that can be accommodated by the suction unit. Of necessity the work at this stage is slow and carefully performed because we are detaching the membrane from the underlying brain structures and must avoid inflicting further damage. It is most important that the patient remain completely immobile."

Hellishomar spoke for the first time in nearly three hours. It said, "I will not move."

"Thank you," Conway said.

More time passed, slowly for the operating team and interminably for the watchers, until finally all activity on the main screen ceased and the Diagnostician spoke again.

"The last of the skinsticker material has been withdrawn," Conway said. "You can see that the interfacing brain structures displaced by the growth have been seriously compressed, but we have found no evidence of necrosis due to impairment of the local circulation, which is, in fact, being slowly restored. It is unsafe to make categorical statements regarding the clinical condition of a hitherto unknown life-form or a prognosis based on incomplete data, but my opinion is that minimum cerebral damage has been done and, provided the effects were not due to heredity factors, the condition should rectify itself when the pressure which is artificially maintaining this working cavity is gradually reduced to zero. There is nothing more that we can do here.

"You leave first, Lesk-Murog," Conway ended briskly. "Seldal, hop back into the pouch. We will withdraw and close up."

Lioren watched the main screen as they slowly retraced their path, and worried. The operation had been successfully accomplished and the great mass of foreign matter within the Groalterri's brain had been removed, but had it been the only cause of Hellishomar's trouble? The Groalterri had carried that foul thing in its brain for most of its life, and it could never have become a highly respected Cutter had there been any impairment of muscular coordination. Was it not more likely, as Conway had suggested, that the missing telepathic function and all the mental distress which had stemmed from it was due to an untreatable genetic defect and incurable? He looked around for Prilicla, intending to ask it how the patient was feeling, then remembered that the emotion-sensitive had been forced to leave. As a species Cinrusskins lacked stamina and required frequent rest periods.

He should ask the question of Hellishomar himself, Lioren thought, instead of waiting for the patient to signal its private distress by calling his name. But suddenly he was too afraid of what the answer might be. Conway and Seldal had replaced the massive osseous plug and sutured the flap of cranial tegument and were removing their operating garments, and still Lioren could not drive himself to ask the question.

"Thank you, Seldal, Lesk-Murog, everyone," Conway said, looking all around to include the OR and technical support staff. "You all did very well. And especially you, Lioren, by making the patient remain immobile when it was most necessary, by discovering the growth characteristics of that skinsticker, and by warning us in time about the effects of air and light. That was very well done. Personally I think your talents are wasted in Psychology.''

"I don't," O'Mara said. Then, as if ashamed of the compliment it had paid, the Chief Psychologist went on, "The trainee is insubordinate, secretive, and has an infuriating tendency to . . ."

Lioren.

They were all listening to O'Mara and seemed not to have heard. Lioren's hand moved instinctively to his communicator to switch to the private channel, wondering desperately what possible words of comfort he could find for this vast being who must again have lost all hope. Then, with his finger on the key, he stopped as a great and joyful realization came to him.

His name had been called but it had not been spoken.

Chapter 26

ONCE again it was a private conversation, but this time without the deep cranial itching that had preceeded his telepathic contact with the Protector of the Unborn. The answers were given before the questions could be uttered, the other's reassurance negated his concern as soon as it was felt, and the nerve and muscle connections between Lioren's brain and tongue became redundant. It was as if a system for exchanging messages chiseled laboriously on slabs of rock had been replaced by the spoken word, except that the process was much faster than that.

Hellishomar the Cutter, formerly the flawed, the mentally deficient, the telepathically deaf and no longer the Small, was cured.

Gratitude washed over him in a bright, warm flood that only Lioren could see and feel, and with it came knowledge, incomplete and simplified so as to avoid damage to his relatively primitive mentality, that must be his alone. The people who had contributed to the unique and wondrous cure of a mentally disabled Groalterri should not be repaid with knowledge that would cripple their own young minds. Hellishomar had touched the minds of every thinking being within the hospital and the occupants of vessels orbiting beyond it, and knew this to be so.

The entities who had contributed to the success of the operation would be thanked individually and verbally. They would be told that Hellishomar felt very well, that a significant change for the better had already taken place in the quality of its mentation, and that it was anxious to return to Groalter, where its recuperation would be aided by the greater freedom of physical movement that was not possible in Sector General.

All this was true, but it was not all of the truth. They were not to be told that Hellishomar needed to leave the hospital quickly because the temptation to remain and explore the minds and behavior and philosophies of the thousands of entities who came to work, to visit, or to be cared for in this great hospital was well-nigh irrestistible. For Lioren had been right when he had told O'Mara that to the gross and planetbound Groalterri the universe beyond the atmosphere was the hereafter that they would need all eternity to explore, and Sector General was a particularly intriguing microcosm of the Heaven that awaited them.

Lioren's concern over the possible effects on the other Groalterri culture of Hellishomar's off-planet experiences had been justified at the time. But now Hellishomar was not returning as one of the Small destined to remain a telepathic mute and crippled by a permanently occluded mind for the remainder of its life. Instead it was returning with all of its faculties restored, as a near-adult who would speak of this wondrous thing only to the Parents. It did not know how they would react to the knowledge he bore, but they were old and very wise and it was probable that the proof that Heaven was as wonderful and mind-stretching as they believed, and even that a small part of it was peopled by short-lived creatures whose minds were primitive and their ethics advanced, would strengthen their belief and cause them to strive even harder for the perfection of mind and spirit that was needed before the Going Out.

A great debt was owed to the Monitor Corps and to the hospital staff who had made Hellishomar whole again, and to the single Tarlan entity who had talked and argued and worked with its mind to obtain the patient's agreement to the operation. An even greater debt was owed by the other Groalterri, but neither debt would be paid. The Federation would not be allowed full contact with the Groalterri for the reasons already given, and neither would Lioren be given the answers to the two questions uppermost in his mind.

During all his contacts with patients Lioren had never allowed himself to influence their nonmaterial beliefs, no matter, in the light of his own greater knowledge and experience, how strange or ridiculous they had seemed to him. He had refused to tamper with their beliefs even though he himself did not believe that he believed in anything. In the circumstances Lioren's behavior had been ethically flawless and Hellishomar could do no less. It would not give its Tarlan friend the benefit of the advanced Groalterri philosophical and theological thinking by telling him what he should believe. And an answer to the second question was unnecessary because Lioren was about to make the decision for himself and do something that was completely foreign to his nature.

Lioren was becoming confused by this highly compressed method of communication, and by answers that come before the questions are fully formed.

It shames me to remind you of the debt you owe, Lioren thought, *and to ask that a small part of it be repaid. When you touch my mind I sense a vastness of knowledge, a great area of brightness that you are hiding from me. If you instructed me I would believe. Why will you not tell me from your greater knowledge what is the truth about God?*

By your own efforts, Hellishomar replied, *you have acquired great knowledge. You have used it to ease the inner hurts of many entities, including my former, retarded self, but you are not yet ready to believe. The question has already been answered.*

Then I repeat the second question, Lioren went on. *Is there any hope of me finding ease or a release from the constant memory and guilt of Cromsag? The decision I have struggled with for so long involves behavior shameful to a Tarlan of my former standing, but no matter. It may also result in my death. I ask only if the decision I have made is the right one.*

Does the memory of Cromsag trouble you continually, Hellishomar thought, *to the extent that you would seek your own death as a release from it?*

No, said Lioren, surprised by the intensity of his feelings. *But that is because so many other matters have recently occupied my mind. I would not welcome death, especially if it came about by accident or as a result of a stupid decision on my part.*

Yet you believe that the decision includes the serious risk of major injury or death, Hellishomar returned, *and I find no indication that you are going to change your mind. I will not tell you whether your decision is right or wrong or stupid, or of the probable results, but shall only remind you that no event in this state of existence occurs by accident.*

This much I will do for you, Hellishomar went on. *Your coming action will not be hampered in any way. Since your decision has now been made, I suggest that you avoid prolonging your distress and uncertainty further and leave without delay.*

There was a moment of mental dislocation as Lioren's mind returned to a working environment in which conversations were conducted by laggard speech and meanings were clouded. It seemed that O'Mara had just finished listing its trainee's shortcomings. Conway was showing its teeth and reminding the Chief Psychologist that it had expressed serious displeasure with everyone in Sector General, and especially those who had risen to become Diagnosticians, and it seemed that every being in the ward was watching Lioren expectantly and trying to move closer.

"The patient is well," Lioren said. "It feels no sensory discomfort and reports a significant and continuing improvement in the quality of its mentation. It wishes to use the public channel to thank everyone here individually."

They were all too excited and pleased to notice him leave. Lioren plotted the fastest route to the Cromsaggar ward and tried to push all second thoughts out of his mind.

He had already checked the duty rosters and knew that there were only two nursing staff on the ward. This was normal practice when patients were fully convalescent and under observation rather than treatment or awaiting discharge, but it was not normal to post an armed Monitor at the ward entrance.

The guard was an Earth-human DBDG, with only two arms and legs and less than half of Lioren's body mass, and its weapon was a disabler. It could scramble his voluntary muscle system or cause full paralysis, depending on the power setting, but it would not kill him.

"Lioren, Psychology Department," he said briskly. "I am here to interview the patients."

"And I am here to stop you," the guard said. "Major O'Mara said that you might try to get among the Cromsaggar patients and that you should be forbidden entry for your own safety. Please leave at once, sir."

The guard was showing the consideration and respect due Lioren's former rank as a Surgeon-Captain, but feelings of kindliness and sympathy, however strong, would not cause it to ignore its orders. Surely O'Mara knew enough Tarlan psychology to know that he would not try to escape just punishment by deliberately ending his own life. Perhaps the Chief Psychologist had thought that even this Tarlan could change his mind and his inflexible code of behavior and force himself to commit an act formerly considered dishonorable and had simply taken precautions.

This obstruction, Lioren thought helplessly, had not been foreseen. Or had it?

"I'm glad you understand my position," the guard said suddenly. "Good-bye, sir."

A few seconds later it stamped its feet and, as if to relieve boredom or stiffening leg muscles, began pacing slowly along the corridor. If Lioren had not stepped aside quickly, the guard would have walked straight into him.

Thank you, Hellishomar, Lioren thought, and entered the ward.

It was a long, high-ceilinged room containing forty beds in two opposing rows and with the nurses' station rising like a glass-walled island from the center of the floor. Environmental technicians had reproduced the dusty yellow light of Cromsag's sun and softened the structural projections with native vegetation and wall hangings that looked real. The patients were standing or sitting in small groups around four of the beds, talking together quietly while another group was watching a display screen on which a Corps contact specialist was explaining the Federation's long-term plans for reconstructing Cromsag's technology and rehabilitating the Cromsaggar. One of the Orligian duty nurses was using the communicator and the other's furry head was swiveling slowly from side to side as it scanned the length of the ward. It was plain that they did not see him and, as with the guard outside, their minds had been touched to render them selectively blind.

Whether or not his decision was the correct one, Hellishomar had promised that he could make it without interruption.

Trying to show neither haste nor hesitation, Lioren walked down the ward in a gathering silence. He looked briefly at the seated or recumbent patients he passed, and they stared back at him. He had never learned to read Cromsaggar facial expressions and had no idea of what they were thinking. When he reached the largest group of patients he stopped.

"I am Lioren," he said.

It was obvious that they already knew who and what he was. The patients who had been sitting or lying on the nearby beds rose quickly to their feet and gathered around him, and those further along the ward hurried to join the others until he was completely encircled by still and silent Cromsaggar.

A sharp, clear memory of his first meeting with one of them rose in Lioren's mind. It had been a female attacking him in defense of an imagined threat to infants sleeping in another part of its dwelling, and even though its body had displayed the discoloration and muscle wastage of disease and malnutrition, it had come close to inflicting serious injury on him. Now he was surrounded by more than thirty Cromsaggar whose bodies and limbs were well-muscled and healthy. He knew well the damage that those horny, long-nailed feet and hard medial hands could inflict because he had seen them fighting each other not quite to the death.

On Cromsag they had fought with ferocity but total control, with the intention of inflicting maximum damage short of killing, and with the sole purpose of stirring their near-atrophied endocrine systems into sufficient activity to enable them to procreate and survive as a species. But Lioren was not another Cromsaggar and would-be mate; he was the creature responsible for countless thousands of their deaths and of all but destroying their race. They might not want to control the hatred they must feel for him, or the urge to tear his body apart limb from limb.

He wondered whether the distant Hellishomar was still influencing the minds of the guard and the two nurses, for normally they could not have helped seeing the crowd closing in around him and would have attempted a rescue. He wished that the

Groalterri would not be so thorough in its mind control because suddenly he did not want his life to end in this or any other fashion, and then he realized that his thoughts were clear to Hellishomar and he felt an even greater shame.

That which he was about to do and say was shameful enough without adding to it the dishonor of personal cowardice. Slowly he looked at each one of the faces surrounding him and spoke.

"I am Lioren," he said. "You know that I am the being responsible for causing the deaths of many thousands of your people. This was a crime too great for expiation and it is only fair that the punishment should lie in your hands. But before this punishment is carried out, I wish to say that I am truly sorry for what I have done, and humbly ask your forgiveness."

The feeling of shame at what he had just done was not as intense as he had expected, Lioren thought as he waited for the onslaught. In fact he felt relieved and very good.

Chapter 27

"THE Monitor guard insists that he did not see you enter the ward," the Chief Psychologist said in a quiet but very angry voice, "and the nurses did not know you were there until the Cromsaggar were suddenly standing around and shouting at you. When the guard went in to investigate you told him that he should not be concerned, that they were having a religious argument which he was welcome to join, although he says that he had heard quieter riots. Tarlans are not noted either for their sarcasm or their sense of humor, so I must assume you spoke the truth. What happened in that ward, dammit? Or have you imposed another oath of secrecy on yourself?"

"No, sir," Lioren replied quietly. "The conversations were public and confidentiality was neither asked for nor implied. When you sent for me I was preparing a detailed report for you on the whole—"

"Summarize it," O'Mara said sharply.

"Yes, sir," Lioren said, and tried to find a balance between accuracy and brevity as he went on. "When I identified myself, apologized, and asked forgiveness for the great wrong I had committed against them—"

"You *apologized*?" O'Mara broke in. "That—that was unexpected."

"So was the behavior of the Cromsaggar," Lioren said. "Considering my crime, I expected a violent reaction from them, but instead they—"

"Did you hope that they would kill you?" O'Mara broke in again. "Was that the reason for your visit?"

"It was not!" Lioren said sharply. "I went there to apologize. That is a shameful enough act for any Tarlan to perform because it is considered to be a cowardly and dishonorable attempt to diminish personal guilt and avoid just punishment. But it is not as shameful as escaping that punishment by deliberately ending one's life. There are degrees of shame, and from my recent contacts with patients I have discovered that there are feelings of shame that may be misplaced or unnecessary."

"Go on," O'Mara said.

"As yet I do not fully understand the psychological mechanism involved," Lioren replied, "but I have discovered that in certain circumstances a personal apology, while shameful to the entity making it, can sometimes do more to ease the hurt of a victim than the simple knowledge that the offender is receiving just punishment. It seems that vengeance, even judicial vengeance, does not fully satisfy the victim and that a sincere expression of regret for the wrong committed can ease the pain or loss more than the mere knowledge that justice is being done. When the apology is followed by forgiveness on the part of the wronged entity, there are much more beneficial and lasting effects for both victim and perpetrator.

"When I identified myself in the Cromsaggar ward," Lioren went on, "there was a strong probability that lethal violence would ensue. It was no longer my wish to die, because the work of this department is very interesting and there may be more that I can do here, but I felt strongly that I should try to ease the hurt of the Cromsaggar with an apology, and did so. I did not expect what happened then."

In a very quiet voice O'Mara asked, "You are still insisting that you, a Wearer of the Blue Cloak of Tarla with all that that implies, apologized?''

The question had already been answered so Lioren continued. ''I had forgotten that the Cromsaggar are a civilized race forced by disease to wage war. They fought with great ferocity because they had to try their hardest to engender the fear of imminent death in each other if their formerly impaired sex-involved endocrine systems were to be stimulated to the point where they would become briefly capable of conceiving children. But while fighting they learned to exercise strict mental and emotional control, and refuse to surrender to anger or hatred, because they loved and respected the opponents they were trying so hard to damage almost to the point of death. They had to fight to insure the continual survival of their species, but the wounds they inflicted and sustained were personal to themselves. They could not have continued to fight and respect and love each other if they had not also learned to apologize for and forgive each other for the terrible hurts they were inflicting.

''On Cromsag the ability to forgive is what enabled their society to survive for so long.''

Suddenly Lioren was seeing and hearing again the Cromsaggar patients who had crowded around him, and for a moment he could not speak because his emotions were being involved in a way that any self-respecting Tarlan would have considered to be a shameful weakness. But he knew that this was another one of the minor shames that he was learning to accept. He went on. ''They treated me as another Cromsaggar, a friend who had done a very great wrong and inflicted much suffering in an attempt to save their race and, unlike themselves, I had succeeded.

''They—they forgave me and were grateful.

''But they were also fearful about the return to Cromsag,'' he continued quickly. ''They understood and were grateful for the rehabilitation program the Monitor Corps had planned for them and said that they would cooperate in every way. It is a psychological problem involving a disbelief in their own ability to exist without severe and continuous stress, coupled with a belief that fate, or a nonmaterial presence whose precise nature was the subject of much argument, might not intend them to live lives of contentment in the material world. Basically it was a religious matter. I told them about the racial memory of the Gogleskans, the Dark Devil which tries to drive them to self-destruction, and how Khone is besting it. And about the problems of the Protectors of the Unborn, and gave what other reassurance I could. My report will cover everything that transpired in detail. I do not foresee the Corps psychologists having serious trouble with the problem. An ensuing religious debate, which the Cromsaggar engage in with great enthusiasm, was interrupted by the arrival of the guard.''

O'Mara leaned back into its chair and said, ''Apart from taking that insane risk you have done well, but then fortune often favors the stupid. In a very short time you have also become something of an authority on other-species religious beliefs mostly, I have been told, by studying the available material during off-duty periods. This is a very sensitive area which the department normally prefers to leave untouched, but so far you have had no problems with it. So much so that you may now consider yourself to be a full member of the department staff rather than a trainee. This will in no sense improve my behavior toward you because you have become the second most insubordinate and selectively reticent person I have ever known. Why will you not tell me what went on between you and ex-Diagnostician Mannen?''

Lioren decided to treat it as a rhetorical question because he had refused to answer it the first time it had been asked. Instead he asked, ''Are there any other assignments for me, sir?''

The Chief Psychologist exhaled with an unusually loud hissing sound, then said, ''Yes. Senior Physician Edanelt would like you to talk to one of its post-op patients, Cresk-Sar has a trainee Dwerlan with a nonspecified ethical problem, and the Cromsaggar patients would like you to visit them as soon and as often as you find convenient. Khone says that it is willing to try my suggestion that the transparent wall dividing its compartment be reduced gradually in height and eventually replaced by a white line painted on the floor, and it wants to see you again, as well. There is also the original Seldal assignment, which you seem to have forgotten.''

''No, sir, I have completed it,'' Lioren said, and went on quickly. ''From the information given by yourself and my subsequent conversations with and about Senior Physician Seldal it was clear that a marked change in personality and behavior had taken place, although not for the worse. At first the change was apparent in the reduced number of couplings with female

Nallajims on the staff, and in its behavior toward colleagues and subordinates. Normally members of that species are physically and emotionally hyperactive, impatient, impolite, inconsiderate, and subject to the rapid changes of mood that make them very unpopular as surgeons-in-charge. Not so Seldal. Its OR and ward staff would do anything it asks and will not allow a word of criticism about their Senior either as a surgeon or a person, and I agree with them. The reason for the change, I am certain, is that one of the Educator-tape personalities Seldal is carrying has assumed partial control or is exerting a considerable amount of influence on the Senior's mind.

"I did not realize that a Tralthan donor was responsible," Lioren continued, "until the incident during the Hellishomar operation when the growth was threatening to get out of control and Conway needed help. Seldal had a moment of extreme stress and indecision during which it must have forgotten who it was. The remark about not wanting another set of big feet in the operative field was intended for Thornnastor, who had offered help, and referred to its six overly large Tralthan feet rather than Conway's, because at that moment the Tralthan tape persona was in the forefront of its mind.

"This is an unusual and perhaps unique situation," Lioren went on, "because observational evidence supports my theory that the partial control of Seldal's mind was relinquished willingly. I would say that the Tralthan donor, rather than being kept under tight control by the host mind, has been befriended by Seldal. The feeling may be even stronger than that. There is professional respect, admiration of a personality that possesses the Tralthan attributes of inner calm and self-assurance that is so unlike Seldal's own, and it is probable that a strong emotional bond has formed between the Senior Physician and this immaterial Tralthan that is indistinguishable from nonphysical love. As a result we have a Nallajim Senior who has willingly assumed the personality traits of a Tralthan and is a better physician and a more content person because of it. That being so I would recommend that nothing whatever be done about the case."

"Agreed," O'Mara said quietly, and for a moment it stared at him in a way which made Lioren wonder again if the Chief Psychologist possessed a telepathic faculty. "There is more?"

"I do not wish to embarrass and perhaps anger a superior by asking this as a question," Lioren said carefully, "but I have formed a suspicion that you, having knowledge of the donor tapes in the Senior Physician's mind, suspected or were already aware of the situation and the Seldal assignment was a fitness test for myself. Its secondary, or perhaps its primary, purpose was to try to make me go out and meet people so that my mind would not be concerned solely with thoughts of my own terrible guilt. I have not nor will I ever be able to forget the Cromsag Incident. But your plan worked and for that I am truly grateful to you, and especially for making me realize that there were people other than myself who were troubled, entities like Khone, Hellishomar, and Mannen who—''

"Mannen is a friend," O'Mara broke in. "His clinical condition has not changed, he could terminate at any moment, and yet he is going around in that antigravity harness like a . . . Dammit, it's a bloody miracle! I would like to know what you said to each other. Anything you tell me will not go into his psych file and I will not speak of it to anyone else, but I want to know. Termination comes to everyone and some of us, unfortunately, may be given too much time to think about it. I will not break this confidence. After all, he is an old friend."

The question was being asked again, but his momentary feeling of irritation was quickly replaced by one of sympathy as he realized that the Chief Psychologist was troubled, however briefly, by the thought of termination and the deterioration of the body and mind which preceded it. His answer must be the same as before, but this time Lioren believed that he could make it more encouraging.

"The ex-Diagnostician is no longer troubled in its mind," he said gently. "If you were to ask your questions of Mannen, as an old friend, I feel sure that it will tel' ɔu everything you want to know. But I cannot."

The Chief Psychologist looked down at his desk as if ashamed of its momentary display of weakness, then up again.

"Very well," it said briskly. "If you won't talk you won't talk. Meanwhile the department will have to contend with another soft-spoken, insubordinate Carmody. No disciplinary action will be taken over your Cromsaggar ward visit. Close the door on your way out. Quietly."

Lioren returned to his desk feeling relieved but very confused, and decided that he must try to relieve the confusion; otherwise the quality of his report would suffer. But search as he would, the information he wanted remained hidden, and he was beginning to strike his keyboard as if it were a mortal enemy.

Across the office Braithwaite cleared its breathing passages with a noise which Lioren now knew denoted sympathy. "You have a problem?"

"I'm not sure," Lioren replied. "O'Mara said that it would take no disciplinary action, but it called me . . . Who or what is a Carmody, and where will I find the information?"

Braithwaite swung round to face him and said, "You won't find it there. Lieutenant Carmody's file was withdrawn after his accident. He was before my time but I know a little about him. He came here from the Corps base on Orligia at his own request and managed to survive in the department for twelve years even though he and O'Mara were always arguing. When an incoming ship whose pilot was badly injured lost control and crashed through our outer hull, he accompanied the rescue team and tried to give reassurance to what he thought was a surviving crewmember. It turned out to be a very large, fear-maddened and nonintelligent ship's pet, which attacked him. He was very old and frail and gentle, and did not survive his injuries.

"During his time here Lieutenant Carmody became very well liked and highly respected by all of the staff and long-term patients," Braithwaite concluded, "and his position was not filled, until now."

Feeling even more confused, Lioren said, "The relevance of what you say eludes me. I am neither old nor frail nor particularly gentle, I have been stripped of all Monitor Corps rank, and my arguments with O'Mara are concerned only with the retention of patient confidences—"

"I know," said Braithwaite, showing its teeth. "Your predecessor called it the Seal of Confession. And the rank doesn't matter. Carmody never used his, and most of the people here did not even use his name. They just called him Padre."

About the Author

JAMES WHITE was born in Belfast, Northern Ireland, and re-
sided there until 1984 when he moved to Portstewart on the
North coast. His first story was printed in 1953. He has since
published well-received short stories, novellas, and novels, but
he is best known for the Sector General series, which deals
with the difficulties involved in running a hospital that caters
to many radically different life-forms.